the eli

WRAIH

*Ama,
Great to meet you!
Big love,
Claire C Riley*

CLAIRE C. RILEY

Series reading order:

~~lust~~
~~pride~~
~~wrath~~
envy
greed
gluttony
sloth

Wrath

Copyright ©2019 Claire C. Riley
Cover Design: All By Design
Editor: Word Nerd Editing
Formatting: Champagne Book Design

ALL RIGHT RESERVED. This book contains material protected under International and Federal Copyright Laws, any unauthorised reprint or use of this material is prohibited. No part of this book may be reproduced or transmitted in any form by any means, electronic or mechanical, without express permission from the author.

This is a work of fiction. Names, characters, places, and incidents are either the product of the authors imagination or are used fictitiously, and any resemblance to actual persons, living or dead, business establishments, events, or locals is entirely coincidental.

Series reading order:

#1 LUST
Rhett aka Lust

#2 PRIDE
Mason aka Pride

#3 WRATH
Samuel aka Wrath

#4 ENVY
Sebastian aka Envy

#5 GREED
Micah aka Greed

#6 GLUTTONY
God aka Gluttony

#7 SLOTH
Rush aka Sloth

To the sinners and the deviants.
And the ones who like to fuck with the lights on.
This one's for you.

ABOUT THE BOOK

I'm a motherless son to a father who hates me. Fury has lived and breathed in my black heart for so long, it's a part of my soul now. The only thing that's ever mattered to me is protecting my twin sister, Sabella, from my father's temper.

So, when the chance to join a secret society presents itself, there's no question I'll do whatever it takes to become a member and earn my place in the ranks of only the most Elite. With a taste for the deviant, I'm drawn to the darkest of desires, and no one ever leaves my bed unscathed.

My task: seduce Patience Noelle, St. Augustine's sweetheart and the mayor's beloved daughter—then break her heart.

Sinning is what I live for, and deviance is my passion. Failing has never been an option. But what happens when my sin becomes my curse—when destroying the only woman I've ever wanted is my key to protecting my sister?

Accept your sin wisely, for the tasks given to earn your place are not for the weak…they're for The Elite. This isn't just my chance, it's my legacy and reckoning.

I am Samuel Gunner.

I am Wrath.

UINCENDUM NATUS

PREFACE

the elite seven

Since 1942, The Elite Seven Society has created and guided influential leaders, molding the country into something better. This society was birthed by Malcom Benedict II, who wanted more for Americans. More wealth. More influence. More power. Some leaders have the skills, but not the influence, and that simply wasn't fair according to Mr. Benedict. He invested his own money and time to construct a society that bred the best of the best, year after year.

But to be the best, you must be ruthless.

Good leaders make sacrifices. Sometimes the sacrifices are hard, but the rewards are plentiful. Mr. Benedict made sure to indulge these leaders with their utmost desires. A devout Catholic himself, he designed a society that rewarded his leaders with the sins that were frowned upon. If they were giving up love and happiness and joy for the betterment of the country, they deserved something in its stead.

Pride, Envy, Wrath, Sloth, Greed, Gluttony, and Lust.

Choosing leaders for this society takes intense focus. Only seven are to be selected, and the investment and time are showered upon the new seven chosen every four years. The university's acting dean behaves as a liaison for the society, bringing the applicants to the predecessors so the selection may begin. The society members going out will bring forth a candidate the society votes on and approves.

After they are chosen, the initiates are given a token and an invitation to initiation. The initiation tests their character and ability to do what's right for the betterment of the society. Once the initiates pass their test, they are discreetly branded with the mark of the society and groomed through challenges during the course of their elite education to breed them into the influential people they were meant to be.

Once in The Elite Seven, there is no getting out. The money and power are their reward. Should they choose to stray or break the rules, the society strips them of everything. Anything they once had will be removed. Opportunities will never arise. They will no longer have the support of the society. To this day, there have been no known occurrences of anyone from the society having to be banished. Every young man and woman aspire to be a part of the elite group whispered about amongst the privileged. Anyone who is anyone knows of the group and secretly hopes their son or daughter is selected, for good fortune is showered on the family for decades to come.

WRATH

VII
UINCENDUM NATUS

UINCENDUM NATUS

PROLOGUE

Staring down at my math homework, I can't help but wonder why algebra was ever invented. Does anyone even use this stuff in real life? Or is it just put here for math teachers to torment us with?

"This shouldn't take you this long. Your sister can do this in her sleep," my grandfather sneers, squinting his wrinkled eyes at me. He is such a hateful man. It makes a lot of sense why my father lacks the ability to love us.

He was never taught how.

I slam my pencil down and shake my head. "Well, I'm not her, and it's useless learning this stuff. We can use calculators in school." I slide off my stool, making my way to the refrigerator to grab some juice. Our father is back in town, so of course the fridge is well stocked, and I'm making good use of the food before he leaves again.

Before I even have the carton out the refrigerator, the door slams, trapping my arm, making me howl as pain shoots right through to the bone of my forearm.

My heart races as fear blooms to life inside me. I know not to offend the elders in this family. I've let my temper get the better of me, and now I'll pay for it.

Grandfather doesn't come around often, but our latest nanny quit after she realized my father liked to fuck her when he was back in town, but never allow her to move past the easy lay status. She gave no notice when she left. She was just here one day and gone the next. Our father was away on business, so our grandmother had to step in to look after us until he could hire a new nanny. He returned home five hours ago, but has yet to make his presence known.

The pressure on the door intensifies as my grandfather pushes his weight against it, making me whimper like a fucking dog being scolded. I hate how weak I am. I make a promise to myself that I'll never be this weak again.

"You don't get to help your damn self to anything until this work is complete! You have no pride in yourself, Samuel. It's a trait you inherited from your vagrant mother. She was worthless too."

Pain slices into my heart at his words. I never got to meet my mother, but I know in my heart she was special, not the wretched woman everyone makes her out to be.

He releases his grip on the door, and my arm falls slack at my side, my pounding pulse vibrating right up to my elbow. How the hell am I going to use my pencil now? His wrinkled eyes bore into mine, taunting me, daring me to say something in retaliation.

But I won't.

I can't.

WRATH

And he knows it.

"Samuel."

Turning from the refrigerator, I look around to see my father standing there—all six-foot-two of him. As usual, he's wearing one of his Henry Poole bespoke suits. I don't think I've ever seen my father in anything but a suit. When you have the most exclusive tailor flying in from Saville Row in London to make you them, why would you wear anything else? His gray jacket is fastened in the middle with two pearl buttons hand lasered with our family crest. It's the smaller details that make the man, he always insists. He stares at me, shoving a hand in his trouser pocket. He looks uncomfortable. Hope blooms in my chest that he saw what just happened and is going to do something about it, but it vanishes with his next words.

"Where's Sabella?"

Going back to the table, I sit and attempt to pick up the pencil, wincing when a sharp stabbing pain throbs. I fight the tears threatening to spill over and gulp past the lump growing in my throat.

"I'm not sure. I think she said something about an extra credit project at school," I tell him, trying to keep my voice steady.

"At least one of them has some brain cells," my grandfather grunts, and I see the shame in my father's eyes. I embarrass him.

Sabella and I go to different schools. Hers is an all-girls Catholic finishing school. Mine is whatever school will accept me. I might be eleven years old, but I have a knack for getting into trouble.

My father nods and pulls his hand from his pocket before finding the cuff of his shirt and tugging it down lightly.

Sleeves should finish above the hand and show one-point-five centimeters of shirt cuff at all times. I know the mantra.

"I have someone coming to talk business with me," he says, his dark, brooding eyes holding mine.

My father is a domineering presence. He commands a room and everyone in it, and right now, he's commanding me to listen and obey. "She's bringing her daughter with her, and I need you to keep her company while we talk."

Business. Does he think I'm foolish? I've seen the sort of activity he does with women who come in and out—and the last thing you could call it is business.

"Yes, sir," I reply automatically. You don't say no to my father.

"I need you to behave, Samuel," he orders. "And we're not to be disturbed. For any reason. Your grandfather will be watching over you until your grandmother gets back from her appointment."

Dread prickles my skin.

"Yes, sir," I say again.

He lets out a huff of air, his stare still on me. He looks like he wants to say something more. Something important. But the moment is gone. "Your hair is getting long," he adds dismissively.

I frown, reaching up to touch it. "I'll get a haircut."

"I'll have Maria book an appointment right away," he says casually before leaving the room.

Who is Maria? Just as the thought passes through my mind, my grandfather taps his finger on the sheet of math homework. "Get this done, boy. I'll be informing the new nanny of how useless you are at completing basic math. She can tutor you."

I stare at the space where my father just stood in

confusion. Every conversation I've ever had with my father has been like that: awkward, uncomfortable. We're strangers, and neither of us will make any move to change that.

I'm not sure what I did to make him dislike me so much, but it must have been bad. Though, what could be so bad that becoming a ghost to your own children was the best outcome?

A few minutes later, I hear the doorbell, and I wait, pencil in hand, poised over my algebra.

"Samuel." It's my grandmother's voice. I look up to see the evil bitch's glare. She's really not happy about having to watch over Sabella and I the last couple days. It's been a huge inconvenience for her social calendar. No doubt I'll pay for it next week when my father goes away on another of his work trips. "This is Patience, Mayor Noelle's daughter." She smiles at Patience, but I can see from her tight smile how fake it is.

"Where's Father?" I ask, just to annoy her.

Her eyes narrow in on me. And then my grandfather's firm hand grips my arm right where the bruise is forming. Acid races up my gullet at the intense burn of pain. He tightens his hold, making me whimper.

"He's working in his office and doesn't want to be disturbed. It's a business meeting with Patience's mother, and you already know this. You may be dumb, but you're not deaf," he says, his eyes cutting to my grandmother, who's stroking Patience's shoulder.

Finally releasing my arm, he pats the stool next to me. "Maybe the girl can help you get this finished," he snaps.

My gaze travels to Patience. She's frowning, making her pretty face contort. "You any good at algebra?" I ask, and she nods enthusiastically.

"I'm this year's mathlete champion," she says, matter-of-fact. "Algebra is my jam." She smiles and comes over to join me. My grandfather grunts something under his breath and leaves the room, taking my grandmother with him.

"Well then, sit down, Ms. Mathlete."

I slide off my seat and head to the refrigerator while Patience sits down, dropping her purse on the table. "You want something to drink?" I ask, throwing a snide look to the doorway my grandparents retreated through. "We have orange juice or soda."

Patience smiles over at me. "I'm fine…unless you want to feed me? I'll work better with food in my stomach. Mom didn't stop for something on the way here and I'm starved."

"Now that I can do," I say. "We've got chicken, or shrimp and pork meatballs, some gumbo, or—" I look through the contents of the refrigerator.

"I'd just love a peanut butter and jelly sandwich, if that's not too much trouble."

I smile at her. "That actually sounds perfect." I start dragging all the ingredients out for a peanut and jelly sandwich, making sure to grab the carton of orange juice too. I plan to drink the whole thing.

I make a plate of sandwiches, and Patience teases me for eating like a starved man. She has no idea. This entire week my father hasn't been here, I've been living on scraps. But I won't complain. I never complain. Instead, I make sure Sabella has enough to eat and is blissfully unaware of the tragedy that is our lives.

We both reach for the last sandwich at the same time, causing Patience to knock her hand into my arm. It catches me off guard, making me gasp and cringe as splinters of pain run up my arm. I hiss in agony, gritting my teeth against the throbbing.

"Sam?" Patience queries, reaching forward and taking my hand in hers. I watch in silence as she rolls back the sleeve of my sweater, her eyes widening at the growing purple bruise forming on my pale skin. Her delicate fingers stroke over the mark, taking care not to add any pressure.

"Sam…"

"Don't," I say firmly, not wanting to hear her next words. I already know what they'll be. *Who did this?* I don't want to have to tell her this new mark is from my grandfather, and the old fading bruises are my grandmother's punishments.

I can feel my anger spiking.

The rage building.

I'm only eleven, but my anger is that of a full-grown man.

And why wouldn't it be? I'm treated like dirt every day of my life. There's only so much a person can take before they snap—before they decide enough is enough.

"Sam?" Patience whispers my name, and I glance across at her. She pulls the now snapped pencil from my grip and tugs down my sleeve. I flush in embarrassment. "Do you want to go get some fresh air?"

"Sure," I grit out, pushing back from the table.

Patience and I head outside, and I take in the muggy air. It's been raining, and clouds are rolling in the distance, warning of more rain to come.

"Are you okay?"

I stop my brooding and look at Patience with a forced smile. "Yeah, I'm fine. It's nothing new for me." I shrug.

"But you know that's not normal, right, Sam? You should tell someone," she tells me.

"Who would I tell?" I scoff. Her eyes hold pity, and it

makes me angry. I don't need her pity. I'd much rather let them take their spite out on me than direct it on my sister.

"Your father?" She frowns, and I decide I much prefer to see her smile.

Other than that one time I tried to tell my father what a psychotic bitch his mother was, I've never told another person. Once you realize the people who are supposed to love and care for you will do neither of those things, it seems pointless.

Instead, I'll bide my time until I can get the hell out of here.

"He grew up under their rule, Patience. We can't all have a perfect family like you."

"My family is far from perfect." She stares out into the distance, watching the rumbling clouds building.

"How about we forget about our families and have some fun?" I offer with a smirk.

She moves from foot to foot, studying me. "Why do I get the impression I'm going to get in trouble if I say yes?" She raises a brow.

With a shrug, I reach for her hand. "Because you like me, and you know I'm trouble."

"You think I like you, huh?" she teases, then slips her hand in mine and smirks. "Good job. I'm trouble too."

***

Patience giggles, despite placing her hands over her mouth to stop herself. Her laughter causes her huge brown eyes to expand wide. I hold a finger to my lips, willing her with my gesture to be quiet. We're hidden in the guest room closet

WRATH

where my grandparents have been staying. We came up here to wreak a little havoc with their crap—unscrew the lids on all their products, hide one sock of each pair, add some bugs to their bed…

Patience is a fresh of breath air in this house, and I feel free with her. My fear doesn't have such a firm grip with her close by. But our fun time ends when my grandfather comes back to the room to collect their belongings. It looks like they're leaving.

When Patience doesn't stop giggling from behind her hand, I take my own and place it over hers. She stills, her eyes locking with mine. My chest aches, and I don't know why. I can't breathe in here. The doors suddenly open, and I don't have time to react as I'm ripped from the closet by my hair.

"Stop it!" Patience screeches as I'm knocked to the floor.

"What are you two doing in there?" my grandfather bellows.

"Nothing," I call out, pushing up to my feet.

"Why do you have that girl in a closet?" he growls.

"We were just playing," Patience defends, but it doesn't matter what she tells him. He hates me and has already made up his mind I'm in the wrong.

"Don't you know I'm a bad kid, Patience?" I smirk. "Isn't that right, Grandpa?" I mock, wanting his attention on me and not her.

"Bad doesn't even begin to describe it," he grunts as he comes toward me using his walking cane to steady his steps. He's had to use a cane for as long as I have been alive. Father told us he sustained a poisonous snakebite and nearly lost his life when he was younger. Shame he didn't.

I snort on a laugh, and his eyes narrow on me.

"Something funny, Samuel?"

Patience, sensing the bitter tone in his voice, rushes to step in front of me.

"Nope," I reply.

"I think you should stop hurting him," Patience says, making my stomach fall to the floor.

My gaze moves to her quickly, then back to my grandfather, who's glaring at my feisty little defender.

"It's fine, Patience. Just go downstairs," I say, moving to stand in front of her.

My grandfather is facing us, his mouth pulled into a thin smile.

"No, it's not fine, Sam. It's abuse!" she yells angrily.

Jesus Christ, I think I'm in love with this girl.

But she's going to cause me a whole world of trouble if she doesn't shut her mouth.

"Abuse?" my grandfather sneers. "How dare you! It's discipline, young lady. Clearly you don't get enough of it at home."

He moves toward Patience, all pretences forgotten. I watch in almost slow motion as his hand rears back, but I step in his way and take the blow to the cheek so Patience isn't subjected to his hate. I grunt in pain, ignoring Patience's gasp from beside me.

"Sam!" she calls my name.

My grandfather tries to push past me to get to Patience, but he'll have to go through me if he wants to hurt this girl.

"You little bastard." Lifting his cane, he belts me with it. Pain explodes across my arm and shoulder.

"Get away from him," Patience screams.

"Run, Patience," I bark, grunting as the cane comes down again, hitting me across the back and forcing me to my knees. Fire alights my back.

WRATH

He glares down at me, swinging at me again and again.

My vision blurs, and every part of my body stings like a thousand angry bees have attacked me.

I *should* stop him.

I *could* stop him.

I'm big for my age, and he's old and getting frailer by the day. But, of course, I don't stop him. It's been beaten into me to take my punishments like a man. Like a Gunner. I lift my arms to protect my face as he hits me again, and again, and again.

"I'll get your dad," Patience cries.

I thought she'd already left.

I squeeze my eyes closed and pray it will be over soon as the cane comes down again.

"That's my son, Mother!" my father roars from his office. "My flesh and blood! *Your* goddamn flesh and blood!"

"Oh, please, don't remind me," she scoffs. "Anyway, he must have done something to incense your father like that. People don't just lose control for no reason, Maxwell," my grandmother replies calmly.

"Does it matter? He's a Gunner. No one has the right to lay a hand on my son. Father drew blood, for Christ's sake. And in front of the mayor's daughter no less."

Patience's tear-streaked face as she was ushered out of the house by her mother will haunt me forever.

Sabella squeezes my hand, but my gaze is fixed on the closed door of my father's office.

My grandfather is gone, though it was his own choice.

My father didn't throw him out and insist he never return like a normal father would. Grandmother has been in there for over an hour arguing with him.

"Don't be such a dreamer, Maxwell. Of course, it matters. He's a spoiled brat; they both are. A firm hand now and then never does any harm." I hear the clink of my father's whisky bottle as Grandmother pours herself a drink.

My stomach clenches in anger. Sabella is anything but spoiled. She's a people pleaser. She's kind and pure. She's good, not spoiled.

My father doesn't reply for a long while, but I can't decide if that's a good thing. I look over at Sabella. She's crying again, hot tears silently streaming down her cheeks. I pull her to my chest, wrapping my arm around her shoulders, and kiss the top of her head, ignoring my own pain screaming at me not to have contact with anything.

"It's okay," I say, but it's not.

"You have a meeting in San Francisco tomorrow. Leave everything to me. I'll get it all cleared up by the time you return," Grandmother purrs.

God, I hate her. Almost as much as I hate him.

"I don't think he means to cause trouble," my father says, and I frown. I've never heard him say anything good about me before.

"Now, that, I don't believe," she replies with a dry laugh. "It comes from *her* DNA, not ours."

"Don't start, Mother," he sighs.

"I'm just saying, if you would have married someone of pureblood instead of that vagrant girl, we wouldn't be in this position," she tuts, and I hear the clink of glass again. "And then for her to go die like she did, leaving you with those babies."

WRATH

"I said not now!" he yells, and the sound of glass smashing is loud and clear. Sabella flinches next to me, and I pull her closer. "It wasn't her fault she died, Mother. She didn't choose to leave us!"

"So, whose fault is it, if not hers? Theirs?"

A chill runs down my spine.

Surely she can't be suggesting we could have killed our mother. We were just babies, seconds old and entirely innocent.

"Sammy?" Sabella whispers from next to me.

"It's no one's fault," my father mutters, sounding defeated.

"It's always someone's fault, Maxwell. No one would blame you for getting rid of them. You've played along with this for long enough. You've proven your point to the world. A Gunner never shirks his responsibilities. But whether you like it or not, they are responsible for her death."

"She died giving birth," he says, tired.

"Giving birth to *him*," she corrects. "And look how he's repaid her memory."

"Sammy?" Sabella whispers louder this time, and I turn to look at her. She's still crying, but now, so am I. Her face is blurry through the tears in my eyes, and I realize I'm squeezing her hand too tightly.

"How you can even bear to look at them is beyond me," Grandmother says.

There's silence, then…

"I can't," my father replies, his voice thick with emotion. "They did kill her. They took her from me, and I wish I could forgive them, but I can't. I know rationally it wasn't their fault, but inside, I can't get past it. I still miss her so much."

Sabella is crying, and so am I, but it's nothing compared

to the anguished sounds coming from my father's office. My father is crying.

"There, there, Maxwell."

"They didn't mean to, and I know that," he sobs, his deep voice rumbling through the house—through my soul. "But I hate them for it. For taking her from me."

I stumble to my feet, needing to get away from here, away from him, away from the pain filling this house. I don't need to hear anything else he has to say.

I take off running out of the house into the rain. I don't even know where I'm going, not that it matters. What matters is I'm not inside those walls anymore.

I run until my legs ache and my lungs burn. Until my tears dry up and my clothes are soaked through with sweat and blood from my cane wounds re-opening. I run and run and run.

But I'll never be able to run from the memories or the words that haunt me.

We killed her.

I killed her.

I'm a murderer.

The crushing misery and guilt that drags at my muscles is agonizing. Everything hurts. My fractured mind, my broken body, my tortured soul. I run until I can't run anymore. Until I'm broken down and have to put myself back together as someone new.

I stop running, my legs tired and lungs exhausted. All my tears have dried up, and I make a promise to myself to never let someone hurt me like that again.

I let the pain harden me and give me strength.

If they want someone to hate, someone to blame, someone to be worthy of their abuse, I'll give them just that.

VII
UINCENDUM NATUS

ONE

8 years later

"You disgust me," my father sneers, his salt and pepper beard twitching as he grinds his back teeth together. "I can't even comprehend how we're related." Moving around the large, ornate desk at the back of his study, he shakes his head, his left hand moving to undo his middle jacket button.

He hates me.

Good.

The feeling is fucking mutual.

I smile, and he narrows his eyes. "She'd be so disappointed in you," he says with total and utter disdain for me.

It's my turn to grind my teeth now. How fucking dare he bring her up. "Good that she can't see me then, isn't it?"

I bite out, thrusting my hands deep into my pockets, my chin lifted in defiance.

"Careful, boy." He glares, but the hate in his eyes is nothing new. "If you can't watch that tongue of yours, I'll do it for you." His idle threat is nothing to be afraid of, and he knows it.

The days of being afraid of my father are long over. There isn't anything he can do or say to control me anymore. His words slide off me like oil, and he hasn't raised his hand to me since I was eleven and took the beating from his asshole father. That was the last time I allowed anyone to raise their hand to me. A month after that, he left on a work trip, and when he returned, neither of us were the same people.

Fucker doesn't scare me.

I scare him.

Sometimes, I even scare myself.

I'm a cannon set loose upon the world, filled with anger and demons. There's no backstabbing or behind-the-scenes staging from me. No, I prefer to fight with my fists and see the blood spill for myself. I enjoy the look of shock and horror on people's faces when I lash out at them, beating them into submission.

Submission. I enjoyed submission in the bedroom too. I expected any woman who shared my bed to be a body for me to use as I saw fit, and I never had any problem finding willing participants.

"This is your last warning, Samuel," my father continues, like I'm listening to him when he knows I'm not. "I don't have the time, energy, or desire to keep pulling you out of the shit you constantly get yourself in. It's obvious you like being buried neck deep in it."

WRATH

He stares at me, waiting for a reaction, already knowing he isn't going to get one.

"Are we done?" I ask with disinterest. My father, the great Maxwell Gunner, is a careful man in all parts of his life. Everything and everyone is perfectly calculated and controlled—except me. I'm the untameable. A relentless storm in its pursuit to destroy everything he's worked so hard to achieve. And I love nothing more than pushing him to lose his cool daily.

He's my father, by blood only. This man has never been anything but a dark shadow in me and my sister's life. The hate is vibrant between us.

His dark eyes glare harder, his nostrils flaring. I let a slow smirk crawl up my face at the satisfaction of pissing him off.

"No, Samuel, we're not done yet. Let me tell you this, and listen well, because I won't be repeating it…"

I yawn.

"I put in a special favor with George Griffin to get you into this school."

"Who the fuck is he?"

"He's the Dean of St. Augustine, Samuel," he snaps. "Listen to me. There are no more warnings…"

I pull my hands from my pockets and crack my knuckles. *St. Augustine. It's happening.*

"This is the last time you get to embarrass me and shame the family name. The last school you will get expelled from. I'm not going to continue to waste money on your education if you don't care about it."

"I don't need shit from you," I throw back over my shoulder as I turn to walk away. My lips curl in disgust for him and everything he stands for. I raise my hand up and show him the middle finger.

He slams a hand on his desk, the sound echoing off the wood. "I won't have you ruin her legacy like you've ruined all our lives," he grinds out as I stalk away, letting the door slam closed behind me.

Her legacy.

Fuck him.

Fuck him, fuck her, and fuck that fucking noise.

I've had her death thrown in my face my entire life. For a woman I never had the chance to meet, she sure did cast a black fucking shadow over me.

My father can keep his money and my inheritance. As he's told me a million times over the years, I don't deserve it anyway—it's her blood money. But am I willing to do this to Sabella?

I storm through the large oval foyer and head to the front door, my footsteps echoing around the large space. I had plans, big plans, and soon enough, he won't be able to do shit to control me. Soon enough, my so-called father is going to regret ever pissing me off.

"Sammy!" Sabella calls my childhood nickname as I pass the curved staircase. "Sammy, wait."

I stop and turn back to her, watching as she takes them two at a time, her long auburn hair flowing out behind her in dark waves. She comes to a stop in front of me, and I flinch at the look of disappointment in her eyes.

Sabella, my twin sister—the only person in this world who can make me feel bad for any of the shit I do.

"What did he say? Are you starting at my school?" she asks with concern.

St. Augustine is an elite school for only the very best of society. It was her school, not mine. Because I didn't deserve to go there. She knew it, I knew it, Max knew it. Hell, the Dean of St. Augustine knew it. What none of them knew was I had a plan, and St. Augustine had always been it.

"He says so, yeah," I grunt out. "Ain't any other schools left to send me to." I chuckle.

"Sammy, that's not funny."

I roll my eyes at her, and she tsks me, already moving on from my quip. She never stays mad at me for long. "My little brother is going to make the girls wild."

I'm her little brother by three-point-four seconds, and she likes to hold that over me. She's older and wiser than me and our father—the mom we never got. I hate that I'm going to her school. Hate that I might mess things up for her. There's no doubt I'll find a way to, whether it be sleeping with her friends, getting into a fight, or just tarnishing her reputation with mine. That's what I always did.

Sabella and I are similar in looks—tan skin, dark hair, dark eyes, and full mouths—but that's where our similarities end. While she buries herself in her studies, I barely make it to class. While she helps out at the Humane Society on weekends and fills her evenings with making coffee for anyone who shows up at the homeless shelter, I fill my weekends with parties, women, and booze, and my evenings with illegal underground fights.

We are complete opposites, yet joined by the inexplicable connection only twins have.

She leans over and pulls me into her arms like I'm one of her lost puppies at the shelter, and I let her, allowing her to mother me in the way only she knows best, making me feel both loved and wanted, despite being a complete and utter disappointment.

I finally pull out of her arms to find her smiling, and I can't stop my own smile from mirroring hers.

"I promise, you won't even know I'm there," I say as I realize she isn't sad about me going to her school and potentially ruining shit for her, but excited at the prospect of having me there. Her beaming smile tells me everything I need to know about how she feels.

She pushes my arm, though I don't move even a millimeter. "I have no doubt everyone will know my little brother is there within the hour." She laughs and flicks her hair back off her shoulder. "Just stay away from my friends."

"That depends," I say, "are they hot?"

She punches me in the shoulder, and I play wince, making her laugh. Her face lights up when she smiles, and I wonder if this is what our mom looked like when she laughed. I bury the thought before it gains substance.

God, she's pretty. I hope to hell she meets a good guy who'll treat her like she deserves. She's clever and kind and beautiful, and she deserves the fucking world. Our mom would have been proud as hell of the woman she is becoming. Pity she isn't here to see it.

"What are you saying?" I ask, feigning shock.

She turns and starts to head back up the stairs. "You're not exactly the shy, reserved kind, Sammy. Girls will be fawning over you, and you'll have the female teachers eating out of the palm of your hand."

"If only I had them eating—"

"Sammy!" she laughs, cutting me off. "You're disgusting."

I chuckle and open the front door before looking

back at her, only to find her gazing down at me, her expression sober. Jesus Christ, women are confusing, probably why I liked to fuck 'em and leave 'em.

"What now?" I ask with an almost imperceptible sigh, though I could never be mad at her.

"Just stay out of trouble. Like, real trouble. Fuck who you want, but stay out of fights…for me. Don't give him anymore ammunition than he already has." Her gaze flits to our father's closed door. "He'll just make your life hell."

I suck in my bottom lip and flare out my chest. "Don't worry about him, Sab. I've got that shit handled."

She frowns and nods, but doesn't look convinced.

"You trust me?" I ask, moving toward her. I smile when she nods. "Then trust that I have him handled."

I reach the bottom of the stairs and take her hand in mine, rubbing my thumb over the top of it as I look up at her.

"He hasn't gotten where he is in life by being a pushover," she says, her doe eyes drowning me.

I kiss the back of her hand and let it go as I start to walk away again. "Sab, am I not the great Samuel 'The Machine' Gunner?" I smirk. "Ain't a man out there who's a match for me." I wink at her like the cocky motherfucker I am and leave, heading over to my car before sliding into the driver's seat.

My car is a gun-metal grey Porsche Cayman with tinted windows and red and grey leather seats. She is the only other female in my life I give a damn about.

I start her up, loving the sound as she roars to life, then I speed down our long driveway, hoping I can outrun my demons.

Of course, you can't really outrun something that lives inside you, and my demons are buried real fucking deep.

Soul deep.

Some might even say I'm the devil himself.

VII
UINCENDUM NATUS

TWO

I throw my cigarette to one side and crouch on my haunches, running a hand across the smooth marble of my mother's grave. My fingertips dip inside the indentations of her name, and I follow the lines from left to right.

LOUISA SAMANTHA GUNNER
You shall live forever.

I've read those words hundreds of times over the years, and I still don't really get them. They don't sound like something my grandparents would say, and my father isn't exactly the sentimental type. Besides, love didn't save her. Money didn't save her. Nothing saved her.

My mother is dead. Has been since the day I was born. Lucky fucking me.

I shake my head in annoyance. It's all bullshit and doesn't really matter, but still, that doesn't stop me from coming back here at least once a week in my quest to understand who I am and who she was.

I hate her and love her in equal measures. She's been apotheosized by my father, yet no one else in the family speaks of her. I'm normally a good judge of character, but it's hard to get a feel for someone with such varied responses.

My father talks about her like she was the very embodiment of heaven, yet my grandmother, and anyone else in our family you might care to ask, despises her. They make that obvious by the sheer fact that they refuse to talk about her. And if you dare to even say her name, be prepared to catch shit for it.

I have no idea what my mom did to deserve such hatred, but it must have been real fucking bad for people to continue to hate a dead woman and her children after all these years.

I pull the wilting flowers from the heavy vase at the base of the large marble slab and replace them with new ones before sitting down on one of the three steps. I once overheard my father telling our maid daisies weren't allowed in the house because they reminded him of her, so, once a week, that's what I do—I bring my mom daisies.

My mom is buried away from the rest of the Gunner family, like they are ashamed of her—the shameful family secret. The grave had been in disrepair, unloved, unkempt, and I'd walked past it several times before I brushed the dirt off the marble and saw her name.

As usual, the thought only made me hate Maxwell more.

WRATH

"I've got another fight later," I say to her, the warm New Orleans breeze carrying my words away. "It's a big one. A lot of cash, and a lot of credibility if I win." I chuckle, and add, *"When* I win."

I glance around, wishing she had a prettier view. She's at the far end of the cemetery, away from prying eyes. Her grave faces someone's backyard and their rickety, old, falling down fence. I wish she had a view of something good, something pretty. Not that it really matters. At least she isn't in one of the popular cemeteries or our family crypt, with money-grabbing tour guides constantly snooping around and visitors taking pictures while they learn about New Orleans' dark history.

Yeah, a shitty back fence was better than that.

"I've gotta go." Sighing, I stand up. I grab a handful of the older daisies and take the short walk over to the grave next to my mom's before placing them in the vase there. I dust off a couple of cobwebs that have formed, then head back to my mom's grave. I don't know when exactly I started doing that, but I hate that no one ever comes to see these graves. They were people once, and everyone deserves someone who cares, right?

I kiss my index and middle finger, then place them over her name. "See you soon, Mom," I say, then walk down the steps, turning to look up at the stone angel on top of her grave before I leave. Something about it always makes me feel better, calmer.

I only ever meant to come here once, maybe twice. Curiosity as to why your own father hates you, and your grandparents are ashamed of you, leads you down dark paths. I've never gotten the answers, but I do find peace here…sometimes. Almost like she's here with me, listening to me and telling me everything is going to be all right.

I'm not sure if she's right about that, but I have to grab all the love and peace I can in this world, even if it's from a dead woman I never met.

The crowd is wild tonight. Chants and cheers of my name bounce around the dilapidated basement, making my ears ring and the walls quake. I fucking love it. The stench of sweat, blood, and stale beer. The testosterone that fills the air, thick enough to make my dick hard and the women horny.

"Gunner, Gunner, Gunner, Gunner…!"

I let the excitement of the crowd rest on my shoulders, allowing each roar of my name to sink into my skin as I'm lifted onto Sy, my trainer's, shoulders. I raise my fists in the air and the chanting gets louder.

I won the fight.

Of course I did. There was never any doubt.

I let the calmness flow over me. The rage dissipates. The only time I ever feel relief from the anger that bubbles inside me is when I am fighting, beating another man to a bloody mess, or when I fuck a woman into submission. Right now, I can enjoy the calm that washes over me while my anger is subdued, the blood of André Michaels, my now unconscious opponent, feeding my fucking hungry, tortured soul.

"Can I get a final cheer for the winner of tonight's heavyweight title and seven-thousand in cold hard cash?

WRATH

Let's hear it for Sam *'The Machine' Gunnnnner!"* Daniel, the organizer, hands over the cash in a large brown envelope. I smile and let the roar of the crowd soothe me again. "Sam, do you have anything you want to say before I have to shut this shit down? The police are apparently on their way to ruin our fucking night." He laughs.

Sy drags the metal barrel over into the center of the circle where I'm standing. He scowls at me, and I pull out his cut of the money and slap it against his chest. He takes it before shaking his head and storming away. I can't blame him. It's a lot of fucking money, and I earned it. We all have. But I have a point to prove, and this is the only way I know how to do it.

I've been winning these fights for months, and now it's time to step it up. I need to get someone's attention, and short of killing my opponent, this is the only way left to do it.

The room silences as I drop my cash into the barrel, all seven-thousand, before reaching and taking the mic from Daniel. He looks just as confused as everyone else. I smirk, enjoying the control I have over everyone.

People have their cell phones out and are filming me. Cameras flash all around me. I throw my arms up and let another roar from my fans roll over me.

"Thanks to Sy, my friend and trainer, and of course thanks to André for being such a goddamn pussy." I nod to where André is being carried out, the red blood almost blinding against his brown skin. "And thanks to everyone for showing up to watch me win time and time again." I look down into the barrel, at my money, and force a bitter smile to my face as I flick the lighter in my hand. "But mostly, thanks to me. When it comes to this shit,

I'm better than the best—I'm the motherfucking elite!" I make eye contact with as many cameras as possible, driving my point home.

I drop the lighter into the barrel, and it goes up in flames with a loud whoosh as the gasoline Sy put in the bottom ignited. The crowd gasps, and I push the mic back into Daniel's hands.

"What the fuck?" he yells, his eyes wide as his gaze flits from me to the burning barrel of money. "If I would have known you were gonna burn it, I wouldn't have given it to you!"

I don't have time to answer him, not that I would have, as the guys who run security come charging in. "Police are almost here! Get the fuck out now!"

The crowd starts to run in every direction, dispersing in seconds, me and the money forgotten. At least for now. There's no way this won't be talked about, texted about. My little scene will be all over social media before the hour is up.

Daniel gives me one last shocked look over his shoulder as he makes it to the door. "You comin'?"

Shaking my head, I salute him before lighting a cigarette from the flames coming from the barrel, then I sit down next to my fucking masterpiece with a grin on my face.

I don't run for anyone or anything, especially not when I'm intending on getting caught.

To get out from under Maxwell, and my entire family's grip, I need money. Money not provided through the Gunner name. I want to stand on my own two feet and stare down at Maxwell as he cowers below, watching as I burn everything he's ever worked for to the ground. He

WRATH

didn't think I was worthy of him, his name, my sister's school, and what came hidden within that school.

Lucky for me, I know more than he thinks I do, and all this, the fights, getting noticed, was my plan. I was going to rock the foundations he built his future on.

The Elite Seven is a secret society at St. Augustine, and I plan to become one of them. To prove my worth, be part of something bigger than the Gunner name. Only the best of the best are invited into The Elite. The rich, the dominant, the people in society who make a fucking difference. Whisperings of the power this group wields. The money they have at their disposal. Small clippings of information—of people brought into power, of lawsuits disappearing, of what The Elite can do for a person. It all appealed to me.

It's the real fucking deal. And I want in. This is where I belong.

I can screw my father over with the help of The Elite. Take him down and destroy him if I'm part of them—and he'd be powerless to stop me. He would see he doubted me all my life, but he was wrong.

So, I've worked and researched and fought to make myself known, heard, important—all in hopes they'll take notice of me.

And tonight is the final piece of the puzzle going into place.

The Elite is for the strong, not the weak. The important, not the unnoticed. And I've made sure I'm both of these things.

VII
UINCENDUM NATUS

THREE

My father stares at me from the doorway. "Get up," he grits out as calmly as he can.

I lift my hands up from the table and jangle my chained wrists as loudly as possible. "No can do, Maxwell," I say, biting out his name. "Cops cuffed me. It was real embarrassing. Pretty sure someone might have caught it on camera too. Sorry about that. Hope no one shows Grandma." I fake grimace, knowing how much shit he'll get from the old witch.

He tries to hide it, but I see the spark of anger behind his eyes as he turns to the female officer next to him. "Get those goddamn cuffs off him now!" he bellows.

"I'd watch your tone, Mr. Gunner. I'm not one of your employees you can just order about," she snaps before stepping away from him.

WRATH

"No? Because I'm certain the healthy contribution the Gunner Foundation makes to this precinct every year means I get to do just about anything I want. Now, get those cuffs off him." As usual, even though his tone is sharp and dangerous, he's calm and composed.

The officer is calm and composed, and probably would have been pretty if it weren't for the uptight look that graces her face every time she glances at me. She comes toward me quickly, pulling out the key and leaning over so she can uncuff me from the table. She's close to me, and I make a point of taking a deep breath as she gets even closer.

"Well, don't you smell fucking delicious, officer," I say into her ear. Her hands still momentarily before continuing. "I'd love to have you across my knee," I say as she finally unlocks the cuffs and stands back up, her cheeks burning bright red.

"I *will* taser you," she says through clenched teeth. "In the balls."

The comment makes me bark out a laugh. "Promises, promises."

"Samuel," Maxwell warns.

I'm still only wearing my thin gym shorts and sneakers, my chest bare and bloody. My hands are still bandaged from the fight and blood is splattered across both of them. I look like shit, no doubt smell even worse, yet there's no denying the look in her eyes right now.

I stand up, pushing my chair back, and move around her toward my father. He has his cell in his hand, tapping away at it impatiently, and glances up as I get closer to him.

"Look at the state of you, Samuel," he bites out.

"Have you no pride in yourself?"

I put a bloody hand to my chest. "Sorry, Maxwell, I didn't quite hear that," I mock, knowing how much he hates me calling him by his name, but I sure as shit am not about to call him father, and there isn't a chance in hell I'm calling him sir.

The young police officer moves to my left. "There's some paperwork left to fill out, then you're free to go. I'll meet you both by the front desk."

Maxwell moves to one side as she leaves the room, but his eyes stay glued to me, his furious gaze burning into mine. I sigh and stretch my arms above my head.

"Come on. Let's get going. I need a fucking shower before I head out tonight. I have a party to go to."

Max grabs me, catching me by surprise, and slams me up against the wall so hard, the air gusts from my lungs. His fingers dig into the hard muscles of my shoulder as he stares darkly into my face, his rage matching my own.

"That's the last fight you will *ever* be in. Do you hear me now, son?"

"Not your son," I grunt out.

"Oh, how I wish you weren't my son, Samuel. If I could go back in time and choose her over you, I would. Be that as it may, it looks like, at least for now, we're stuck with each other, so let me make something clear to you."

The world blurs as my anger descends over me in a red mist.

I'm going to kill him.

I'm going to cut his fucking head off and shove it up his ass if he doesn't get the fuck off me in about five seconds.

"You break my rules one more time and you're done.

WRATH

I'm through with you," he continues, oblivious to the fact that I'm an inferno ready to erupt and destroy him. "Your grandfather and grandmother are already through with you. In fact, let's just say the entire family is through with you. All you have left is Sabella, and she just pities you."

I glare back equally as hard, and he smirks at me before letting me go.

"You think you're so smart, that you have everything under control."

I shake my head. "I just don't give a shit about your threats."

"No?" he goads.

I shake my head. "No."

"Then how about this. Sort your shit out or your both cut off. No inheritance, for either of you. You don't care what happens to you—that's fine, so do it for her. Because one more fuck up, and you're both done," he snarls.

I shake my head, the anger surging through me making me shake. "You fucking piece of shit!"

I grit my teeth and keep my features blank. I'll never give him the satisfaction of letting him know when his words get to me.

He steps back, looking me up and down before straightening his suit. "It looks like this is one fight you won't get to win, son."

I squeeze my hands into fists and bite back the words I want to unleash on him. My rage flares to life like fireworks. I take a deep breath, letting my chest rise as it fills with air, then slowly let it out. He wins? I'll show the sorry son of a bitch who wins.

His hard gaze holds mine. "This is the very last time we have this conversation," he says, then turns to leave.

I step away from the wall. "Hey, Dad?"

He turns, a frown on his face at my choice of words. He raises an eyebrow at me. "What?"

"Go fuck yourself," I snarl.

Shock quickly turns to disappointment before he turns away with a shake of his head, leaving me alone.

"Go motherfucking fuck yourself!" I roar, kicking the chair and table, enjoying the screech as they clatter across the floor. "Fucking prick!"

I drag my hands through my unruly hair and take a couple breaths as I try to calm myself down. It's no good. I need to fight or fuck or I'm going to explode. The inferno within me blazes. All I can think about is chasing my sack of shit father down the street and tearing him apart, piece by fucking piece.

I leave the room and head to the front desk to grab my stuff. The female officer is behind the desk with her head down, but she looks up as I approach before reaching down to her side and lifting a brown leather duffle bag.

"You need to sign here for your belongings," she says, pointing to a sheet of paper in front of her as she passes me a clear bag with the few things I had on me when I was brought in. "And your father left this for you," she says, her gaze roving over my bare chest as she hands me the duffle bag. Despite her job, she's eye-fucking me like I'm a stick of cotton candy and she wants a lick of my sugary goodness. I'd fucking let her too. Pussy is pussy.

"You should probably get changed before you head out," she says with a jerk of her chin toward the male bathroom. "We don't want to be arresting you for indecent exposure."

"Care to join me?" I reply bluntly. She scoffs and

WRATH

shakes her head, and I smirk, casting a casual glance around us. "There's no one here to stop you, officer."

She shakes her head again, her jaw hanging down. "Are you serious?"

"About fucking you? Yeah." I nod.

"I'm a police officer, Mr. Gunner, and you are a criminal, in case you've forgotten," she says with disbelief.

My smirk widens, and I lean in. "That's what'll make it feel so good." I take a step away from the counter, grabbing the bag as I do. "Your loss." I shrug with a chuckle and head to the restroom to change.

Good old Dad can't have his son embarrassing him anymore than he already has by walking out of the police station half naked. Clearly, he stopped on his way over to pick them up for me because everything still has tags. I snort a laugh as I slide on the dress shirt, ignoring the stupid as fuck tie he got me. Fucker has dressed me like I'm a lawyer getting ready for court. Actually, maybe that's appropriate after all.

Once dressed, I leave the bathroom and head back out into the station, winking to the officer behind the desk as I leave. Shame she's such an uptight bitch. I could have had a lot of fun with her.

Back outside, early evening has turned into night, my favorite time, and the streets are coming alive. My car is parked just around the block thanks to Sy. He's a good friend and a great trainer. It's a damn shame he's heading out to LA in search of greener pastures. I've always been able to rely on him for just about anything. I'm going to miss him. Still, if things go how I expect them to, I'll have a whole band of brothers by my side soon enough.

VII
UINCENDUM NATUS

FOUR

It's late. So late, some may say it's early. The party I'm at is still going strong, despite the lateness. I didn't really want to party after the day I've had, but Daniel insisted this was *the* party to be at. It's being held in the French Quarter in a beautifully restored apartment building. The whole place stinks to high heaven of wealth and excess. Daniel and one of his friends crashed the gym earlier, fucking around on the high-tech treadmill and almost dropping the heavy weights on Daniel's foot. They'd almost gotten themselves kicked out of the party. Apparently, that's the only room in this place that's a no-go area.

Whoever lives here must be a real boring fuck if the gym is his special place.

The music's still banging. The people who remain sway to the heavy beats booming from the huge floor-standing speakers in the large living room. The lights pulse, giving everything an almost ethereal glow. Or maybe that's the effect of whatever I took earlier. This isn't the sort of party Daniel usually goes to, where red cups and cheap beer prevail. This place is classy as fuck. Expensive liquor bottles line the large kitchen island, and I snatch a glass from the tray on the table and tip some whisky into it before grabbing a handful of ice from the champagne bucket, dropping them in my drink with a splash.

I take a swig of it, humming in satisfaction as the liquid slides down my throat. Fuck, that's good stuff. My appreciation for good whisky is the only thing Maxwell and I share, so I'm used to drinking decent stuff, but this is so much better than even the most expensive whisky I've imbibed.

I pull my cell from my pocket and stare at the twelve missed calls from Sabella before pushing it back into my pocket.

I'm pissed off.

Pissed off and high.

Now is not the time to talk to her.

I've heard nothing about, or from, The Elite since burning my seven grand and getting myself arrested yesterday. I'm beginning to think I imagined the whole Elite bullshit. That maybe they were a figment of my imagination. It was only an overheard conversation that had set me on this path anyway, so I've obviously fucked up my facts somewhere along the line.

I take another sip, thinking back to that day.

"I want Sabella in. She deserves this. She's the perfect candidate," Maxwell's voice rings out in a hushed tone from his office.

"I don't think she could stomach The Elite. The things that are required are made for a particular type of person, and I don't see that perfect daughter of yours having any of the desired qualities required, Maxwell," a woman's voice I don't recognize replies.

I scowl and move closer to the door so I can hear better. Elite? What the hell is The Elite?

"Sabella may be an innocent, but that doesn't mean she won't be suitable. I have the funds, and she'll be ready to pledge when the time comes. I really—"

"What about the boy? Samuel? He seems like more of an Elite fit," she says, cutting him off. My attention piques even more, and I glance around the lobby to make sure no one is near. *"I hear he's rebellious. A wild one, as they say."*

Maxwell laughs. It's deep and rumbling and grates on every one of my nerves. My hands clench into tight fists, and my jaw ticks with annoyance.

"Samuel isn't Elite quality," he says simply, as if that's enough of an explanation.

"No?"

"No."

"And why's that?" she replies. I hear the click-clacking of her heels as she walks around Maxwell's office. The sound cuts off her next words to me, but the slam of Maxwell's hand on the desk is easy to distinguish.

"I said no!" he yells. *"He's not good enough."*

"Says you."

"He's too rash, too reckless, and he can't be trusted. Sabella is the one you want. The one The Elite needs."

The other woman laughs, the sound like a witch's cackle.

WRATH

"Let me make something very clear to you. The Elite don't need anyone, Mr. Gunner. People need The Elite. We'll take Sabella, but only if we get the brother enrolled at St. Augustine too. I have a feeling he'll be useful to us. Maybe not Elite, but useful all the same."

There's silence for a long time, and I scowl at the closed door, wishing I was inside to see this other person, but mostly so I could see the look on Maxwell's face. I've never met anyone who held anything over him, but this woman—this Elite—clearly does.

"I'll need to think on it," he finally replies.

"Don't think too long, or the choice will be taken from you. The Elite don't wait for anyone," she bites out. "The Elite is for just that—The Elite. The top of society. Samuel is already on our radar, but Sabella...well, she's done nothing to stand out to us. Nothing to catch our attention. My favors extend to you for a limited time only. My brother can never know of this offer."

"Fine," Maxwell replies.

Her shoes click-clack on the floor again, coming toward the door, and I dart back up the stairs, making it to the top just as she opens the office door and leaves.

I try to catch a glimpse of her, but the most I get is long black hair pulled back in a hairband.

I head out to the balcony, taking in a lungful of New Orleans' air. I feel antsy, despite the concoction of drugs and drink in my system. My mood is dark, and the more I'm left to think, the darker it gets.

Laughter erupts from farther down the balcony, and I

look across at the two guys talking. They look like they're sharing some inside joke, their friendship clearly strong. I've never had that—a real friendship. I've never really wanted it, but tonight, for some reason, seeing these two makes me yearn for something more than the bleak existence I live in.

Two women make their way over to the two guys before draping themselves over them and giggling. Their dresses are so short and lowcut, their asses are practically hanging out, and their huge tits bulge from the top. One of the guys grabs a woman by the waist and drags her body to his. He leans in, gripping her face in his hands, and plunges his tongue into her mouth. She practically melts at his contact. Looks like someone has the Romeo touch.

"Samuel," Daniel calls my name and gets up from the wrought iron chair he's sitting in. He grabs the hand of the girl he's with and starts walking toward me. He doesn't belong here, in this place, with these types of people. He stands out by a mile with his scruffy clothes and bedraggled hair. Not to mention, the guy's out of his head, his skin pale and sweaty, and his eyes practically rolling.

He places a hand on my shoulder as he reaches me, pulling to a stop as he drags the girl he's with against his chest. "This pretty little thing's been staring at you all night," he slurs, kissing the top of her head. "Can't seem to get her to believe I'm the better man, though." He shrugs and laughs.

The girl's petite. She smiles up at me through thick, dark lashes that can't possibly be real.

"That's because you don't know what you're talking about," I say, side-eyeing Daniel. "Every man and woman in here knows I'm the better man."

"Is that so?" he replies.

"Brother, you know I only ever speak the truth," I reply darkly.

Daniel lets out a high-pitched laugh. "That's true." He turns to the girl. "Casey—"

"Connie," she corrects. "It's Constance, but my friends call me Connie."

"Connie, this man right here will answer any question honestly."

She lets out a nervous laugh, and I light up a joint, watching her.

"What's so weird about that?" she asks, shrugging out from under Daniel's weight as he leans on her heavily, too drunk to stand up on his own accord anymore.

He sways and stumbles back into a patio chair with another laugh. "Ask him. Ask him anything. It's fucking hilarious."

Connie turns to look at me, puzzled. She chews on her bottom lip in thought for a moment before finally deciding on her question. "Okay, what day is it?"

I roll my eyes. "Tuesday."

She giggles. "I don't get it."

Daniel reaches for the joint in my hand, and I let him take it. "No, no, you have to ask him a real question. Watch." He looks up at me, and I shake my head.

"Don't do it, man. You know you never like the answers you get," I warn.

Daniel's smile falls, but he still asks his damn question. "Why are we really friends?"

The thing with Daniel is he's actually a good guy—deep down, beneath the bullshit of being the perfect little criminal. Both his parents are assholes. His sister is a slut. He never graduated high school and has no plans for college. His main way of earning a living is selling drugs, arranging fights, and doing practically anything else he wants to score some quick cash.

"We're not," I reply, my expression blank, because I refuse to feel sorry for what I'm saying. It's not like he doesn't really know.

"Why did you come to this party with me then?" he says, a small frown on his face.

"You have really good weed."

"Why else?"

"I felt bad."

"For what?"

Reaching over, I pluck my joint from between his fingers and take a deep drag. I fucking hate playing this game with him. People always think they can handle hearing the truth until it comes down to it, and then they fall apart.

Daniel holds my gaze, a feeble attempt at showing me he doesn't care that I burned all that money after the fight—that he doesn't really give a shit it took him all month to scrape that kind of cash together and I just set fire to it and laughed like it was fucking nothing.

Connie laughs as she looks between us. "Okay, okay, I get it. Erm…do you think I'm pretty?" she asks flirtatiously.

I hold Daniel's gaze for a beat longer before turning my attention back to Connie. I look her up and down. "Yeah."

Her cheeks heat, and she grins wider. "Okay," she says, raising an eyebrow as her courage grows. "How big are you?" she asks, surprising the hell out of me.

WRATH

I raise an eyebrow back. "Six-foot-five," I say carefully, playing her at her own game.

She laughs loudly. "No, I mean...how big are you?" Reaching over, she cups my dick over my jeans, the alcohol and weed in her system making her bold. She has no fucking clue what she's in for.

"I knew what you meant," I reply, and she opens her mouth and sighs.

Daniel leans back in his chair and pulls a joint from behind his ear. "I keep telling her you're no good for her, man." He lights it and blows out a smoke ring, though I barely hear him as Connie continues to stroke me hard beneath my jeans, her drunken gaze on mine.

"Room down the hallway. Door to the left," Daniel says, and closes his eyes as he takes another drag. "You clean up your own mess."

I take Connie by the hand and pull her along behind me as we head inside, passing drunken people passed out in the hallway or talking quietly. This apartment is filled with luxury and excess. No expense has been spared. And the people who come here to party are the untouchables. The rich and spoiled. The ones who look down their noses at people like Daniel while simultaneously buying his drugs from him. I step over some college kid who's sneakers look like they're worth more than Daniel's entire house and tut. Rich or poor, alcohol fucks us all up the same.

I head into the spare room at the end of the hallway, closing the door behind us, and turn to Connie.

"You should know something before you do this," I say, slowly unbuttoning my shirt.

"What?" Connie replies, pulling her tight red t-shirt

over her head, her thick afro bouncing around her shoulders. She reaches around and unclips her bra, freeing her breasts, and my gaze falls to her hard, brown nipples. I lick my lips as she grabs her breasts in her hands and squeezes them, giving a fake groan.

"I'm in charge. You do what I say, when I say it, and how I tell you to do it. Understand?"

"What?" She stops undressing as I slide my shirt off and hang it on the door handle. She stares up at me, her gaze dipping to my firm chest. "What do you mean?"

"I mean," I reply, stalking forward and unbuckling my belt before sliding it out of the loops of my pants, "you listen, you learn, and you do what I say. In return, I promise you the best night of your life."

I hold out one of my hands, and she stares at it uncertainly before lowering her hand into mine. I nod toward her other hand, and she does the same.

"We got a deal?" I ask, and she nods, all too eager to agree even though she doesn't really understand what she's agreeing to.

I bring the belt up and wrap it around her wrists before buckling it tight so her hands are bound, then I make an extra loop at the other end of the belt. Her chest heaves as she looks between me and her bound wrists and licks her tongue along her bottom lip, fear and excitement dousing her features.

I reach out and cup her cheek before stroking my thumb across her bottom lip. "It's okay. I'm not going to hurt you, Connie."

Taking hold of the loose end of the belt, I pull her toward the wall where a punching bag hangs, then let go of her for a second to reach up and unhook it before laying it down on its side. Then I grab the belt loop and slot it on to the hook. She's on her tiptoes, and hugely uncomfortable, going by the grimace and wide-eyed expression on her face, as she tries to keep her balance.

I start to unzip my pants. "Keep still," I order. She continues to sway and fret, and I scowl as I grab hold of her, stilling her instantly. "I said keep still," I demand. She stops moving, her stomach muscles taut as she uses everything she has to keep herself from swaying. She nods, her eyes on mine.

I let her go. "We need a safe word."

Her eyes go wide. "A safe word?"

A small smile lifts the corners of my mouth. "In case it gets…a bit much for you."

Relief floods her features, and she bites on her lower lip flirtatiously. "How about Budweiser?" She laughs, though I can see the strain on her face from standing like that. Her breathing is becoming rapid through arousal and nerves.

I pull a condom out of my pocket and push my pants and boxers down my muscled thighs, watching as her gaze falls to my heavy cock. She swallows, her chest rising and falling so much, I'm surprised she isn't hyperventilating. She licks her lips, her eyes still on my throbbing cock.

I take a step toward her before reaching out to stroke a hand along her waist. "How about…titilate?"

"Titilate?" She giggles, her gaze moving up to meet mine.

I tear open the condom with my teeth, throwing the wrapper to one side before sliding it down my throbbing shaft. I look up at her hungrily. "Yeah, titilate."

Her mouth hangs open like a fish out of water, and I

drop to my knees less than an inch away from her pussy.
"Okay, okay," she agrees quickly.

"Titilate it is then," I say with a smile before grabbing the back of her ass and lifting her so her legs hook on to my shoulders and her wet pussy is on my face. I bury my tongue in her folds, lapping at her juices as I crook a finger inside her and begin strumming her body.

Connie bucks against me, grinding against my face and hands as much as she tries to pull away from the intensity. I use both my hands to spread her thighs wider, sliding my tongue along her and dipping it into her hot center before sucking on her clit. She cries out, panting as she continues to grind her throbbing pussy against my face.

"Oh God, yeah!" she moans into the air.

In a sudden move, I stop and look up at her. I drag a hand across my mouth, wiping away her juices, and smile darkly.

"What? Don't stop!" she pleads, looking down at me. "I'm so close, don't stop!"

I drop her legs off my shoulders and slowly rise to my feet. I slide my tongue up her stomach to her breasts where I suck each one of her dark nipples into my mouth and grab her ass firmly in my hands. I stand to my full height, bowing my neck slightly so we're face to face.

"You don't control this, I do. I decide if you get to come or not, got it?" I say, my lips against the side of her neck. I slide my tongue up her throat until I reach her earlobe, then suck it into my mouth, letting it back out with a loud pop.

I reach between us, slowly sliding two fingers into her, my eyes boring into hers as she gasps. "I said, got it?"

WRATH

I move my fingers in and out of her, the pad of my thumb pressing against her clit.

She nods quickly. "Yes!" She leans in to kiss me, and I pull away from her mouth.

"I don't kiss," I reply.

She looks hurt, but I don't give a fuck. "Don't be silly. It's just a kiss," she says before trying to kiss me again.

"You do what I say, and how I say, remember?" I reply coldly, my fingers playing her body faster. "Now, be quiet. I don't want to hear anything from you unless it's your safe word, got it?"

She looks confused and hurt, but nods anyway.

I pull my fingers out and spin her to face the wall. I run my large hands up and down her body, gathering some of her moisture from between her legs and rubbing it against her asshole before slowly sliding a finger inside of her on my way up. She grunts and rears against me, but doesn't make a sound.

"Good girl." I press myself against her back, fisting my hard cock in one hand and wrapping my other arm around her waist to keep her still as I push against her tight, wet entrance. "I'm not a gentle man, Connie," I growl into her ear, swiveling my hips so I dip the head of my cock in and out of her, teasing her body to perfection.

"But what I lack in gentleness, I make up for in pleasure." I push myself all the way into her, and she gasps against the intrusion. I let my thickness settle inside her, allowing her tight pussy to adjust to my size. I grip her hips roughly in my hands and nip at her shoulder.

"Do you remember your safe word, Connie?" I ask.

She nods frantically.

"Tell me what it is." I nip at her again, the head of my

cock pulsing at her entrance.

"Titilate," she groans as I start to slide out of her slowly.

"Don't forget it," I murmur as I pinch her clit between my fingers. She groans again, and I slide myself almost all the way out of her body before plunging back in to her depths. She whimpers and bites down on her fat bottom lip to stop herself from crying out as I begin moving inside her. I hold on to her hips as I thrust in and out of her harder and harder, trying to reach the peak of the mountain before the volcano erupts, before the hatred and anger that lives and breathes inside me ruins everything.

I fuck Connie, feeling her body engulfed in orgasm after orgasm as I thrust into her over and over, my dick so far inside her, we're almost one person. I'm grinding my hips, swiveling them to hit every delicate fucking spot in her that will light her body on fire so it tightens around me and pulls the pleasure from me.

"Titi..." she starts to groan as her body shakes with another orgasm, her pussy squeezing me, milking my cock. "Titil...oh God, oh God!" she screams as I slam myself in so hard, I lift her off the ground.

I come suddenly as she trembles under the strain of taking so much, and she sobs and cries out loudly, her body squeezing every last drop from me. Milking my cock as I throb and shoot my cum like a fucking machine gun.

"Titilate! Titilate! Titilate! Oh God! Oh my God, titilate!" she screams out at the top of her lungs as I slide out of her body slowly, dragging my length along her already oversensitive pussy, and she unfathomably has another orgasm all on her own like a fucking champ. "Titilate!" she screams.

WRATH

I'm panting and sweating as pleasure hums through every nerve ending just as Daniel and the two friends from earlier throw open the door.

"What the fuck?" one of them yells, his eyes going wide as he looks over at us. He has a knife in his hand, and he stares between Connie and I with a shake of his head before starting to laugh.

I cock my head as they continue to stare. I put my hands on my hips as I catch my breath and give a mock salute. The two friends cheer me on before turning and heading back out to the party with their girls trailing after them, clearly fucked out of their heads. Daniel drags a hand down his face and laughs.

"Fuck me, we thought you were fucking killing her," he says with a dark chuckle.

I grin and look up at Connie, still hanging from the punching bag hook, her head to one side and her eyes closed, her pleasure sliding down her inner thighs.

"Fuck, *did* you kill her?" he asks seriously as he comes farther into the room.

I reach up and unhook her before carrying her limp body over to the bed and laying her down on it. I place a blanket over the top of her to protect any modesty she might have left and check her pulse before looking back at him.

"She's just passed out," I reply before pulling the condom off my now flaccid cock. I tie it and throw it in the trash before grabbing my pants and boxers and sliding them back on.

"Another one ruined for the rest of mankind," he mutters, and I raise an eyebrow at him in question. "They're never the same once you've had them." He turns and leaves the room, and I crack a smile as I button my shirt back up.

I check on her again before I leave the party. She's still out cold, but her breathing is even, so I figure all the adrenaline and alcohol finally hit her. She'll be fine. Nothing a good night's sleep won't solve, though she might be walking like she's been fucked raw for a couple days. I make sure to leave her a glass of water and some aspirin on the nightstand, just in case.

I might be a bastard and heading out before she wakes, but I'm not a total animal.

VII
UINCENDUM NATUS

FIVE

My head is banging when I finally wake up. I crack an eye open, noting the sunlight streaming through the pool house windows, which means I didn't even make it to my bedroom last night.

I stretch and yawn, reaching out for the bottle of water I'm hoping I had the good sense to grab before coming in here.

"Looking for this?" Sab asks, and I crack open the other eye.

Everything's blurry, but slowly comes back into focus. I reach for the bottle of water she holds hostage, groaning when she moves it out of my reach. She smirks and finally lets me grab it.

"You're like an angel," I mumble as I twist the lid off and down almost the entire bottle in one go. I sit up, noting I'm still fully dressed and half slumped over the futon in the lounge of the pool house, a movie paused on the television in the corner. I snort as I realize I'd been watching *Fight Club*, probably for inspiration. What an asshole.

"And you're a mess," Sab says, sounding almost angry.

I glance over at her with a raised eyebrow. "Who ate your cake this morning?" I reach into my pocket and pull out my cigarettes before lighting one. It tastes like ass, but I need the nicotine.

"Dad told me what you did," she replies, and I shrug, taking another drag. "Do you want him to cut you off? Is that what it is? Because I don't get it. You're purposefully goading him, Sammy."

I stand up, swaying on my feet as I walk to the small kitchen area to grab another bottle of water and get a little reprieve from her nagging. She doesn't understand what I'm trying to do for us, and I can't tell her. Not that it seems to matter. I still haven't heard anything from The Elite, so I obviously blew my chances, and I'm all out of ideas on how to get their attention.

"Sammy, will you talk to me?" Sab follows me into the kitchen, and I let my cigarette hang from my lips as I lean down and grab another cold bottle of water from the small fridge. "What's this big plan of yours? Let me try to help you. You know I'd do anything for you, right? If you're in some kind of trouble, maybe I can help."

I groan and look up at her. "I'm not in any trouble. That's all I can say. And I know that sounds like bullshit, but it's the truth. I do have a plan. A plan to get that asshole off our backs for good, you just have to trust me."

She frowns. "You're acting irrationally. You're

drinking too much, getting high, you get kicked out of every school you start at, you fight with everyone, I just..." She looks away.

"What? You just what?" I yell, my own voice hurting my ears.

"I'm worried about you," she says softly.

I sigh and drag a hand down my face. "I'm fine. How many times do I have to tell you that you don't need to worry about me? I can handle myself. I can handle our prick of a father. I can handle whatever life throws at me. So just give me some fucking credit. I've taken care of you and I for this long, haven't I?"

"I just—"

"Enough!" I yell, louder this time, startling both of us. "Just give me a fucking break, Sab, okay? He's a prick and I hate him. I've always hated him—this isn't new information!"

"But this is different," she says.

I laugh darkly and shake my head. "Is it? Is it different?"

"Yes!"

I shake my head again. "The only thing that's different is he can't do shit to hurt me anymore."

Normally, Sab just accepts my bullshit for what it is. She's pure and good, innocent and kind, and sees the best in everyone. However, today she's clearly not willing to brush everything under the carpet and forget about it.

"I don't get it," she says softly. "I know he's never really been there for us, but I don't get why you hate him so much. He's never been around long enough to do something so bad that you could hate him this much."

I drag my hands through my hair and push it back so it's slicked from my face. "Just leave it," I plead.

"No, not this time, Sammy. This time, I want to know what's going on." She comes closer, and I hold a hand up to stop her in her tracks. "Talk to me. Please."

I glare over at her. "You want me to talk to you? You want to know why I hate that piece of shit so much? You want to know how those slutty nannies he left us with would treat us like shit when he wasn't around. How he was so blind to it because he was sinking his dick into them night after night—because *that* was all he cared about. Not whether they were capable of looking after two little kids, but whether they were hot enough for him to fuck."

Sabella scowls and takes a step back. "What are you talking about? That never happened."

I let out a dark, bitter laugh. "Not to you, it didn't. I made sure of it."

Her eyes glisten with tears as her skin pales. "What are you saying?"

I sigh. "It doesn't matter."

And it doesn't. What's done is done.

"It does matter!" she yells at me.

Our eyes connect across the room, and I wish I would have kept my goddamn mouth shut. But I didn't. Maybe it is time for her to learn the truth.

"Those nannies hated us, Sab. They treated us like shit because they wanted to be more than just a fuck buddy to our dad and saw us as a complication—the reason he never stuck around. So, they were cruel to us. They pinched us and slapped us, just made sure not to leave any marks. They left us in our rooms and locked the doors so they didn't have to deal with us. They deprived us of love, of hugs and kisses, of any affection—the affection our dad fucking *hired them* to give us! Until one day, I figured out

WRATH

if I kept them busy by being a little shit, they'd leave you the fuck alone. If I was the little bastard child of the family, they'd take it out on me and not you, because you'd look like some little saint and maybe they'd love you and be kind to you. Maybe they'd see a place for you if they ever managed to pin our dad down. I made sure you got to be the golden child while I played the part of devil incarnate."

Sabella stares at me, tears brimming her eyes. I hate that I've hurt her, that I've burdened her with this, and yet it feels good to get it off my chest. That makes me cruel, but I've held it in for so long, I can't help but find some relief in sharing it.

She's everything I'm not, and she deserves better than to have a brother like me and a father like Maxwell Gunner. She deserves a mother, grandparents who give a shit about her, and a life so much better than this.

Her eyes are glassy as she backs away. "I've got to go."

I stare after her in surprise and shock.

"Sab? Please don't go," I plead, remorse burning in my gut along with the stale alcohol and drugs.

"I need to go. I'm meeting Dean Griffin. He's helping me go over some notes for class. I'll talk to you later, Sammy." Sabella walks away, leaving me alone with my guilty conscience.

"Fuck," I yell, throwing the bottle of water across the room. It explodes somewhere, and I slink down to the kitchen floor with my head in my hands wishing I could be anyone else but me right now.

After a cold shower to wake myself up, I down an espresso shot and walk to my car, my shoes crunching over the gravel. Maxwell's car isn't here, which means he isn't home. Probably why he hasn't given me shit for getting in so late last night. At least I've had a reprieve from him so far today.

This is how it goes with Maxwell and I. He gives me two days of bullshit out of every month, then he's gone for the rest of it, working or screwing, or whatever the fuck he does with his fucking life.

I climb into my Porsche and start the engine, not sure where I'm actually heading until the wheels hit the road. Twenty minutes later, I pull up to the cemetery with a bunch of daisies on the passenger seat. I never come more than once a week, but today, it's almost like she's calling me to her. I make my way to the back of the cemetery, seeing the angel on top of her grave rising above all the others as I approach, and I stop in awe.

The sun is setting already, the entire day lost to my hangover. It dips below the angel, creating an orange halo around her head. I gulp, my arms hanging limply by my sides as I watch, mesmerized by the spectacle. I know it's nothing more than the earth turning and pure coincidence, but it feels right, like this is where I need to be right now. The ball of anger I always have inside me loosens its grip as the sun drops completely below the angel and the spell is broken.

I make my way to the grave, climbing the three stone steps as I stare at her name like I do every time.

Today, there are no words for her. I have nothing I want to tell her. Nothing I want her to know. Today, I just want a mom—my mom. I just want to sit with her. Be near her. Today, for some ungodly fucking reason, I really want to know her.

Sitting down, I lay her flowers next to me and light a cigarette. I smoke it in silence, watching as the dark shadows fall over the cemetery. My heart thuds in my chest, slowly, methodically, like it's waiting for something. That's what it feels like. Like I'm waiting for something to happen.

I glance back around at her name again, but it's the same as it always is, just letters strung together to make up the name of a stranger. A woman I don't know and never will. A woman no one ever talked about. A woman my father claims to love, but never speaks of. A woman who means everything and nothing to me.

I grimace and rub at my chest as a shooting pain threads its way past my ribcage. I finish my cigarette, throwing the butt to one side, and stand back up. I tear the wrapping away from the daisies before dropping them into the water with the ones I left only yesterday.

As I turn to leave, I see something.

A piece of card…an envelope sticking out from under the vase.

I frown and look around, making sure I'm completely alone before lifting the vase and taking the envelope. I jog back to my car, turning on the overhead light so I can see what it is. I half expect it to be a letter from the groundskeeper or something telling me to stay away from other people's graves. And rightly fucking so, I guess.

But it isn't a letter—it's an invite.

"Invitation to Deadly Sins," I murmur as I read it.

A smile crawls up my face. I've heard of this club. I know what it means.

I've been noticed by The Elite.

VII
UINCENDUM NATUS

SIX

"**F**uck," I grumble, dragging clothes out from my closet.

I've seriously let my shit slide the past couple months in my desire to attract the attention of The Elite. It was an added bonus that it pissed Maxwell off too, of course. My father is a stickler for always dressing smart. The man doesn't believe in smart-casual, and I'm pretty certain my grandma bought him his first suit before he was in kindergarten.

Since finding out The Elite existed, I've been playing a part as I slotted myself into the world of underground fighting by wearing jeans and leather jackets instead of the bespoke Brioni suits I'd been brought up in. True that even my jeans and leather jackets were more expensive than most people's monthly salary, but that didn't matter.

WRATH

Not to Maxwell, and not to The Elite.

The Elite was all about money and power. Exclusivity and upper-class privilege. They saw men like me every day: rich men living off old money. I was nothing special to people like them, so I made myself different, forcing myself to stand out from others. I used what I knew—what I was deep down inside. I used my rage and my skills with my fists to push myself out into the limelight, into a place I hated being so I would be seen and heard—so The Elite would find me instead of me finding them.

And it worked.

But tonight, despite how comfortable I've become in my new skin, tonight is a night for the old me. Not Samuel "The Machine" Gunner, but Samuel Louis Gunner, heir to the Gunner fortune and black sheep of the family.

An hour later, I'm sliding on the five-thousand-dollar suit jacket, newly ordered and hand delivered to my door, and buttoning it up over matching suit pants. I slick back my hair away from my face, revealing my strong jaw and dark eyes before slipping on my Rolex and sovereign ring. I barely recognize myself. I'm a mix of Samuel and Maxwell, and I loathe it. Staring back at me is the man who was supposed to grow into someone like my father—the man who hated me—the man I hated back with every fiber of my being. I swallow as I stare at myself, the bob of my Adam's apple moving up and down my throat.

Maxwell Gunner was supposed to love his children and be there for them, but he'd been a ghost for most of our lives, only showing up once or twice a month and then destroying everything about us he could. He'd come home, fuck the nannies, then tear me apart for not being good enough.

I wasn't smart enough.

I wasn't dressed right.

I wasn't behaving how I was expected.

Maxwell left us to the nannies who didn't give a shit about me or Sab, who only wanted to bag themselves a rich husband, then he broke us down so we'd be as miserable as him—and now I looked just like him.

I sigh. At least the suit feels damn good on.

"Check you out," Sabella whistles from the doorway of the pool house, where I decided to move into to avoid my father even more. "My brother looks hot." She laughs.

"I'm a regular pussy magnet," I grin, and she grimaces, making me laugh.

"You're disgusting." She fake gags. "Seriously, though, you look good."

I straighten my cuffs as I turn to look at her and smile. She's wearing sweat pants and a knotty bun thing on top of her head, but even studying in her casual clothes, my sister is stunning.

"Unlike you," I tease. "Looking more and more like the help every day, Sab." I cock an eyebrow, and her jaw drops.

"Rude, little brother. That's just rude."

I bark out a laugh, and fuck, it feels good. I can't remember the last time I laughed with meaning. I'm glad she's not bringing up the other shit I told her. I don't think I'm ready to talk about it anymore. In fact, I wish I could go back and not tell her. The relief of unburdening myself was short and bitter.

"I like this look on you," she says as she walks farther into the room. She comes and stands in front of me before leaning over and tightening the knot on my tie. She smiles

WRATH

approvingly and smooths her hands down the front of my jacket. "It's nice. It reminds me of how things used to be."

I cock an eyebrow at her, feeling my features darken. I know where this is going to lead. That's the thing with Sab—she's like a dog with a fucking bone that just won't let go. She is good, pure-hearted, beautiful, and intelligent, and she wants me to be just the same as her. But I'm not like her. There's a darkness inside me that doesn't live in her, and hopefully never will.

"Leave it," I warn.

"What? I'm just saying, it's nice seeing you like this again. More like the old you."

My smile falls away completely. "Who says I want the old me back?"

"Sammy, don't be like that."

I sigh. "Things change, Sab."

"And things can change back!" she says, sounding exasperated. "I'm just saying, he's not all bad."

"Did you not hear a word I fucking said earlier?" I bark out bitterly.

"If he would have known—" she starts, but I cut her off with a sneer.

"He wouldn't have done shit. He wouldn't have believed me. He was too busy getting his dick sucked by the help and traveling the world to give a shit about us. And when he wasn't doing those things, he was bowing down to our grandmother, who also despises us, or have you forgotten about that?"

Her eyes look away from me, because yeah, there's no denying the disdain our grandmother felt for us. She never approved of our mother because she came from a humble beginning, and she never approved of our father keeping us. I'd heard her once arguing with him about putting us up for adoption so he could start fresh.

I prayed to any God that would listen that night that he'd do just that. Anything was better than living that life—a life of being unloved and unwanted by everyone who was supposed to care about you.

Our grandmother's feelings toward us were the same as each slut of a nanny who came to work in our house. She blamed us for our father not being around. Funny thing was, I blamed us too. I turn away from Sabella, scooping up my keys and the invite off the coffee table. "You know she's not even buried in the family tomb, right?" I say indignantly, the resentment I feel toward him bubbling in my gut and turning the food I ate earlier sour.

Sab frowns. "Who?"

"You know who. They buried her away from the rest of the family. Like she's some dirty little secret," I say, the flames of rage licking at my insides the more I talk about it.

She looks hurt, confused, and then she shakes her head. "Why does that even matter now?"

I huff out a breath, my nostrils flaring. I should have kept my goddamn mouth shut. "You're right, it doesn't matter. Not to him, and not to the rest of the family. But I thought it would to you," I reply, my tone clipped and cool. "She was our mother, Sab."

I stride past her, needing to get out of here before I say something I really regret. Spilling my secrets is the last thing I can afford to do right now. Especially when I'm so close to achieving everything I've worked so hard for.

"Sammy!" Sab calls after me, but I ignore her, feeling guilty for drowning out her voice with every step toward my Porsche.

WRATH

I open the door and climb in, settling into my seat and starting the engine. I let out a slow breath and force myself to relax. I need to be calm tonight—not my usual charge in and destroy shit style. I look out my window toward Maxwell's Ferrari 812 and smile.

"Sorry, sweetheart, I need to stray to the dark side tonight." I rub my hand across my car's dashboard before cutting her engine.

I walk over to Maxwell's Ferrari, letting my gaze move along her soft red curves.

"He'll kill you if you drive her," Sab says from the doorway of the house. She's followed me, and by the way she's chewing the inside of her cheek, she feels bad for what she said. "You know that's his baby."

I look over to her with a grin, all anger between us dissolving. "That's exactly what makes it so tempting, sister."

She shakes her head at me and purses her lips. "You're incorrigible." She throws the keys to me and smiles, her way of an apology—of telling me she loves me no matter what and always have my back.

The feeling is mutual. Sabella is the only person in this world I care about.

I catch the keys in my left hand and give her a nod. "Thanks."

"What should I say if he asks?" Sabella turns to go back inside.

"Tell him his lady in red wanted a real man for the night."

Half an hour later, I give the keys to the valet of the nightclub and head to the entrance. A security guard scans my invitation and directs me to a mirrored elevator instead of the main party. I keep my expression guarded, taking in my surroundings when the doors slide open.

This place, club…whatever the hell it is, is even more decadent than the one downstairs. Bodies fill the dance floor, moving to the rhythmic beats. I stand at one of the tall glass poseur tables, grabbing the attention of one of the waitresses walking around the place with a nod of my head.

She comes straight over, every curve of her lean body accentuated in the tight black pantsuit she wears. Her hair is pulled back from her face, revealing high cheekbones, clear eyes, and red lips. She smiles as she comes closer.

"What can I get you, sir?"

"Sazerac," I reply as I pull out my wallet.

She smiles at me. "That won't be necessary." She turns and leaves, heading toward the bar area, and I put my wallet back away.

The waitresses are carrying trays loaded down with cocktails and bottles of Dom Perignon. I watch as they deliver drinks, then walk away. Fuck, this place really is high-end if all the drinks are free. Who are these people?

"Care to dance?"

I look up as a stunning brunette comes over to where I'm standing. Her dress is tight and short, but not slutty. There's something classy about her. The waitress also comes back with my drink, offering the brunette a smile.

"Can I get you a drink?"

The brunette doesn't take her eyes off me as she replies. "Dry martini."

WRATH

The waitress leaves again, and I pick up my drink and take a sip. Fuck, that tastes good. It burns away at the nerves of apprehension and excitement in my stomach, making me feel more relaxed. I scan the club, my eyes resting on a well-dressed man sitting in a roped off section. Guards are standing to attention like fucking dogs. There's an air about him. Importance. Money. It's almost regal.

"So?" the girl presses, her tongue flitting out to dampen her bottom lip.

I cock an eyebrow at her in question, and her smile widens.

"Dance?"

I smile and take another sip of my drink. "Not much of a dancer. Besides, I'm waiting for someone." I gesture with a head jerk to the guy. "Who is that?"

She doesn't even have to look to know who I'm talking about. "That's Mr. Benedict the Third." She bites her lip.

"He important?" I query, and she frowns and fights a smirk.

"You could say that. Now, how about that dance?"

I take one last look at him, watching how his hands trail over the bare shoulders of the woman next to him. She's young, so young, I'd think she was still in high school, but there's no way if she's working here. This club's too important to make stupid mistakes like that. Still, it gives me an idea of this man's particular tastes.

"How about I dance and you watch?" she offers.

I run a hand over my chin like I'm thinking about her offer, and she pouts. "Go ahead," I reply with a flick of my hand.

The brunette starts to sway her hips in time to the beat of the music. She's mesmerizing to watch. I put my drink down and let my heated gaze wash over her as she smiles at me and dances.

"Would you like a private room?" the waitress offers as she comes back over with the martini. "We have several available for your discretion."

"I think that would be a good idea, don't you?" the brunette says, her smooth as silk voice washing over me. "Oh, but you're waiting for someone," she pouts again, and I chuckle.

I'm waiting for someone. I just don't know who. The invitation didn't give me any clues as to who I was meeting, what was expected of me, or what time they'd be here. I look the brunette up and down. She's stunning. The sort of stunning that tells me she's here for my pleasure.

"I think a little privacy would be good," I finally agree, deciding whoever I'm meeting can wait.

We pick up our drinks and follow the waitress through the crowd, passing the bar where a couple men my age stand, ordering drinks. I recognize them from the party the night before, but I don't let on to them. This isn't the time for niceties. Fuck, it's not time for private lap dances, and I'm already making an exception for that. The waitress stops outside a large, ornate wooden door on the opposite side of the room.

"Room three is free. I'll have a bottle of champagne sent in, but please help yourself to anything you'd like." The waitress opens the door and gestures for us to go inside.

We walk into the lavish room, the muted lighting

setting an atmosphere that seduces you just by being surrounded by it. I have another sip of my drink and unbutton my jacket with my other hand before turning back to look at the brunette.

"Well?" I say, taking a seat on the cream colored sofa that curves into a semi-circle. I drape my arms over the top as I stare at her. The drink and adrenaline is already going to my head. I have a feeling it's going to be a long night and things are going to get better as the night wears on.

"Well?" she replies, placing her martini on the small table next to the sofa.

"I thought I was going to see you dance." I gesture with one hand to where she stands, and she lets out a flirty laugh. "So, dance."

She lifts her drink in front of her, and I do the same with mine. "To tonight," she says, then throws the drink to the back of her throat.

I grin, more than happy with the toast. "To tonight." I swallow the rest of my drink and put down the glass. She turns the music up using a switch by the door, then turns back to me, taking slow steps forward. She sways her ass and hips as she runs her hands through her long hair, her gaze on mine the whole time.

My eyelids grow heavy as I watch the door open and the waitress come in with a bottle of champagne. The brunette doesn't stop dancing, and the waitress pours me a glass before handing it to me. I think I say thanks, but I can't be sure. I'm lost in the moment of watching the woman in front of me and the fuzzy feeling in my head.

Jesus, I'm hot. I reach up and loosen my tie before unbuttoning the top button on my dress shirt. The room is warm and blurry as I take a sip of the champagne, feeling the gold flecks slide down my throat and the bubbles fizz on my tongue. Fuck, this is good stuff.

The brunette leans in close to me, her breath warm on my face as her hands reach for my belt.

"Everything okay, Samuel?" she asks.

"Superb," I slur.

VII
UINCENDUM NATUS

SEVEN

I wake up worrying I'm dead.

Going by the way I feel, I think I would have preferred to be, because death couldn't have been this painful. My mouth is so dry, my tongue feels like sandpaper, and I'm pretty sure I must have rubbed sand in my eyes to make them this gritty and bloodshot.

My heads pounds with the pain of a hangover from hell, and my stomach heaves when I start to move to sit up. I clutch a hand to my head and wince as I force my eyes open. The world blurs and spins until it finally comes to a stop and settles.

"Fuck," I grumble, and dive up from my bed. Tripping over my bedsheets and almost falling on my face, I stumble to the bathroom and throw the lid open of the toilet before hurling into it. The sound and smell of sick hitting the water makes me feel even worse. I flush as I continue to retch, drowning out the sound and smell of my own vomit.

When I'm done, I slump back down on the cold porcelain floor, feeling dizzy and achy all over. I'm cold. So cold, I'm shivering, my teeth chattering like I'm standing in an artic wind. I crawl over to the shower, reach up, and turn the hot water on before clambering inside on my hands and knees.

The water pounds down on me as I lay in the fetal position, trying to work out what the fuck is going on. I don't remember much about last night after meeting the brunette. There were many drinks, sex, and by the way I'm feeling now, drugs, but the memories are hazy at best.

I can only hope I didn't fuck up my chance with The Elite by being a complete asshole.

I lay there until I finally feel warm enough, then I sit up slowly before peeling my clothes off. Because yes, I slept in my own clothes too, shoes and everything. The dizziness begins to pass, and I slowly stand and wash myself.

I'm supposed to start school today, but I'm not sure I'll even make it to my first class. I'm already registered thanks to Maxwell, and he's even had the curtesy of leaving me my class list and a pile of paperwork that needs to be signed and taken to the counselor's office. Money can buy you whatever you want, and despite the term already starting, Maxwell made sure his money bought me a place at St. Augustine .

WRATH

I'm dressed and trying to force some eggs and coffee down my throat when Sabella comes into the kitchen. She pauses in her steps and grimaces at me, and I give her the middle finger. I'm in the main house since there's nothing to eat in the pool house, and she slows her steps as she comes up to me.

I'm back to wearing my jeans and leather jacket again, my hair flopping over my eyes because I couldn't be fucked to do anything with it.

"Wow," she says, continuing toward the coffee pot.

"Wow?" I reply dryly.

"Yeah, wow. You really look like crap, Sammy. That's going to be a great first impression."

I turn in my seat to glare at her. "Why, thank you, sis. That was just the look I was going for today—crap with a splash of go fuck yourself." She raises an eyebrow at me, but doesn't say anything. I turn back to look at my eggs.

My stomach still feels queasy, but the painkillers are starting to kick in and ease the headache. I know I'll feel better once I eat something, but actually getting the eggs from the plate to my mouth is a whole other story. I can normally handle my booze, so I can't fathom what the fuck made me feel so bad today. I hear Sab rummaging around behind me, but choose to ignore her in favor of poking my eggs around my plate and trying not to throw up.

She finally sits down opposite me and slides a glass toward me. "Drink it."

I grimace as I look at the raw eggs cracked into the glass and push it back toward her. "I think I'll pass."

She smirks and tuts. "Little brother, trust me on this. If Dad sees you looking like that, he's going to drop you straight off at an AA meeting. No passing go, no collecting two-hundred dollars. You're done for. Drink the eggs and get to school. Do what you need to do today, get an early night, and remember drinking on a school night is never a good idea," she says with a smirk and a wag of her finger. She's trying to keep it light, but there's worry in her tone. I don't blame her. Everything I'm doing, I'm doing for her. Maxwell is a bullshit father, but as long as his attention is focused on me, he's leaving her alone.

She stands up before I can reply and walks back out of the kitchen.

I scowl after her, then reach for the gruesome egg concoction. There were at least three raw eggs in it, but I can't look too closely without feeling queasy again. Picking it up, I throw the contents of the glass to the back of my throat and force myself to swallow the slime without gagging.

Fifteen minutes later, I'm by my car, ready to go to school, and feeling a little more alert thanks to the eggs Sab gave me. Always knew she was the smartest out of us. I look across, seeing Maxwell's Ferrari back where she rightfully belongs, and wonder how she got back here. There's no way in hell I would have driven fucked up on booze and drugs. That's just something I won't ever do.

Come to think of it, how the hell *had* I gotten home?

I assumed I jumped in a cab, but that wouldn't explain the Ferrari being back. I drag a hand through my hair and decide to think on it some more later. Right now, I need to get to school before I screw up my first day and let Sabella down.

I slide my hand into my jacket pocket to pull out my keys when something falls out and lands by my shoe.

WRATH

Reaching down, I pick it up and look at the gold coin with the skull embossed on one side with a frown. I turn it over in my hand, seeing the words THE ELITE SEVEN embossed on the other side.

"Fuck," I murmur, looking around me. For who or what, I don't know.

A slow smile creeps up my face as I turn the coin over and over in my hand.

I'm in. I'm fucking in.

At least I hope that's what the coin means.

Shoving it back into my pocket, I feel something else in there and pull it out. It's a small white business card with some coordinates and a time on it. I turn it over, but there's nothing else.

I drag a hand through my hair and try to stifle the huge, shit-eating grin on my face in case I'm being watched. I unlock my car and climb inside before setting off for school in a better mood than when I woke up.

VII
UINCENDUM NATUS

EIGHT

I pull up into the parking lot of St. Augustine's and get out. My hangover has all but dispersed, though I still have major fucking blank spots in my memory of last night. But I practically have a fucking skip in my step as I head across the grounds, barely taking in the huge building and many students milling about. I missed the start of term, but good old Maxwell had everything smoothed over for me to start late. It's only a couple weeks, but I'll no doubt have a lot of catching up to do if I don't want to get thrown out. And If I'm in The Elite, I need to be here.

I head into the main school building, nodding to a couple girls who're staring at me like they want to choke on my dick in the middle of the hallway. I smirk and continue to my first class. Maybe this school isn't going to be so bad after all. The school grounds are huge, with several

WRATH

buildings all across the campus, but the counselor's office and all faculty offices are in the central building.

I've never had a problem getting laid, but these past couple months, I've been even more of a pussy magnet. Dressing like the ultimate bad boy is apparently every rich girl's wet dream. Fucking suits me too.

My backpack is slung over one shoulder, and I shrug it farther up and look at the sign on the wall to make sure I'm going the right way. This school is huge. Ridiculously so. With three tennis courts, its own stables, and an indoor pool for the swim team, it's out of this world. Something most people will only ever dream about. I should be grateful to be going here, yet all I can think about is the chunk of gold in my jacket pocket and the fact that I'd rather be anywhere but here.

When I look back down, I almost walk into another guy who's stopped to look at his phone.

"Shit. Sorry, man," I say, and he turns slowly and looks at me. His gaze moves up and down, almost like he's checking me out.

"Sam 'The Machine' Gunner," he drawls, giving me a slow smile.

I lift my chin, my game face automatically back on. I didn't expect anyone here to know me, and I can't deny it unnerves me that this guy does.

"Who's asking?" I say with narrowed eyes.

His smile widens, his green eyes sparkling in amusement. "Steady, just a fan."

I look him up and down, taking in his smart clothes, perfect hair, and freakishly bright green eyes, but it's his expensive as fuck watch that my eyes focus on and the way he swivels it on his wrist.

"I normally win money for my fans. Can't see why you'd need the cash," I reply dryly.

He chuckles darkly. "Funny you should say that. You actually lost me a lot of money."

My eyes widen, and I can't help but laugh back. "You bet against me?" I shake my head. "Well, that was your first mistake."

"And my second?" he replies.

I smirk. "Thinking we were gonna be buddies." I turn and start to walk away when he slaps a hand on my shoulder.

"Name's Sebastian," he says, carrying on like I didn't just blow him off. I glare when he holds a hand out to me. "Come on, don't be a prick," he laughs.

I shake my head at him in shock, then take his hand, giving it a firm shake. "For the record, I'm always a prick," I retort dryly, and it's his turn to smirk now.

"You heading to class?" he asks.

"Yeah, Professor Pulliver apparently thinks he can teach me more about business management than I already know." I shrug. I was already planning on sitting in the back and sleeping through the class.

Maxwell chose my subjects since I continued to put it off just to piss him off. I guess the joke is on me now.

"Ahhh, you unlucky bastard. Professor Pulliver is an asshole!" Sebastian laughs. "Word around campus is he has little dog syndrome."

"Not that I give a shit, but why are you telling me this?"

Sebastian slings an arm over my shoulders, and though I want to shrug out from under the weight of it, I don't. He doesn't seem like he's trying to be overbearing or assert his authority on me, and despite the fact that something about him freaks me the fuck out, and I sense something a little amiss with him, I decide he's just a friendly fucking guy. I also like the fact that he came right out and told me he hasn't even bet on me. It was ballsy. The guy deserves at least five minutes of respect from me for that alone.

"Why? Because I have that sorry son of a bitch too and I'm trying to help you out," he chuckles. "Come on. He hates tardiness and he'll make people stay after class to clean if you're late."

He lets me go and gestures for me to follow him toward class. Even going so far as to hold the door open for me when we arrive like I'm his bitch. I frown as I pass him, but all he does is chuckle again. I'm starting to wonder if I've misjudged him completely when he catches up to me on the steps that lead to our seats. He leans in, and I scowl harder at him.

"I like pussy, Samuel, stop panicking. I wouldn't want your cock even if you offered it to me."

He moves past me and sits down before gesturing to the seat next to his. When I don't move to sit down, he stands up. "Yo, Samuel, I got you a seat," he bellows, his hands around his mouth to make his words travel further.

He ignores the looks from the other students like he doesn't give a fuck who's watching and sits back down, raising an eyebrow at me and smirking. People must have been used to him though, because only a handful turn to look. Even so, my attempt at sliding into the back of the class and sleeping through the lecture is diminishing by the second.

I grumble and start toward him, sitting in the seat he's

saved for me. I turn to him, and he opens his mouth to speak, but I cut him off with a scathing look.

"Listen, we're not buddies, you hear me? I don't fucking know you, and if I'm honest, I don't think we'll be hanging around in the same circles, so don't get too attached. I know I'm an awesome fucking guy, but you're going to have to find yourself a new BFF." I wink and turn to face the front as Professor Pulliver walks in. "Jesus Christ," I grumble.

Professor Pulliver barely scrapes five foot tall. A thin, wiry man with graying cotton candy hair on his chin and the bushiest eyebrows I've ever seen. He looks like a fucking caricature or some shit.

"Attention, students!" he all but screams, his nasally voice traveling all the way to the back of the room. "Eyes front, pens poised, and brains switched on, or you'll be staying after class."

I've never been one to judge people by their looks, but this guy is the weirdest motherfucker I've ever met. I hate Maxwell even more for putting me in this class now.

"What did I tell you?" Sebastian whispers, "little dog syndrome. Like one of those chihuahuas." He laughs quietly and leans back in his seat, and despite my better judgment telling me there's something very wrong with Sebastian, I can't help but laugh along with him.

After class is finished, I grab my bag and head to the door. Professor Pulliver has all but put me to sleep. The guy might be the most weirdly boring man I've come across, but it doesn't help that my hangover is beginning to make a reappearance.

"You heading for lunch?" Sebastian asks as he walks in step with me.

I turn and glare, but decide I'm feeling way too shitty to even tell him to fuck off right now. "I told you, we're not friends."

"Never said we were. We're just two guys going for lunch. Kinda like a date, but one where neither of us end up sucking cock at the end of it." He smirks, and I shake my head, giving up.

"Sounds like a shit ending to a date if you ask me," I reply with a raised eyebrow, and he snorts on a laugh.

"Food," I say. "I need food. And coffee." I drag a hand down my face, pushing my hair back from my eyes.

Sabella's eggs got me through that first class, but there's no way I'll make it through the rest of the day. I need food, coffee, and sleep before I head to the meeting tonight. I need to be alert for whatever happened. But there's no way of ditching class without Sabella losing her shit on me.

Sebastian leads me to the cafeteria, though it could barely be called that. It's more of an upmarket, self-service, five-star restaurant. I stare at the food, my stomach grumbling, wishing I could just have a burger and fries. Right now is not the time for Var Salmon or Beef Wellington. Seriously, what the fuck is with this place?

Sebastian slings an arm over my shoulder again. "Go grab a seat. I've got you covered."

I turn and head to a table, more than happy to be sitting down and not staring at the food anymore. I've attended a lot of schools the past couple years, all of them expensive, but none of them like this. This school is for royalty or some shit.

Sabella has always been the golden child in our family, and he obviously repaid her by sending her here. St. Augustine's is regal in its decadence, and no expense has been spared—not even in the fucking cafeteria.

Cherry walnut panels line the room, a far-cry from the magnolia painted walls of my last school. Even though it's still early for lunch, a lot of students gather around, sitting around on their stuck-up asses and drinking their espressos while talking bullshit politics they don't really give a damn about or understand and how to spend their family fortune. I hate them all. Every last one of the fake motherfuckers.

"Shit, not going to kill someone, are you?" Sebastian laughs as he sits down opposite me and slides over a plate. I look down at the cheeseburger and fries on my plate, my stomach growling in appreciation.

"I'd kiss you in thanks, but you already told me you prefer pussy." I smirk, and he sits back in his chair smugly, his hands playing with the watch on his wrist. "Gotta say, you don't seem like Augustine's type." I pick up my burger and take a huge bite. Almost come in my pants at the taste of it too. Best damn burger I've probably ever had.

"Looks can be deceiving," he replies mysteriously, still fiddling with his watch.

It's my turn to laugh now. "You mistake me. You fit in just fine if you're going to be the cover boy for this school, but..." I pause and stare at him, wondering how far I can push him, "you don't seem like you have all your tickets to ride the train, if you don't mind me saying."

I bite into my burger while another slow grin spreads

WRATH

across Sebastian's face. I can't decide if I've actually offended him and he's covering it or if he really doesn't care. I finish off my burger in one more mouthful and wait for him to reply, not giving a shit either way.

"You see a lot, but you don't really get it, do you?" he finally replies, like the mysterious fucker he is.

I swallow the lump of meat and bread and lean back in my chair. "Get it?"

"Yeah." He looks around the room before pointing at a guy who could be the equivalent of a Ken doll. "See that guy?" I nod. "He's captain of the swim team. Plays tennis on Thursdays at his daddy's club to keep up appearances. He likes to take his girlfriend out on the family yacht on weekends, even though he actually hates the water. But Tuesdays are his special days. Just for him."

I frown at the Ken doll wannabe. Seems like he has the perfect life. For him at least. "What's so special about Tuesdays?"

Sebastian leans forward. "On Tuesdays, he likes to go get a massage by one of the little Thai women down by the Monastery club, and afterwards, he likes to fuck his masseuse up the ass while she wears a pig mask and calls him by his mother's name."

I stare at him, wide-eyed and shocked to hell. "What the fuck?" I say, and Sebastian stands up before pushing his chair back in under the table.

"Like I said, you see, but you don't really get it. Enjoy the fries. See you around, Sam."

He turns and walks away, leaving me sitting at the table like a fucking loner. I stare between him and the Ken doll guy wondering how much of that story is actually true.

Or maybe it's just like he said. I see a lot, and that part is true at least. I *am* an observant guy. You have to be when you like to fight, because you have to see the smallest of movements so you know what your opponent is lining up to do next, but maybe I don't really get it.

I look around in frustration. Fuck, Sebastian has really gotten in my head. No one has ever done that to me before.

I push my tray of half-eaten food away and stand up. None of this even matters. All that matters is tonight. The meeting. The Elite. And getting Sabella and myself out from under Maxwell's grip once and for all.

VII
UINCENDUM NATUS

NINE

Pulling up to the building just after dark, I cut the engine on my car and get out. Reading the wrought iron sign hanging on the wall, I see it used to be a nunnery. I parked a little farther away and walk so I can watch from a distance as everyone arrives, but there isn't much to see without going inside. The nunnery has a brick wall at least twelve feet high all the way around it, so unless I go through the gate, all I can see are dark shadows.

I look around me. The flutter of nerves similar to those I get just before a fight tremble in my stomach, making me aware of everything I have to lose if this is some sick joke someone's playing on me.

I light a cigarette to steady my nerves as a large hand comes down on my shoulder, making me drop my cigarette and reach around to grab whoever it is. I've got them in a headlock before their next breath, and he's tapping out on my arm as I squint down into his face.

"Sebastian?" I scowl. "What the fuck are you doing here? Did you fucking follow me?" I tighten my grip as he grins up at me. He taps on my arm again, and I let go and shove him away. So much for my discreet entrance. "I asked you a fucking question," I grit out, feeling the pull of rage in my chest.

"Guess we're both interested in The…Elite," he says with a smirk as the color in his face turns back to a normal shade. He pushes his hair back and starts fiddling with his watch. His eyes are wide with excitement, not an ounce of nervousness or apprehension.

Fucker is crazy, that's for damn certain. I knew something was a little off with him earlier today, and now I get it. I see it in his freaky green eyes and the way he doesn't even seem fazed by me almost choking him out.

"You know about The Elite?" I ask, my eyes narrowing. It's all too fucking convenient. I don't believe in fate or chance, and I'm not about to start believing in it now.

"Of course I know about them. I see fucking everything in this town." He reaches down, picks up my cigarette, and offers it to me, but I shove away his hand.

"You expect me to believe that? What are the chances of that?"

"Of what?" he asks.

"Of running into you twice in one day. The second time here." I gesture around us as I fight the anger bubbling inside me. "At a top secret society."

Sebastian taps the side of his nose and leans in. "First rule of fight club is you don't talk about fight club." He glances over to the gates as another shadow slips inside.

WRATH

"Come on. Don't wanna miss all the fun, do we?" he says with sarcasm as he starts to walk away.

When I don't immediately follow, he looks back over his shoulder. "Samuel, this is our big chance. Don't blow it by being a suspicious motherfucker like usual." Then he turns and walks away again.

I stare around us. The evening is dark. A sliver of moon slips out from between the clouds, but all too quickly passes back behind them as the wind picks up.

"Fuck it," I mutter, starting toward the walkway.

This is it.

I'm in.

I'm in the fucking Elite.

Everything I've done over the past couple months has been leading up to this moment. Every dollar earned with every fist thrown, every bloody knuckle and bruise—it's all been for this. For my title—Wrath. And my title couldn't be anymore fucking perfect for me.

I'm still in a daze thinking about it when I realize the guy Baxter, whom I overheard one of the other guys call God, is speaking. He's standing next to Pride with a card in his hand, but I missed what he said.

Sebastian leans over. "Sins of the body, huh? This should be fun."

"Sins of the body?" I ask.

He grins wider. "To bond the brotherhood, we have to indulge in the sins of the body. I'd say this secret society is starting out just perfect, wouldn't you?"

"Yeah," I agree. "I would."

"Unless we have to fuck each other, that is," he laughs. "I ain't taking dick for no one." He punches me in the arm lightly. "Not even for you, brother," he says as he raises his eyebrows and stalks away.

Sins of the body—sex.

Other than fighting, sex is my domain. My dark domain. I like my sex like I like my fights—dark, bloody, and full of cries of pain.

I wonder how my so-called new brothers are going to feel about that. Deep down, we all have dark desires, but none are as dark as my own, and most don't act on those urges. But I'm not most people.

I'm Samuel "The Machine" motherfucking Gunner. Wretched brother to a twin sister, shameful son to a dead mother, an undefeated champion in the ring, and a master of sin in the bedroom.

VII
UINCENDUM NATUS

TEN

I'm not sure what was in the chalice we drank from when we arrived, but whatever it had been was spiked. I've taken enough drugs to know the difference between drunk and high, and I was most-definitely fucking high. High enough not to worry about what my newfound brothers would think of my dark desires anymore.

In the lobby of this huge house, women outnumber us ten to one. Each woman is more delectable than the last, beckoning us farther into the house.

I didn't know what to expect when we arrived, but a huge house surrounded by heavy security wasn't it. I was just glad I remembered to bring the skull embossed coin with me. We needed to show it to gain entry, though I was surprised when the guy asked to see our tattoo before settling for the coin. I'll dwell on what the tattoo is later.

Right now, I'm flying. My head is fucked, and my body is loose and ready to go.

I blink sluggishly, and my view changes from the bar area to me walking into another room, my steps heavy and body feeling foreign to me. I have no clue where I am now, but none of it seems to matter as the door in front of us opens wider and we step into another world—a world of writhing, naked bodies, their moans and cries resounding throughout as they beg to be touched or fucked harder. A world of lust. A world of fucking sin.

Jesus.

Fucking.

Christ.

I swallow, my nostrils flaring at the sights and sounds around me, my dick coming to life.

Sebastian slaps me on the shoulder, forcing me to turn to look at him. I narrow my gaze on him. His pupils are really fucking wide, making those freaky green eyes look even freakier. Are they swirling? I swear they are. Fuck, my head is a mess.

He's saying something, his lips moving real slow, but I can't focus enough to understand. The words are disjointed and slurred. There's so much noise around us, it's impossible to hear one person. I think I try to tell him so, but my tongue feels heavy and too big in my suddenly dry mouth.

"Is this what I think it is?" God, aka Gluttony, asks from in front of me. His eyes roam over the naked scene before us, his hand rubbing over his chest like it's tight.

"Yeah," I reply, reading his mind.

A sex den, or maybe a dream. I'm not sure which anymore, but I don't care either. I'm not complaining either

WRATH

way, and neither are the other guys.

Venturing inside, I pass a masked woman bent over the arm of a red sofa, her huge breasts swaying as a man takes her from behind. His hands on her hips leave finger-shaped bruises on her pale, perfect skin as he thrusts into her over and over. She moans and hangs her head, letting the euphoria take over her body. My cock stiffens in my jeans, begging to be let free.

Another masked woman on all fours on the floor writhes in pleasure as two masked men take her at the same time. In fact, we're the only ones not wearing masks. A realization I don't like. There's a man underneath the woman, taking her pussy, and a woman behind her, her mouth ravaging the other woman's asshole with her tongue. She grunts as cock and tongue thrust into her in unison. I'm pretty sure I hear God laugh nervously from somewhere in front of me.

"I want some of that," one of my newfound brothers says, though I don't know which one.

"That one's mine," Micah, aka Greed, groans with a sneer.

The room spins, a myriad of colors, shapes, and sweaty, naked bodies as we continue to move through it. My hands reach out to touch the flesh of women as we pass by, stroking along smooth thighs and taut stomachs as they moan up at me while being fucked. One woman lays on her back across a circular bed. She crooks a finger at us all as we pass and laughs. We stop in front of another door, and God knocks once before opening it and beckoning us all inside.

Sebastian sways a little in the doorway, and I slap him on the back as I squeeze past him.

"Messed up," he mumbles, and I laugh in agreement.

We are messed up indeed, and it feels fantastic. In the center of the room, there are seven chairs all set out in a sacrificial circle—at least, that's what it looks like. I sway on my feet before choosing a chair and collapsing into it. Dragging a hand over my face, I try to clear some of the blurriness from my head and gather my thoughts as I look around the room, but barring my fellow sinners, there isn't much to see. Dim lighting. Deep crimson walls. Flickering candles lining a large, walnut sideboard beside a wall of paddles and whips.

I hear the sound of a door opening from somewhere behind me, but I don't have the energy to turn and look. I didn't need to either as seven naked masked women walk into the center of the circle, a different woman moving to stand in front of each of us.

I drowsily stare up at the woman in front of me. A beautiful mixed-race woman with golden eyes and huge, firm breasts. She glances to the left of me as she talks to someone about a camera, then looks back down at me and smiles before dropping to her knees.

"You okay, baby?" she purrs. I am now.

Reaching out, I stroke her soft curly hair, my dick straining in my jeans, and I nod. I want to speak, but my mouth feels dry, my tongue heavy. The only thing that seems to work is my cock, which isn't necessarily a bad thing.

"I'm going to make you feel real good, baby," she coos, working the zipper on my jeans expertly before pulling out my hard length. I sigh as her hands wrap around the girth, and she begins gently running her hand up and down it.

WRATH

My head lolls back, too heavy for my shoulders. It feels good—real fucking good.

Scanning the room, my gaze falls on the chair next to me—God, aka Gluttony. The woman in front of him is working his dick with her mouth, her head bobbing up and down rhythmically as he grips her hair in his hand and surges up into her throat repeatedly. I look to the other side of me to find a slender blonde straddling Sebastian. He grips her hips, helping her climb his cock before anchoring her to him so she can slide her sexy little body down onto his hard length, pumping into her with enough force, the chair grinds over the floor. Every time she closes her eyes or looks away, he grabs her face and forces her to look him in the eyes. Jesus, even when he's fucking he's a freak.

I look back to my woman as she leans over to take my dick in her mouth. I want her to, of course I do, but I also have better plans for her body. I grab her chin between my thumb and forefinger and squeeze so she'll look at me.

"What's wrong, baby?" she asks in a seductive purr.

"Shut up," I order, my eyes narrowing. "You talk when I tell you to talk."

Her cheeks rise into a smile behind her mask, and she nods.

"Eyes down, thighs apart, wrists together," I say, finally finding my voice.

She averts her gaze and drops her chin to her chest.

Standing from my chair, I shrug off my jacket and throw it to the floor. Moving to her, my hands rub over her back, sliding up to her neck. I crouch behind her, tilting her head to one side so I have better access to her throat. I trace her neck with kisses, my hands smoothing over her soft skin to reach around to her nipples and pluck them one at a time. They're hard and pert, and I reach down between her legs, happy to feel the arousal dowsing her pussy lips.

"Stand up," I order, and she complies straight away. Good girl.

I turn her around and run my hands over her flat stomach and round ass before finally reaching over to suck one of her dark, pebbled nipples into my mouth. She groans loudly, and my gaze hit hers hard.

"Quiet," I bark, and she nods. "Good girl," I soothe, moving behind her again, my large hand flaying over her naked flesh.

Grunts and groans grow louder all around me. The sound of flesh slapping against flesh and the chorus of moans coming alive are turning me on so much, I think my dick might explode any minute. I need to be inside her, sinking full hilt until my balls slap against the apex of her thighs.

"What's your name?" I slur in her ear, wishing I wasn't feeling so dizzy and messed up. I like to be in control, especially when it comes to sex, and this is too close to being out of control for my liking.

"Courtney," she replies breathlessly as I plunge a finger deep inside her hungry pussy without warning. She yelps, then softens against the intrusion, her head falling to one side.

"Courtney what?" I ask as I strum her pussy with my fingers, the heel of my hand rubbing against her clit in circles.

"Courtney, sir?" she says hesitantly, and I nod.

I put a hand on her back and gently push her forward,

WRATH

until she's gripping the back of the chair with both hands. "Hold on," I order.

"Sir?" she whimpers, her head still low.

"What?"

From somewhere, she produces a condom and holds it out to me. Fuck, I almost fucked her without wearing anything. Not cool at all. The room is spinning, and everywhere I look is full of sex and depravity. Sebastian's mouth fucking his girl's pussy like she's a plate of caviar. Greed is dripping hot wax on his girl's tits. The guy, Rush, who I think was given the sin Sloth, is slouched down in his chair while his girl rides him, her hips thrusting back and forth as she plays with her tits. I'm not fazed by anything, but something about the situation feels wrong, off.

Courtney stands up and turns to me, disobeying my direct orders. The beast in me roars to the surface. I grip her chin tightly, my nostrils flaring at the sight of her eyes widening in surprise and shock.

"I never told you to move," I grit out.

"I'm sorry, sir," she says, her heady gaze betraying how sorry she really is.

"Now you have to be punished," I say. "Stay there." I stride to the back wall, stepping between fucking bodies, and take a paddle down from it.

I stroke my palm along the wood, testing its strength and texture before deciding it's not the right one. Putting it back, I pick up another one and do the same thing.

This is the one.

I turn back around, looking down as Lust now feasts on his woman's cunt. He's hooked her legs over his shoulders, his hands strumming her body to the brink of orgasm before nipping at her clit.

I stride back toward Courtney, who's bent over the chair with her hands on the arms of it, her ass just waiting for its punishment from me. Good girl.

I smooth my hand over her ass cheeks a couple times, loving the feel of her warm, soft flesh beneath my palm. But it isn't warm enough. Not yet. I want it hot. Burning with fire and pain before I strike pleasure into her center.

"Stay still," I order.

"Yes, sir."

This isn't her first time playing, and I like that. It saves me from having to teach her. Lifting the paddle, I slap it down against her ass cheek, then wait to see if she makes a sound, praying she does. Not that I would have been able to hear anything with Rhett fucking Masters, aka Lust. He must be the pussy magician, making his girl scream as she comes hard against his mouth.

My cock strains, more than ready to fuck Courtney, but I'm not done with her yet. And the pleasure is always in the preparation. I lift the paddle and hit her ass again. Her skin turns rosy and hot where the paddle hits her, and I smooth my hand over the fiery flesh, noting the way she hisses. I smile, enjoying her pain, and decide she needs one more slap with the paddle before I fuck her, just so she knows who's in charge.

I smooth my hand over her ass again before standing upright and rearing back, smacking the paddle across her for a third time. She whimpers, and I almost cum in my jeans at the sound of her cries. My balls draw up, ready to blow their load before I've even been inside her.

"That looks like fun." Sebastian grins, looking across at me as he fucks a lean blonde woman. Dude barely looks out of breath, despite the trickle of sweat trailing down

WRATH

the side of his face. "I mean, seriously, don't stop. That shit is hot. Next time, do it harder," he continues talking as he thrusts into her, watching me the entire time like it isn't weird as fuck. Scowling, I ignore his laughter and give my attention back to Courtney.

I drop the paddle and use my hand to smooth over her hot skin before slapping my palm down. Her muscles clench, and my nostrils flare in desire for her. I run my hand up across her pussy, sliding a finger inside, then back out before I slap my hand across her again. She lets out a strangled cry of pleasure. I repeat the process—soothing her tender flesh, strumming her cunt to the edge of orgasm, then slapping my hand across her ass, over and over, enjoying each stroke of my hand on her. The way small welts appear on her reddening skin and a bright red handprint is left behind from my abuse, and the way her muscles tighten around my fingers as I plunge inside her.

She still hasn't moved from her position, but she wants to. She's a simpering wreck, her body quaking with need and pain. My dick is painfully hard. If I don't fuck her soon, my balls are going to explode.

Tearing open the condom, I roll it down my thick cock before lining myself up with her entrance. Gripping her hair like reigns on a pony, I stroke the smooth skin of her back, calming her over-sensitized body, before abruptly slamming into her.

My cock surges forward, filling her as I pull her hair back. Her body is being pulled and pushed in two different directions as she moans something into the air around her. She cries out, her eyes watering as she tries to look back over her shoulder at me. This woman—whoever the fuck she is—is a pro at taking cock. Her body quickly adjusts to my size as I slide out of her tight cunt before sliding back in.

Fuck, this feels good.

She feels good.

So good, I can ignore Sebastian still talking to me while he fucks his girl.

So good, I can ignore the dizziness in my head.

So good, I hold back my own orgasm because I refuse to let this be over yet.

This sex is dark, dirty, and sinful. It's everything I like.

I know her name's not really Courtney, and I know this is a job for her. But right now, I don't give a fuck about any of that. I don't care that all the women are wearing masks and we're not. I don't care that there's some darker motive to this evening. Whether it's the drugs, the atmosphere, our brotherhood bonding—right now, all I care about is fucking Courtney until I can't see straight.

I hold on to her hips tightly, but unlike others, my touch isn't bruising. It's controlling and forcible enough to mold her body, keeping it in the exact position I want without harming her. Because when I hurt a woman, mark her flesh with my touch, there's nothing accidental or needy about it.

And just like when I fight, my anger and rage begins to slide away. I get lost in the sensations of sex. Of desire and lust. Of giving and taking. Of fucking someone and taking their control away because we both know I have all the power in this situation. That they are completely at my mercy.

They'll come if I let them.

They fuck how I tell them.

They'll stand or kneel—suck or fuck.

WRATH

They'll submit to my every punishment and desire.

I am the master of this situation, and it's my favorite place to be.

At some point in the night, I come, hard. And then I take my seat like I'm king of the fucking room while we swap partners and I fuck the next girl in line, submitting her to the same ritual as Courtney. Only…instead of a paddle, I use a rider's crop.

The night is a blur of sex.

Of naked bodies.

Of groaning men and women.

Of pleasure and pain.

Of coming so hard, I see stars.

Of comradery, brotherhood, and bonding.

Somewhere in it all, there's a camera. But in this moment, I just don't give a fuck.

VII
UINCENDUM NATUS

ELEVEN

I take another toke on the blunt, inhaling and holding the smoke in my mouth for several seconds, feeling the heaviness float over my tongue before letting it out slowly. The bitter aftertaste is the most delicious thing I've tasted in weeks. Fuck, this shit is strong. I'm beginning to see why Sloth's always so chill about everything. It's hard to feel anything when you're stoned all the time.

Sebastian runs and jumps into my pool, splashing everything with water. Normally, I would have lost my shit at something like that, the red mist dropping down like a blanket over me, but today, I laugh hysterically. And fuck, it feels good to laugh like this.

Life is fucking good.

Maxwell is away on business again, but as soon as he's back, that dipshit is going to see exactly who's in charge

WRATH

around here. Things have changed, and there's no going back now. Not for me, and not for him. I'm going to grind that motherfucker under my heel until he's dust and get Sab and I away from him and the black memories he's shoved down our throats our whole lives. Then, I'm going to set about destroying everything he and our grandmother have worked for their whole lives. I'm going to take down the Gunner Foundation from the very roots, because none of these fuckers deserve it.

Fuck him, and fuck this family.

No longer will I be the black sheep of the family. Very soon, I'm going to be an entire fucking flock of black sheep and the motherfucking shepherd to boot, just because I fucking can.

"I like your pool," Sebastian says as he swims to the edge of it. He leans against the side, and I sit up before leaning down to hand him the blunt. "Way too good for the likes of you."

I smirk. "Jealous much?"

"Always," he replies, and the look in his eyes gives me pause. He takes a long pull on the joint and gives a couple coughs, which sets me off laughing all over again. "Fuck, that's good. What did you put in this?"

I glance over at Sloth where he lays on one of my loungers with his shirt off, his eyes closed behind his dark shades. The guy is either always sleeping or looking like he wants to go to sleep. He smiles, though, showing us he's awake, and reaches out blindly for the blunt.

"My special recipe." He smirks.

This is exactly how I expected it to be in The Elite—no pressure, no one giving me orders on what to do, where to go, or who to be. Fucking perfect.

"Well, your special recipe is perfect," Sebastian says.

"Like I don't already know that," Sloth replies arrogantly.

We've been hanging out all afternoon. I'm not really sure how it happened, but when I woke up this morning, Sloth had been lying on one of the sun loungers around my pool like it was perfectly normal.

I hadn't asked any questions, and he pulled out a baggy of weed. At some point, Sebastian showed up with some liquor, and the rest, as they say, is history.

After nearly committing a felony two nights ago helping Lust with a little daddy issue, we need this. It feels good to be around them all just chilling. I hadn't expected, or even thought about this when I decided to join The Elite, but it was a brotherhood, and I was quickly beginning to trust these men—these brothers.

"Can I ask you a question?" Sebastian asks as he swims on his back around my pool, the joint still dangling from his lips.

I take a shot of whisky and glance at Sloth. Other than Sebastian who I met before all The Elite shit, I pretty much refer to my brothers by their sin names. It's the only way to keep them all straight in my head. I think Sloth's eyes are still closed behind his shades, but I can tell he's listening regardless.

"What?" I ask.

"What's in it for you?" Sebastian asks. He flips the joint around in his mouth like he's about to give someone a shotgun, then submerges himself under the water. I'm not sure if it's to buy me or him several seconds to think of my next words, but I'm glad for it all the same.

He swims to the opposite end of the pool, then kicks

WRATH

off the wall and swims back. When he finally surfaces, he pulls out the joint and blows out a plume of thick smoke.

"Well?" he asks, eyeing me.

I look over at Sloth, who's actually showing some interest in my answer. He sits up, blinking behind his glasses.

"What's in it for you?" I ask Sebastian. "Or you?" I say to Sloth. "What's in it for any of us? Power. Freedom. Control," I reply, answering honestly.

"But you've got everything." Sebastian drags his hand through his wet hair. "Just look at this shit. You've obviously got money, and you've clearly got the freedom to do whatever the fuck you please. What more could a man ask for?"

I smile. But it's not friendly. It's dark and sinister. Sebastian's smile falters.

"Revenge," he says, matter of fact.

"Now that, I can drink to," Sloth replies. He pours us all another shot of whisky, handing one to me, then to Sebastian. "To revenge," he says with a smirk.

I drink, but I don't feel comfortable doing it. I've let too much information out, given too much away. I'm not used to trusting other people, to relying on anyone but myself. I look over at my brothers who are talking and laughing, and realize things are different now. I have to trust these people. That's what I've signed up for with The Elite.

We're a brotherhood, and we've bonded.

We're in this—*whatever* the fuck this is—together.

Sabella chooses that moment to walk around the corner of the house, her short dress grazing the tops of her thighs and ruining my good mood. I already know what's coming. I saw it on Sebastian, God, and Rhett's face a couple days ago when they first saw her on campus. My sister is hot, smoking hot, and it's the bane of both of our existences. The amount of boys, then men, I've knocked out for staring at her the way my newfound brothers are is too many to mention. I don't want The Elite world fucking with my family. She'll always come first. After all, this is all for her.

Sebastian lets out a long whistle, and I turn and glare at him, my attention moving to Sloth as he lifts his shades to get a better look at her.

"That's your sister?" Sloth asks in disbelief. "Fuck me, there'd be a whole Princess Leia and Luke Skywalker thing going on if I were her brother." He chuckles, and I snarl at him.

"Watch your fucking mouth," I bite out, my good mood evaporating like a balloon on a sharp pin. "Or I'll watch it for you."

"Luke didn't know she was his sister, man. Don't be putting that shit out there and ruining the biggest twist in cinematic history." Sebastian scowls, but Sloth only shrugs and takes another hit from the joint.

"I'm just saying, sister or not, I would tap that ass. She's fucking delicious." Sloth leans back on the lounger before blatantly rearranging his hardening cock.

"Like I said, shut your fucking mouth or I'll shut it for you. Permanently," I snarl again. I take a deep breath and try to get control of the rage growing inside me. Neither of these assholes seem to realize how close they are to being drowned in my swimming pool if they don't stop undressing my sister with their eyes.

"That's what I said the first time I saw her. She gave me the look," Sebastian says, a smirk still firmly on his

WRATH

face. "Seriously, she's too beautiful to be your twin sister, Samuel. Maybe you're adopted."

Both men start to laugh, but all I can do is glare at them and grind my teeth. I crack the knuckles on my hand, more than ready to end them both.

"Shut up or get the fuck off my property, both of you," I grit out, all humor gone.

"Easy, Sam. We're just fucking with you," Sebastian replies, giving me a slow smile.

"I'd rather be fucking with her," Sloth says, and my gaze shoots to him.

"That's it. Get the fuck out of here. Now," I yell.

I stand up as Sabella walks over to me, taking off her shades and pulling out her ear buds. She looks between the three of us, her gaze taking in the pot and beer scattered around us. Sebastian lifts himself out of the pool as Sloth picks up his beer, neither man making any move to get off my property.

"Why weren't you at school today?" she asks me sharply, her gray eyes moving from me to Sebastian, who's grabbed a towel and is wiping down his chest. He's strong and lean, and she clearly likes what she sees, which sours the drink in my stomach even more. "Sammy, you said you weren't going to mess it up this time," she says, looking back at me.

"And I'm not," I bite out. "But things have changed." I fold my arms across my chest, suddenly feeling like her father. Could I ground her? Burn all her dresses and skirts and make her wear baggy jeans and my old sweaters for the rest of her life? Technically, she is older than me, but that doesn't really mean shit.

"It doesn't look like it to me," she says with a wave

of her hand at the little party we were having before she showed up. "Clean this mess up, and yourself, before Father sees."

"I'm a big fucking boy, Sab. I told you I have this shit handled, and I do. Now, go cover your tits up before I have to kill one of these fuckers."

She puts a hand on her hip and cocks her head at me, her cheeks glowing pink in embarrassment despite her feisty attitude. "You're unbelievable, you know that?"

Sebastian comes to stand next to me, and I glare over at him, though he ignores me in favor of staring at my sister. He holds a still damp hand out to her.

"Well, this can't be coincidence," he says with a smile, and Sab's scowl falters.

"What can't be coincidence?" she asks, her tone frosty.

"I'm warning you," I grit out. There is only so much I'm going to let slide. We're Elite brothers so I'm giving him the respect of not beating him to a bloody pulp, but that respect will only grant him so many passes.

I want to rip his head off.

"Bumping into you again. This is twice in a week," he drawls. "Since your brother is too damn rude to introduce us, I'll introduce myself. I'm Sebastian Westbrook, and you're the better-looking Gunner sibling I see."

She takes his hand, even though I know her well enough to know she doesn't like him—at all. She might find him attractive, but he's being too forward, too arrogant, and too fucking self-assured for her liking. She's into more of the shy, nerdy type.

"Well, Sebastian, I don't think you're the best influence for my brother. And since this is my house as well, I'd like you all to leave." She lets go of his hand and crosses her arms over her chest. She looks back at me. "You promised me, Sammy. You promised me you'd give this a real shot." She shakes her head, her anger dissipating into sadness. "I don't know why I always believe you. You always end up letting me down."

She turns and walks away from me, and Jesus fucking Christ, she's our father's daughter all right. She knows just how to make me feel like a piece of shit with only the bare minimum of words.

Sebastian's smile falls as thunder rolls in the distance and I feel the first drops of rain land on my bare shoulders.

"Thought I told you to get the fuck out," I snarl at Sloth. I look over at Sebastian. "You too, motherfucker."

Sebastian nods and turns to get dressed, his green eyes sparking with something akin to anger, which is unusual for him. Of all the things I know about Sebastian, anger isn't one of them. He's weird as fuck, overly-friendly to almost everyone, but I don't think I've ever seen him angry yet. My cell pings in my pocket, and I pull it out and read the message.

Fuck. This is it.

I drag a hand through my hair and suck in my bottom lip.

"What is it?" Sloth asks as he walks over to me.

"My task," I reply. "Tonight's the night."

He slaps my shoulder. "Have fun. Just remember to wrap it up if you've gotta fuck a horse or some shit." He laughs before walking away.

Sebastian is slipping on his Oxford shoes when he looks up at me. "What does it say?"

I push my cell back into my pocket as the rain starts to come down harder. "It just says to meet at the old nunnery tonight at eight."

He comes toward me. "If you need anything, any help at all, one call is all it takes." He pats my shoulder, and I nod.

I'm still pissed off at him, but I have bigger things to think about than Sebastian ogling my sister.

Tonight is it. My task. The final seal to get me into The Elite.

One stupid task stands between me and breaking Maxwell Gunner's hold over my sister and I. One stupid task and he'll see who's really in charge around here.

I can't fucking wait.

VII
UINCENDUM NATUS

TWELVE

The rain is coming down hard now, great sheets slicing through the night sky and drowning out the light of the moon shining through the old nunnery's windows. It's fucking glorious.

"You got it?" Pride asks, his expression unreadable, as usual.

I look at the card again, memorizing every word of it.

The coin given to you by The Elite offers one trade of future favor. If you cash it in to forfeit your task, you won't be given a choice on the second task. You will need to follow it through or be expelled as a candidate. Using your coin leaves you no future favors shall you ever need something not freely given by The Elite. Think carefully about your choice. You only get one.

WRATH
Your task is the sin of seduction.
Patience Noelle, Mayor Noelle's only daughter & St. Augustine's' sweetheart
For the girl who doesn't believe in love.
Your task is to break her heart.
The Elite giveth, and The Elite taketh away.

I frown, but nod, and Pride reaches over and takes the small piece of card from me before holding it up to one of the candles and setting it on fire.

I know Mayor Noelle. He's been to our house for dinner several times over the years, and I know his daughter, though I haven't seen or thought about her in years—not since we were both little kids trying to find some fun when instead she witnessed me getting a beating. I didn't see her again until we were in our teens at stuffy dinner parties our fathers threw. She went from pretty little defender, to an awkward buck-toothed, frizzy-haired, slightly underweight teenager with no tits. But there was always a connection between us, that one day that bonded us forever.

I drag a hand through my hair. This is going to be easy and embarrassing all in one. I've broken enough girls' hearts over the years not to let that shit get to me. What was one more?

He moves around the room, blowing out the candles. "You look deep in thought," he says as he blows out the last one and we make our way across the cold concrete floor to the door. The storm hasn't let up, and I'm beginning to wish I'd worn my boots instead of my sneakers. I'm going to get soaked just getting to my damn car.

"I know her," I reply as we stand in the doorway

looking out at the rain.

I don't know much about Mason, or should I say Pride, but Sloth said he's a trustworthy guy. Dependent and loyal, or some shit. I guess that's why he was chosen to run our group—which clearly pisses off God aka Gluttony.

God is the type of man you don't tell what to do. None of us are, but where the rest of us don't take our sins too seriously, he clearly takes great offence at not being Pride. His father is like the third richest man in the world or some shit like that, so there's never been a problem he couldn't fix with money—until now. It's almost too funny that the most arrogant man in our group has been cast the sin of Gluttony.

"You know who?" Pride asks, swinging his car keys around his index finger.

"My task," I jut a thumb back over my shoulder. "I know the girl it's about."

"Does it change things for you?" he asks seriously, a frown tugging at his hard features, making him look almost concerned. I'm not sure what it is about this guy, but it's almost like he doesn't want this—The Elite. He hates his given sin, that much is obvious, and there's no missing the air of guilt surrounding him right now.

I shake my head. "No, I guess it makes it easier."

"Good, because The Elite don't want you wasting any time. Get started with it straight away," he replies.

I chew on my bottom lip for a moment. I haven't seen Patience in a long time. Not since the night I kissed her and ruined everything.

I stumble through the dark house, wondering where the low music is coming from. My father sent Sabella and I to bed as soon as the dinner party was over. She's fast asleep, but I haven't been able to. Instead, I stayed awake, doing push-ups, sit-ups, and working up a sweat. I'm only thirteen, but I'm determined to become a man as fast as I can. My life revolves around men in suits coming into my home and shutting doors on me. Men with muscles bigger than my entire body. Men in expensive suits, with women dripping from their arms. Men and money—that's all I know. And I'm determined one day I'll command their respect, one way or another.

I stand on the stairs in the dark, listening to the soft music coming from my father's study, wondering if I should make sure he's in there and hasn't just left the music on.

Voices murmur from within, and I realize he's inside talking to someone. I should go back up to my room, but I'm curious. Father never had anyone around after the servants went home. I creep farther down the stairs and tiptoe toward his door before placing my ear against the wood and listening.

At first, I can't hear anything, just the low beat of the music vibrating through the air, but then, there's a sound. Moaning and the sound of slapping. Hands on flesh and the soft cries of a woman.

My heart pounded in my chest, a sick feeling building in my gut.

My father is beating someone—a woman no less—and she's crying.

I'm not sure what to do. I've always known there's something dark about him, secrets he keeps from Sab and I. And the way he looks at us both sometimes is enough to make anyone fearful. Especially the way he looks at Sab. But I never thought this.

WRATH

I've been working out, building my muscles and strength, and the fear I always feel when he's home from one of his trips has slowly been evaporating. It's now or never. I have to stand up to him. To protect whoever he's hurting and show him I'm not a little kid anymore—that I won't just stand by and let it happen. Not in my house.

I roll my shoulders and crack my knuckles before pressing down on the handle of his door and pushing it open. I'm lucky. He's facing the opposite way and doesn't hear me. I look around for something to hit him with, my gaze falling on a long paddle on the chair next to the door. I pick it up with a frown, my hands stroking over the hard wood as I wonder what it is.

The woman yelps, and my gaze shoots to her. She's bent over my father's desk, her skirt lifted up to show her bare ass, her pink cunt flashing at me as Father moves to the left and strokes a hand over her lower back.

I swallow, transfixed. Her hands are bound with black cord, and her ass has red welts across it.

"You've been a very naughty girl. Don't think I didn't see you at the table touching yourself, pressing your fingers inside your greedy cunt. I told you that you had to wait until I was ready to give you pleasure." My father speaks in his usual domineering tone, sending shivers down my spine. "This punishment is your fault. Remember that." His arm rears back as he lifts something up, then strikes her ass with it.

She yelps, again, and Father leans down next to her ear. "Silence."

"Yes, sir," she whimpers.

He rears back once more, hitting her ass and causing more red welts to appear on her skin. My pants feel suddenly tight, too tight. Reaching down, I adjust my semi-erect dick.

This is wrong.

He's hurting her.

And yet I can't stop the way my heart races and my dick tingles as I watch.

Father smooths a hand across her ass again. "Good girl." I listen to him unbuckling his dress pants before letting them, and his underwear, drop to the floor where he steps out of both and kicks them away.

Now, all I can see is my father's white ass and her beautiful one, now welted and red from the sting of whatever he's used on her. My father goes to stand behind her, and I know what's coming next. I've seen porn, I'm not stupid.

I want to walk away, but something keeps me here, glued to the spot as I watch him fucking her. She never makes a sound, never moves unless he rearranges her body to suit his needs better, and when he comes, he comes with a loud groan, grabbing her hips and slamming into her so hard, the large walnut desk he normally works at screeches across the floor, startling me out of my reverie.

I look down at the paddle in my hand, my gaze falling from the wood to the wet patch at the front of my jogging bottoms where I just came while watching my father bang a woman.

"Are you okay?" he asks, moving to untie her hands.

"Yes, sir," the woman giggles.

He reaches for a pot of cream and begins to smooth some over the welts. "That better?"

"Much. Thank you."

She stands up, and my father leans in, kissing her, his hands tugging on her hair as she wraps her arms around him. He pulls out of the kiss first, and she opens her eyes, her gaze falling to me since I'm still standing, slack-jawed in the doorway of his office.

"Shit, Max," she hisses, grabbing for a scrap of material

WRATH

from the floor to cover herself with.

My father turns around, his dick still dripping with their cum, his gaze roving over every inch of me, from the cum stain on my pants to the paddle in my hands.

I swallow and opened my mouth to say something, but he looks furious—more furious than I've ever seen him. I slam my jaw shut before any words come out.

My father stalks toward me, his gaze hard, dark, and scary as hell. "What the fuck are you doing out of bed, Samuel?" he barks. I shake my head, still not having words. "Speak!"

I realize I'm trembling, shaking from head to toe as I try to make sense of what I've just seen and why he's so angry at me. His face is red, and his dark eyes are cold. He doesn't even seem embarrassed by his own nakedness.

"Did you just watch all of that?" he bites out, and I nod, my gaze going to the woman still standing at the desk as she gasps. "Are you a little pervert, Samuel?"

"No, Father," I mumble.

But I am.

I just watched what my father did and there's no denying I liked it. I liked it a lot.

"You disgust me. Get out of here, and don't ever speak of what you saw again. Do you hear me, boy?" he yells.

I nod and turn to leave.

"Samuel. Give me the paddle."

I turn back and hand over the paddle to him, a feeling of grief washing over me at its loss. I stare at it in his large hands, jealousy surging through me as I wonder if I'll ever feel its touch again.

"What is it?" Father asks, sensing I have questions.

I bravely look up into his face, thinking, stupidly, that he'll like me being a man and asking my question. "Did it feel good?"

I hate him with every inch of my being. I have done for a long time now. Yet I'm thirteen and curious. I have questions that only he can answer.

He frowns and briefly glance over at the woman—a woman I now recognize as Marie Noelle, a woman who had been at our dinner table earlier tonight. And Patience's mom.

"Did what feel good?"

"When you hit her with it," I reply, my jaw flexing. I know instantly I should have kept my mouth shut.

My father's face goes blank and he stares at me for what seems like an hour or more before replying.

"You don't speak of what you just saw to anyone. Do you hear me?" His voice is calm, but there's something chilling in his eyes.

"Okay," I reply, then turn away, feeling angry. "I won't mention it to anyone. Not even the Mayor."

I've only taken one step away from him when his big hand comes down hard on my shoulder. "What did you just say to me?"

"Maxwell! Sort this out!" Marie scolds from behind. "If he says anything..."

"He won't!" he yells before spinning me back around to face him. The back of his hand hits the side of my face and I grunt in pain. "Did you just threaten me?" he sneers. I shake my head no, feeling dazed. "If you think you've got the balls to threaten me, then at least have the balls to follow the threat through, Samuel." He shoves me out into the hallway, slamming my back against the wall.

"I'm sorry," I grunt as he knees me in the stomach.

But I'm not sorry, I'm angry.

Angry at him for fucking the Mayor's wife because I know it could hurt Patience if she finds out, and angry because he has

WRATH

information that I want.

"You little bastard. Don't you ever threaten me. You keep your mouth shut or I'll make sure I shut it for you!"

He pushes me away, and I stumble and fall to the floor. I stare up at him, his flaccid dick hanging limply between his big thighs.

"Just remember your place, boy. If it weren't for me, you'd be nothing. A nobody. A little orphan boy with no mommy or daddy," he sneers, but his expression suddenly changes, his rage dissipating in seconds. He swallows, guilt filling his features. "Just get out of my sight," he says, his voice thick with emotion, shame flaring on his cheeks. He pulls his hands through his hair and turns away from me. "Don't speak of this to anyone."

I jump up and run.

I know where I'm going as soon as my feet hit the ground outside the house. I'm going to see Patience. It's the same place I visit every time I need to find peace.

By the time I arrive at her house, I'm soaked from the rain and out of breath, the damp patch on my pants no longer visible. A crack of thunder and lightning illuminates her house and I run harder.

I see a light on in her window and throw a stone up at it like I do every time. Seconds later, she looks out at me with a frown before nodding and turning away.

It's raining even harder now, and I stand under the large beech tree in her backyard to stay dry. I watch as she comes outside, glancing left and right for me. I whistle to get her attention. She closes the door quietly behind her and runs through the rain to me. By the time she's travelled the short distance, she's soaked too. Her thin cotton nighty clinging to her body.

"What is it?" she asks, wrapping her arms around herself to keep warm. Her dark eyes look me over, small frown lines

pulling between her eyebrows. "Are you okay?" she reaches over to touch my cheek her eyes showing sincere concern. I guess there's a mark from where my father has hit me.

"I'm fine, I just wanted to see you," I say, wondering why I've really come here.

Patience is my friend. My confident.

I never told her about the things my father had said that night, and we never talked about my grandfather or any of the cruel nannies that came in to our home and treated us unkindly. She's just Patience, and I'm just Samuel. We're friends—she's my only friend.

But standing under the beech tree, both of us wet from the rain, I see something in Patience I've never seen before. A spark of something as she pulls off her glasses to wipe the rain away from the lenses. As she goes to slide them back on, I reach out and touch her arm, stilling her, thoughts of her mother's cunt still vivid in my head.

"What is it?" she asks, concern flushing her cheeks.

I step closer to her, needing her body heat. I'm trembling from the cold, desire still burning in my gut. I'd come to tell her about her whore of a mother, but now that I'm here, it seems irrelevant. I reach out, wrapping a hand around the back of her neck, and gently pull her to me.

She whimpers automatically, leaning into me like I'm the sun and she's ice melting to my touch, her dark eyes wary but full of hope. I swallow before placing my mouth on hers and kissing her hard.

I can feel her braces.

I can feel her tongue.

I can feel her body rigid next to mine.

But mostly, I can feel something I've never felt before. Need. Desire. Urgency. And something else that feels good. Something

WRATH

that isn't fear.

I feel powerful.

I feel in control.

I run my hands over her body, my pants tightening as my palm moves over her ass and she groans in my mouth as I squeeze. My dick is hard in my pants and I press myself against her, desperate to hear the sounds her mother had made for my father come from her mouth.

Patience suddenly pulls out of the kiss and steps back from me. "Samuel?" she says, my name a whisper on her pink lips. "What's wrong?"

I fold my arms across my chest, scared of the weird feelings I'm having and embarrassed by the way my wet pants cling to my heavy erection. Her eyes are closed, her lashes thick and dark against her pale skin. She slowly opens her eyes, and it feels like she sees me, the real me.

The frightened boy.

The boy who just wants love and affection.

The boy with no mother.

The murderer.

The boy who's so fucking confused by what he saw tonight, he feels sick to his stomach, yet equally turned on.

And it scares the shit out of me.

I push her away. "Get off me."

"What?"

"You're such a cock tease," I snap angrily.

My words cut her and pierce her worse than any sticks or stones ever could.

"Why are you saying this, Sam?" she asks, her forehead creasing in confusion and pain.

I've never felt so powerful in all my life. I have the power to hurt, to control someone with my words. "I said, you're a slut, just like your whore of a mother."

"Sam!" *my name escapes her lips. One of her hands flies to her mouth to hold in her sob and I suddenly wish I could take them back. But I can't.*

"Patience—"

"Stay away from me!"

I grab for her as she tries to run back to the house. "Please, I'm sorry!"

She turns and slaps me, hard across the face. "Stay away from me."

And then she leaves me there, standing under the tree alone.

"You okay?" he asks, interrupting my thoughts.

I swallow, thinking about Patience, the girl I hadn't seen since the night under her tree where I kissed her, then called her a slut.

"What?" I ask, taking a drag of my cigarette.

"You went all…" he shrugs.

He looks deep in thought, like he actually gives a shit about this story—about Patience, me, and the outcome of it.

"I'm fine. Just thinking about shit."

He looks out into the rain. "You ever think this is all bullshit, Sam?"

I throw my cigarette to the ground. "I think most things are bullshit, brother," I reply without looking at him. "Whatever. I need to go."

I don't wait for him to reply before jogging to my car, becoming drenched again by the time I reach the door.

WRATH

Pride drives a shitty Chevy Impala that looks like it's about to fall apart, yet he doesn't seem to notice. The man could be driving a Lamborghini and I doubt he'd even blink. He's all business and no pleasure.

He starts his engine, and I watch him drive away until I can't see his lights anymore, then I look out into the rain beyond my window, thinking of that night with Patience.

I'd pushed that memory, and that night, to the back of my mind, and now it was going to bite me in the ass.

VII
UINCENDUM NATUS

THIRTEEN

I look up Mayor Noelle as soon as I get home. Research is everything with this task. I've seen Patience a handful of times since that night, but nothing after she turned fifteen. Someone once said she was being home-schooled, but I never cared to look into it. I was too busy fighting, fucking, and taking drugs by that point.

A quick search on Google shows Mayor Noelle still lives in the same old plantation house, half a mile from here. But there aren't any discussions on the whereabouts of where Patience is now.

I bring up some photos from a recent charity benefit, hoping to spot her, but the creep is constantly surrounded by women—young women who should have better sense than allowing this prick to fuck them.

My cell vibrates, and I pick it up, reading the message

from Sebastian.

OPEN YOUR DOOR.

I frown at the message. I'm not in the mood for company right now. I have shit to be getting on with and making small talk with him isn't important right now. I head out of my room to the front door of the pool house and sure enough Sebastian is stood there, his green eyes cutting through the gray day.

"What?" I bark.

"Gotta watch that temper of yours, Sammy." He grins as he uses my nickname from Sab.

"What did you just say?" I scowl. I look past him, seeing Sabella moving around in the kitchen of the main house. "Have you been talking to my sister again?"

"Stop acting like such a pussy. We were just talking." He twists the watch on his wrist, and I continue to scowl at him. "I came to find out about your task—do you need any help with it?"

I scowl harder. "No."

He rolls his eyes and pushes past me. "You know I'm good with technology, right? If you need something, let me know, use me."

"You sound like a cheap porno," I snicker, and he joins in.

I watch him moving around the pool house, picking up my shit and putting it back down.

"What do you want?" I ask, closing the door since he clearly isn't fucking leaving anytime soon. I walk into the kitchen to grab an energy drink. I've been up most of the night thinking about Patience and Maxwell and Sabella and the fuck up I've made of my life.

"I told you, I came to help," he says as he looks down

at my laptop. He glances up at me. "You looking into the Mayor?"

"Can't say," I reply.

"Can't say or won't say?" he smirks back. "Ooooh, a mystery! We're like the Scooby Doo crew. You can be Shaggy and I'll be the tall blond dude that gets all the hot chicks." He winks.

I'm actually not sure if we can talk about our tasks since we haven't been specifically told not to, but I have a feeling it would likely be frowned upon.

"Either. Both," I reply with a shrug. "Have you gotten yours yet?" I ask, curious.

The task hadn't been what I'd been expecting, and I was interested to know what everyone else's had been. Mine seemed…wrong, fucked up even. Why do this to a girl? What did The Elite hope to gain by hurting her?

He sat down at my computer and started clicking buttons, his hands moving over the keyboard too fast for me to comprehend. "Nope, not yet. Bored as shit waiting for it, though."

I pull out two energy drinks and pop one open before downing most of it in one chug. Fuck I'm tired. And I'm supposed to go to school today. A meeting has been booked with the school counselor, courtesy of my dickhead of a father.

"Here you go," Sebastian says. He's looking at my computer screen and he gives a whistle. "She's fucking hot. Not as hot as your sister, but sill incredibly bangable."

I scowl at him. "Watch yourself."

He laughs as I head over to the laptop. I expect to see porn or some shit, but what I see makes me drop my can. Thank fuck I drank most of it.

WRATH

On my computer screen is Patience. At least…I think it's her. I pick up the can from the floor and throw an old t-shirt over the wet patch before moving to the laptop to get a better look.

It *is* her, but not like I've seen her before. No wonder I hadn't instantly recognized her.

Patience is beautiful. Really fucking beautiful.

Nothing like the gangly kid I once knew.

Her hair hangs long, dark, and shiny down her back. Her lips are big and pouty, and behind them are straight white teeth. Her skin is pale like milk, and she fucking filled out. Her tits look big and firm, her legs long, her waist narrow. Things just got a whole lot more complicated.

"Fuck," I murmur as I scroll through pictures of her.

"You gonna tap that?" Sebastian asks from over my shoulder, making me practically jump out of my skin because I'd been so lost in thought that I forgot he was even here.

"Motherfucker, I will knock your fucking teeth out if you do that to me again!" I yell, but then I can't stop myself from laughing as he feigns innocence.

"What can I say? I'm quiet."

"Quiet? You're like a fucking stalker the way you creep about."

"It's my crazy ninja skills," he jokes.

I shake my head, ignoring the weird look on his face as I look back down at a picture of Patience. This time, she's laying on a beach with some friends wearing a tiny white bikini that barely covered her large tits. *Jesus, she needs to cover those up*, I think darkly. *Preferably with my mouth.*

"So, she's your task?" Sebastian asks.

I glance back over at him, trying to decide whether it will be okay to talk about it or not. He'll probably find out anyway, I decide.

"Yeah," I look back at the photo of her smiling, her hair tied in a messy bun as she splashes in the sea.

"You gotta fuck her?" he ask. "Because I've gotta say, not that I want us to become life partners or anything, but you're a good-looking guy so I don't think you'll have any problem. She doesn't have a boyfriend. She's been traveling the past year after graduating high school early. Not that she actually went to high school. In fact, it looks like—at least from what I quickly read—she was homeschooled from the age of fourteen. Probably going to do the same when it comes to college too. She's been living off and on with her mother in California too."

He leans against the desk, picks up my unopened energy drink, and pops it open. "I'd say she's probably still a virgin too—despite that tight ass of hers. Something spooked her when she was a kid, and I reckon she's never gotten over it."

I stare up at him in shock and wonder. "You got all that from a couple pictures?"

He laughs and drinks from my can before grimacing and putting it back down. "Dude, that shit will rot your insides." He starts to walk toward the door.

"Sebastian!" I call angrily, standing up.

He stops and turns around. "No, I got that from the quick search I did on her. I sent it all to your printer, man. Give me a call if you need anymore help. And calm the fuck down. You're like a pot of boiling water ready to bubble over all the time. It makes me fucking jumpy."

He leaves, and I look at my printer, seeing two or

WRATH

three sheets of paper printed off. Dude is a fucking genius, despite—or maybe because of—his weirdness.

I reach over and grab the print-outs before reading through them quickly, knowing immediately what spooked her all those years ago.

Me.

Guilt burns in my veins at the thought of this beautiful woman feeling like shit all this time because of me. And then I grit my teeth. No, not because of me, because of Maxwell. Because of that night and what he'd done.

Motherfucker ruined things for me and her.

God, I can't wait to ruin him.

My cell phone rings in my jeans, but I ignore it in favor of watching Patience from across the room. Besides, I already know who it is. It's the same person who's been calling since I missed my first counselor session at school.

Patience leans back in her chair and picks up her coffee mug before taking a sip. I intended to go over as soon as her friends left for class, but instead, I've been sitting here for an hour, watching her like some weird kind of stalker.

But I can't stop.

The more I watch her, the more I worry about going over.

Jesus fucking Christ, I'm turning into a pussy.

I was a kid back then, and I fucked up, surely she'll understand that?

She reaches up and stretches her arms above her head,

her little t-shirt lifting to reveal a smooth flat tanned stomach beneath. A barista stops by her table and she orders another coffee and picks up her pad and pen before continuing to write.

From the stuff Sebastian printed off for me, she has a tutor who comes to her house three times a week. She's a psychology major and currently has an essay due in. She is beautiful and clever. Sab would love her. Shame she isn't ever going to be more than a quick fuck.

I shake the thought off. This isn't about a relationship or finding someone Sab will approve of. I don't intend on making her my girlfriend and living happily ever after as we ride off into the sunset. This is about a task. Fuck her, make her fall for me, and then break her heart. I'm guessing The Elite wants her to fail her course or something, though I don't see understand why they want to do that to a girl like her. She's traveled the past year, helping build orphanages in South Africa, digging wells in Cambodia. I mean, she's as fucking pure as they come.

"I'm a Man" by Black Strobe comes on the radio, and I chuckle to myself. I fucking love this song and I definitely need to draw on my inner man to get this shit done.

Okay, pussy, it's now or never. This is a fucking sign.

I stand up, threading between the tables and ignoring the brazen looks from other women. I have a target, and just like in the ring, I'm not going anywhere without my pound of flesh.

I stop next to her table and look down at her. Her top is low cut, revealing the swell of her breasts in her bra. Makes me wonder how pink her nipples would be after I made her wear nipple clamps for an hour. Fucking hell. I groan.

WRATH

I clear my throat as she slowly looks up, her dark eyes taking in my legs and moving up my hard body all the way to my face. Her eyes widen slightly.

"Patience Noelle," I say, "it's been a long time." I smile, flicking my tongue out to dampen my lips.

She takes a deep breath and stands up, coming toe to toe with me. I think she's going to smile, maybe even kiss me. Fuck me, she's prettier in person than her pictures. How that's even possible, I'm not sure, but it's true.

Her eyes narrow as she rears back, her hand coming down hard to slap me across the face. The sound echoes between us. It's like a gnat bite to the cheek, but that isn't exactly the point.

She turns her back on me and picks up her things before looking back around and glaring at me. "Not long enough," she hisses, her fat lips practically spitting venom as her eyes narrow.

She squeezes past me, and like the bastard I am, I let her walk away, too shocked and too turned on to stop her. Because if there's one thing I like more than anything, it's a feisty woman I can teach to submit.

The jangle of the bell above the door signals her leaving, and I stare after her, rubbing a hand along my cheek and giving a low chuckle.

This task just got a whole lot harder, but I'm going to enjoy getting her in my bed.

VII

UINCENDUM NATUS

FOURTEEN

I walk into the retirement home, a huge bunch of flowers under one arm and a bag of candy in the other. I'm dressed in my best smart-casual attire, because jeans and a leather jacket won't do for this type of place if I want to win her round.

The woman working reception looks up sharply, her gaze taking in every inch of me as she gives me a warm smile. "Welcome to Nouvelle nursing home, can I help you?"

I step to her desk, leaning on it and giving her my best panting-melting smile. "I'm actually looking for Patience Noelle, I believe that she helps out here?"

The receptionist's face falls. "Yes, she's already started. Are you here to volunteer?"

I nod, and she hands me a sign-in sheet. "We're all

going to be here one day, you know? We have to look after our elderly."

Her cheeks turn pink as I throw her another smile. "Yes. Exactly."

I slide a check over the counter to her. "Hopefully this will help."

Nouvelle Nursing Home is in financial trouble. Sebastian got me that information within thirty seconds of looking. He downloaded an itinerary of all the places Patience frequented, and with every line I read, I disliked this task more and more. If Sabella ever finds out I fucked this girl up, she'll never forgive me. She is so like Sabella, it's freaky. She is good and kind, honest. She gives up her time, money. Jesus fuck, she's everything I'm not.

The receptionist opens the envelope, and her smile grows wider. "Oh my," she murmurs, her gaze fixing on me. "Let me take you down there."

She starts to stand up, but I hold up a hand. "No need. I'll find it."

I sign in and head down the corridor, feeling the receptionist's eyes on my ass the entire time. I grimace as I look around. This place is in dire need of repair and redecoration. The paper is curling in the corners, the carpet is greying and a funky smell hangs in the air that reminds me of death. Not to mention that there are large cracks in the walls.

I'd rather die than end up in a place like this.

The door to the coffee room is open and I look in, my gaze scanning everywhere for her, finally finding her pouring coffee for a guy who reminds me of the skeleton dude from Tales from the Crypt Keeper. The old perv is staring right down her top as she pours him a coffee, but instead of feeling angry, I chuckle, knowing I would do the same damn thing.

I can't help my smile as I look at all the happy faces. This place might be a shithole, but no one here seems to care. Another girl walks over and speaks to Patience, and she nods and smiles, placing her hand on the other girl's arm. God, what I wouldn't fucking give to have her touch me like that…and more.

I straighten my shoulders and walk in, heading straight to the oldest lady in the place and handing her one of the flowers from the bunch I'm carrying. She gives me a gummy smile as a little light enters back into her gray eyes.

"Oh, I haven't been given flowers since I was thirty-two years old," she coos. "Thank you, young man. You've made this old lady very happy."

I shrug and look around. "I don't see any old ladies around here," I reply with a wink, and she laughs as I move to the next old broad and do the same thing. It's around the eighth old lady when Patience comes over to me, hissing in my ear.

"What are you doing here?" she bites out.

I turn to face her, looking surprised. "Wow, what a surprise. I didn't expect to see you here."

She rolls her eyes at me. "Cut the crap, Samuel."

I give her a half shrug and walk away, and because I'm an arrogant bastard, I know she'll follow me. She comes to stand in front of me, blocking my view of an old lady wearing a head scarf, her hair fluffing out the sides of it like an old Romanian woman.

"Do you mind?" I ask with a scowl. "I'm trying to put a little light back into these people's lives."

WRATH

Her mouth drops open, and she stumbles over the words that don't quite make it past her tongue. She glances to the side, then back to me before letting out a frustrated sigh.

"I need you to leave," she finally says, her tone clipped.

"I'm not sure what to say to you, Patience, I'm just here trying to do something nice," I say calmly. She hates that I'm here, but she's going to have to fucking get used to it. I'm going to follow her everywhere, until she finally caves and gets the fuck in my bed.

Tears fill her eyes, and shit, I think she's going to cry, but then something in her settles and she pulls her shit together. I like that. I like that she's not fooled by my bullshit and being a pushover.

"Really? So this is just a coincidence then?" she asks, her voice softer and hands on her hips. "You've really been here before?"

I can't lie. Or...I won't lie. It's a promise I made to myself when I was a kid. I've never broken it, and don't intend to now, but I can't admit the truth to her or she'll be fucking furious with me.

There's a tap on my shoulder, and I'm relieved for all of two seconds until I see the receptionist with my check in her hand and a flirty smile on her face.

"Excuse me, the manager asked me to come over and personally thank you for your donation. You have no idea what this means to us." She smiles again, and I nod my head.

"Yeah, it's fine, don't worry about it," I say.

"We hope this isn't the first and last time we'll be seeing you around here. I know I personally would enjoy getting to know you more, Mr. Gunner."

I look over at Patience. Her soft expression has turned hard. She shakes her head at me, her cheeks burning red.

"You're unbelievable!" she bites out, then walks away.

"Fuck," I grumble. I jog after her, catching her in two easy strides, aware everyone in the room is watching us. "Patience," I say her name, and realize I like the feel of it on my lips.

As kids, I always loved her name, and as a man, I love it even more.

"Go away," she snaps, continuing to walk away.

I jog in front of her, stopping her in her tracks. "Will you just listen to me?"

"No!"

"Please?"

Her eyes narrow. "No!"

"Patience," I say her name right about the time she rears back and slaps me hard across the face. Again. Fuck me, it doesn't hurt anything but my pride. She really needs to know who she's dealing with.

I rub a hand over my jaw in fake pretence. She looks shocked that she's just hit me again, and I think I can use it to my advantage.

"You deserved that," she says softly, her cheeks flaming red as everyone looks at us.

I look up at them and nod. "I did."

"Don't do that," she says.

"What?"

"Don't pretend you're saving me when we both know you're an asshole who's only out for himself."

I have to admit, that hurt a little. Mainly because it's the truth.

"That's just mean," I say to her, and doubt flashes

across her face. "You know, I like you, that's all. I thought maybe I could do something nice while getting to see you."

She shakes her head and walks away.

Shit. I thought I'd gotten through to her.

She heads out of the room, and I look around, not sure what to do now. The receptionist has gone back to her desk, and the old lady I'm stood next to looks at me expectantly.

"This is better than Days of Our Lives," she says with a smile. "Go after her!"

I nod and dump the rest of the flowers on her lap before following Patience out into the hallway, but when I get there, she's gone.

Fuck.

VII

UINCENDUM NATUS

FIFTEEN

The sound of Maxwell's shoes slapping across the floor as he walks through the foyer draws my attention. I look up from the computer I'm working at as he stops in the doorway.

"School called," he growls, "you missed your appointment."

I put down my pen. "I've already spoken to them and rescheduled the appointment."

He sighs. "You're missing the point, Samuel."

"Am I?" I glower. "Because I thought the point was to go to school and not get in any fights, and that's what I'm doing."

His eyes narrow on me, finally taking in the papers spread over the desk like confetti. "What's all that?"

"Homework," I bite out. "Apparently, the most boring

teacher in the world with a voice that sends you to sleep isn't enough torture. They also want to make sure we're bored as fuck when we get home too." I drag a hand through my hair, noting the way his lips raise in a half smile at that comment.

"Mr. Pulliver," he chuckles. "He's got little dog syndrome, but he knows his shit if you can get past how boring he is."

I laugh back, then force myself to stop. His own laughter dies off. "If it's all right with you, I'm going to take this evening off. I could use a break. My brain isn't used to doing all this work." I lift an eyebrow.

He frowns, confused by my admittance and me asking him for anything.

Don't get used to it, fucker.

"Sure," he replies before turning from me. I smile, but drop it quickly when he glances back around to face me again. "I have a charity function tonight your grandmother is throwing. Sabella is coming." He scratches at his beard, a harsh scowl on his face. "I have another ticket if you want to come with us."

I soften my features and nod. "Yeah. That would be good."

He grunts something else before walking away, and I smile again. I already knew about the charity event tonight, thanks to Sebastian, and I had no doubt The Elite could have gotten me a ticket if I'd asked, but I needed to go with dear old Daddy and my sister. Patience is going to be there, and if I'm going to win her over, my bad boy image isn't going to cut it. She's had boyfriends, and they've all been the type who try to date Sabella: good, wholesome family men—the opposite of everything I am.

I can't change or hide the fact that I've been kicked out of so many schools, or deny my police record for fighting, so changed man is what I'm going for. Showing up with my sister, father, and grandma is imperative to win her over.

"Sammy?" Sabella says as she comes into the room. "Are you okay? What happened?"

"I got into a stupid fight at school," I lie. "It doesn't even hurt," I lie again, and shrug like nothing happened, despite the fact that my legs feel like melting jelly.

"Really?" She peers into my face, which by now must be starting to bruise, or at least swell. "It looks painful," she says as she reaches up to touch the cut.

I force myself not to react when she touches my bloody, tender lip, and I'm rewarded with a smile from her. I smile back, glad I didn't tell her the truth.

"See," I say. "I'm fine."

She nods, but frowns. "I don't understand why you're always fighting, Sammy. Why you're so angry all the time."

I shrug, because what can I say?

Our father hates us. He hires nannies to look after us, but when they realize they're not going to be the next Mrs. Gunner, they take their frustrations out on us—on me, because I take the beatings for you.

I'm bad because then you get to slip under the radar.

But if I'm good, we'll both get hurt.

And I'd rather die than let something happen to you.

"I don't know. I just feel angry all the time," I say, which

WRATH

isn't a complete lie.

I do feel angry all the time.

I feel angry that we have to live this way.

I feel angry that we don't have a mother.

That we barely have a father.

But mostly, I feel angry because I'm so damn sad all the time. Because I don't understand why my father can't love us—love me. How he can't see the shit going on right under his nose.

"People suck," I say. "They annoy me, and I can't help but let my fists do the talking."

I hate lying, to her especially, and I vow when I grow up, I'll never lie again.

Sabella sighs at me. "I wish you'd at least try to be good, Sammy. Promise me you'll try."

We're twelve, but we're both older in our heads.

"I'll try, Sab," I lie again.

It's better that I lie than tell her the truth.

I head upstairs to shower and change. I already had a new suit and shoes delivered this afternoon, and I find I'm actually looking forward to putting them on. It's not bespoke, and not from my usual tailor. Instead, God hooked me up with one of his contacts. As much as I've always hated wearing suits, there's something to be said for how wearing one makes you feel and look powerful.

After my shower, I towel dry my hair and slick it back from my face before sliding on my dress shirt and buttoning my pants. The gray suit God's tailor picked out for me fits like a glove. I'm used to bespoke, but this is as good.

Silk lined, wide lapels, and real horn buttons. I stare at myself in the mirror, feeling like a fraud, but quickly brush the feeling away. I pick out a pair of gold cufflinks and fasten them before sliding on my jacket and spraying on some five-hundred-dollar cologne.

Back downstairs, I wait by the door. The limousine pulls up as I open the door and light my smoke. I call up to Sabella.

Tonight is going to be fucking horrible. I despise spending time with Maxwell, but spending time with my grandmother is even worse. The old hag is just that—a judgy old bitch who looks down her nose at everyone and everything. Nothing is ever good enough for her, not even her only grandchildren.

My father joins me by the door, side-eyeing the cigarette in my hand. He doesn't smoke. And he hates the fact that I do. That's one of the reasons I originally started. Petty? Yes. But I don't give a fuck. Anything I can do to make his life as unbearable is worth it in my book.

He looks me up and down appraisingly, his salt and pepper beard twitching as he takes in my new suit. "That's not from—"

"No. I got my own tailor," I reply, cutting him off.

He nods. "It's good. You look..." he hesitates, trying to find the right word, "smart."

I want to laugh. He could have said anything, because anything at all that would have been better than smart. I look more than smart. I look fucking impressive. My frame has bulked out since the last time he's seen me in a suit. I fill it now instead of just wear it. But of course, he can't just come out and say that to me. Say he's proud I'm turning my life around. Or he's glad I'm coming tonight.

WRATH

No. Instead, the fucker thinks I look smart.

Prick.

Sabella comes down the stairs, her tight black and silver dress clinging to her hourglass figure. Her hair is pinned up high on her head, soft curls trailing down each side of her face. Both Maxwell and I stare at her with a frown.

She looks like a Hollywood star. Like Marilyn Monroe or some shit.

"Go change!" Maxwell barks.

"Right the fuck now!" I bite out.

She looks between us both, her gray eyes going wide before she starts to laugh. "I will do no such thing."

She pushes between us and heads to the limo, and I turn to stare at Maxwell. "You're not seriously letting her go out like that, are you?"

He stares after her with a look I've never seen before on his face. "She looks so much like her mother." He smiles, the hard lines of his face softening. His gaze is still on Sabella as the driver opens the door for her and she climbs inside.

"What did you just say?" I ask, my throat feeling tight.

He turns to look at me, the fog clearing and his features hardening again. "Keep an eye on her tonight," he replies, his tone tense and uncomfortable. He looks away from me and heads toward the limousine. I stare after him, wondering what the hell just happened.

"Come on, Sammy. We're going to be late," Sab calls out the window, a huge smile on her beautiful face. She's basking in this—her little brother and her father traveling in the same limousine—and to a party, no less. We're acting like a real family instead of enemies for a change. It's something none of us are used to.

No, all I've ever had is Sabella and the grave of a mom I visited once a week to confess my sins to. But this… family…I can see why people want it, crave it so much. A mother, a father, a sister, a life that's not about anger and violence, hate and rage, but maybe about love and laughter. The light instead of the dark.

I swallow and bury those pathetic thoughts down deep. That will never be me. I won't let it.

I start walking to the limo, my shoes crunching over the gravel. I slide inside to play the part of loving brother and respectable son. I smile at Sab, and she hugs my arm. I catch Maxwell's gaze on us, his look unrecognizable to me.

Perhaps there is an ounce of love there after all. A speck of pride trying to surface through all the years of bullshit he's put us through. It doesn't matter. It's too late for any of that now.

I give him a tight smile and watch as he returns it tersely before looking at Sabella, pride in his eyes. What is it he said? She looks so much like our mother? I look across and smile at her, wishing I could see what he does. Know what he knows. But I can't.

Maxwell Gunner destroyed every photograph of our mother.

He's blotted her out of our lives like a bad memory. I've never seen what she looks like, and I never will. I can't help but wonder how much of her he sees in me.

I hope it's a lot.

I hope when I ruin him, he'll see her ruining him too.

Because I can't imagine anything could be more painful for him. And pain is my speciality.

VII

UINCENDUM NATUS

SIXTEEN

"Oh, you brought him with you," my grandmother says, not even trying to hide her distaste for me. She accepts Sabella—Sab worked damn hard over the years to win my grandmother's acceptance—but me…well, she despises me. More so because I won't play her bullshit game. "He's not going to cause a scene, is he? I have the Mayor here tonight, and some friends from the pony club, Maxwell."

"I won't be any trouble. I promise," I say with as much sincerity as I can muster.

She looks me up and down in disfavor. "Yes, well, I've heard that one before."

She turns and walks away, and I try to hide my laughter as best I can.

Stupid old cunt.

She's right, though. She has heard that one before. The only thing I enjoy more than pissing off Maxwell is embarrassing my grandmother. I got drunk at her sixtieth birthday and fucked her best friend's niece in the cloakroom, making sure she climaxed loudly right in the middle of the speeches. That took some fucking skill, let me tell you, but I played that girl like the fucking Pied Piper.

But my favorite memory was at a charity fundraiser she held for the victims of Hurricane Katrina. Not survivors, victims, and that was my first problem with her piece of shit charity event. The second being that the so-called victims were rich bitches who lost their fur coats to the storms.

My grandmother didn't give a shit that people had lost lives, homes, their belongings. No, she cared that she and all her rich bitch friends had lost their fur coats.

"It's not funny," Sab says, elbowing me in the side.

I raise an eyebrow at her, realizing I must have been snickering to myself.

Maxwell's already excused himself to talk to one of the local counselors, leaving us alone.

"You wanna drink?" I ask.

"Sammy," she warns.

I hold up my hands innocently. "What? It's just one little drink."

"Fine," she replies warily. "Champagne. I'm going to say hi to some friends."

"I'll bring it over," I say.

I notice a piece of shit man-boy with more gel in his hair than is reasonably acceptable for someone his age staring at her. I glower at him until he looks away.

WRATH

"Yeah, that's right, fuck face," I mutter, "look the fuck away."

At the bar, I order a whisky sour and a glass of champagne with a curt nod before taking my time to look around the room. I haven't seen Patience yet, but I know she's here, somewhere. Hopefully, she won't see me and try to run away like she did today. Otherwise, this task is going to be longwinded and annoying as fuck.

My eyes fall on a man talking in hushed tones with an officer in full uniform, an array of badges adorning the breast of his jacket. *What a pretentious prick.* The other man is one I recognize, though. It's the guy I saw at The Elite nightclub, and just like that night, tonight he has an air of authority and superiority surrounding him like a visible aura. "You have an eye for spotting the power in a room," a sultry voice purrs, coming to stand beside me. An intoxicating scent wafts into my nose, burning the nostrils, and overused sickly perfume. I drop my eyes to her. She's pretty. Pitch-black hair falling like a sheet of silk over her shoulders, resting over a pair of perky tits in a revealing black number, but she has a fake look that's never appealed to me. Why do women think they need to do all that shit to their faces and bodies?

The woman from The Elite club told me who he was, but I want to know who he really is. He clearly holds power given the places and people he mingles with.

"Who's he?" I ask, giving him another look. He's tall, real fucking tall, and broad, a pristine suit, tailored and expensive. He surveys the room, taking in everything and everyone while allowing the police guy to do all the talking. But he's the one in charge of the conversation, that much is very clear.

"That's my brother, the king of New Orleans," she scoffs, picking up a drink I didn't notice her order. She takes a sip and moves closer to me until we're almost touching.

"And the uniform?" I query.

"Ah, that's our chief of police." She smiles tightly. "It's not what you know in this town, Samuel. It's who." My eyes snap to hers with her use of my name.

"You have me at a disadvantage," I growl.

Her eyes spark wide before she tells me, "Oh, that I know."

"Lillian." Maxwell announces his presence, "I see you've met my son. I hope he's behaving himself." His expression would seem impassive to anyone else, but I see the tightness around his eyes as he looks between us.

Knocking back my drink the barmaid finally set in front of me, I gesture for another.

"He was just telling me about his classes," she says with a smile, her eyes still trained on me. "He says he's been putting all of his efforts into the *tasks* laid out to him. It's nice to know he takes these things so seriously and intends to see his duty through to the end," she tells Maxwell, her eyes are still fixed on mine. Her double meaning doesn't go unnoticed by me.

She's something to do with the fucking Elite.

Maxwell grunts at her words like they're laughable. "Sabella, my daughter, I'd love for you to meet her. She's the one I spoke to you about."

Reaching forward, she pats Maxwell's arm. "Maybe later. I'm being summoned by the almighty. Excuse me." She waltzes off toward her brother, who's scowling at her.

"How do you know her?" I ask Maxwell, who's busy

watching Lillian's ass as she makes her way through the crowd.

"She's your counselor, Samuel, and a very influential woman. It would be a good idea to keep in her good graces." With that, he fucks off, leaving me wondering what the hell a school counselor would have to do with The Elite.

I hear a loud laugh, and when I look over, I notice God and the fattest man I've ever seen in my life standing next to him. God looks acutely uncomfortable. In fact, I don't think I've ever seen him look as uncomfortable as he does right now as the fat guy shoves some shrimp in his mouth.

God keeps his cards close to his chest. Out of everyone in the group, I know him the least. He's used to getting his way, either by buying whatever it is he needs or using his family name. If I'm honest, he's the sort of guy I can't usually stand to be around. He's far too fucking self-assured and obnoxious, just like my grandmother and her hag friends. But no doubt having him on my side has its benefits. Like the suit I'm currently wearing for instance.

He sips on a glass of wine while the fat guy stuffs his face with a tray of shrimp and avocado appetizers. The more he eats, the more uncomfortable God looks. I'm about to look away because watching it is making me feel sick, but God looks up and catches my eye. I can't decide in that moment if he's relieved to see a friendly face or even more embarrassed.

Either way, we've seen each other now. I leave Sabella's champagne on the bar and head over to him.

"God," I say, shaking his hand. "How are things?" I ask, trying to feel him out and see if he's had his task yet.

He shakes my hand. "Good," he replies, not giving anything away. "Nice suit."

I smirk, but don't get to reply as the fat fuck next to him pauses in his eating to look between us. He wipes his hand down the front of his jacket and holds it out, and I reluctantly shake it.

"Baxter Goddard the Fourth. Better known as Four. And you are?" He narrows his eyes, his bulbous cheeks making them turn into slits as he ponders his own question. "Maxwell Gunner's boy, right?"

I nod. "Yes, sir."

This is God's father. Jesus, no wonder he looks like he wants the ground to swallow him up. I'd be embarrassed too if that was my father. It just goes to show money can't buy you everything. You can be the third richest person in the world and still be a freakshow who's own son is embarrassed by you.

"We don't normally see you at these get-togethers," he states, matter of fact, his fat tongue flicking out to lick his greasy lips. He looks between God and I, and his eyes widen. "Oh, I see," he replies, giving us both an oily-mouthed smile. "Off you go then. I know how these things work. Time to get to work, no doubt." He returns to eating before I can reply, and I take that as my cue to leave, grateful for the escape.

"Pleasure to meet you, sir," I say, practically gagging on the word "sir." I'm not a "yes, sir," "no, sir" type of man, but I'm playing a part, and Baxter fucking Goddard the Fourth can blow my whole act if he decides he doesn't like me. Or, more likely, he can tell The Elite he doesn't want me in.

He may be a fat fuck, but he's as sharp as a pin. It's

WRATH

obvious nothing gets past him. He knows who's who and what's what. I guess you can't be too careful when you're as rich as he is. I bet he has a stream of people ready to screw him over at every turn.

He sucks the grease off his fingers and shakes my hand again, and my nostrils flare in disgust. I start to walk away, and God steps in line with me. I side-eye him.

"Don't say a fucking word," he bites out.

"Wasn't going to," I reply seriously. What's there to say? Clearly there's more than just me with the daddy issues in this little group, and I'm not about to judge him based on his fat as fuck father, just like I wouldn't expect him to judge me on my prick of a dad.

We pass a waitress carrying a silver tray of appetizers, and I grab a shrimp on a cocktail stick. I bite it off before placing the empty stick back on the tray. God watches as I chew, but quickly looks away. God likes to look good. Going by his physique, he treats his body like a temple. He exercises, eats well, and doesn't splurge on what goes into his body unless it's drugs or drink.

We're similar in shape and size, though I eat and drink whatever the fuck I want. My build is all down to the many fights I've put myself through and not through denying myself anything. I didn't win my fights by being disciplined or training hard; I win them on pure rage alone. Hence why most of the people I fight give up their little hobby when I'm done with them.

I should probably feel some shame in that, but I feel pride.

"So, is this business or pleasure?" God asks, grabbing a glass of champagne from one of the waitresses. She gives us both a seductive smile, but she could have been an

Amazonian goddess for all I care. She isn't Patience. And Patience is the only woman I want right now.

"Business," I reply, quirking an eyebrow at him, and he nods. "Hopefully leading to some pleasure along the way."

He chuckles darkly, his gaze on the waitress. "That's the best type of business." His cell phone beeps in his pocket, and he pulls it out to read the message.

While he types out a reply, I take my time to look around again for Patience. I still haven't seen her, but I see Mayor Noelle talking to my grandmother by the bar, so I know she has to be here somewhere. They're deep in conversation, neither of them looking particularly happy as their discussion becomes more heated. The mayor looks my way, a small frown tugging between his eyes before he looks back at my grandmother.

"I need to go handle something," I say to God, and he glances up from his cell to see where I'm looking.

"Problem?"

"Let's just say I didn't leave him with the best impression of me, and I really need him and his daughter to think I'm a motherfucking prince right now." I take a sip of the whisky sour in my hand.

"My father is pretty friendly with the mayor. If you want me to, I can put in a good word," he offers.

I'm tempted to say no. Mainly because I'm used to handling my own shit, but then that's what The Elite is for—to back each other up. We're supposed to be a brotherhood, and that means letting people help me. The thought is less than appealing, but if I can be polite to my fucking bitch of a grandmother, I can accept a little help from God.

WRATH

The irony of that statement isn't lost on me.

"Sure. That would be helpful," I reply grimly.

"Don't look too pleased about it," he retorts dryly.

Sabella walks into the room at that moment, and I notice several men turn to look in her direction. Jesus fuck. I'm going to end up killing someone tonight.

"That's your sister, right?" God says, and I glare at him. He smirks, unaffected by my protective big brother shit. "Don't worry, I've already been warned off her by Sebastian, and she's not my type anyway" he deadpans.

"I'm gonna fucking kill him if he keeps this up. She's not interested in him," I grit out.

I like Sebastian. Well, as much as you can like someone you barely know. But I have no qualms over knocking his teeth out if he keeps chasing Sabella. She's off limits to all these motherfuckers.

"He'll get the message," God says, slipping his cell back into his pocket. "Come on." He starts to walk toward Mayor Noelle, and I follow.

"Mayor," God says, holding his hand out. The Mayor takes it and gives a curt nod of his head. "Mrs. Gunner-Antoine." He takes my grandmother's hand in his and kisses the back of it. She blushes and gives a giggle that belongs more to a schoolgirl—not a seventy-year-old lady.

"Mr. Goddard, I'm happy to see you here tonight," the mayor says.

"Wouldn't miss a charity event to save—" He looks around for one of the banners hanging on the wall.

"Extra funding for the women's bridge club," my grandmother cuts in with a smile.

"Ahhh, yes, that's the one." He snorts, making my grandmother narrow her beady eyes on him.

Jesus fucking Christ, I need to get out of here before I lose my shit. Of all the self-righteous things my grandmother could have brought these people together for, it's for her fucking bridge club. She has more than enough money to pay for this herself, so the whole thing is just to get in the same room as these people and be flashy. God, I hate her.

"I'm sure you know Samuel Gunner, Mrs. Gunner-Antoine's grandson." God nods in my direction, and both my grandmother and the mayor give me tight smiles. "I hope there's no hostility against him since he's such a good friend of mine and my father's."

I almost bark out a laugh as the mayor physically shrinks at God's words and my own grandmother looks at me in shock.

I smile at them both politely. "Good evening, Mayor."

He glances between God and I, taking the hint from God, before holding out a hand to me. At least he's learning his fucking place. "Good evening, Mr. Gunner. I was just telling your grandmother how much Sabella has grown since she used to play with my Patience."

I was there too, prick. She was mine then...

I don't really know the man, but no doubt he knows a lot about me from Patience, and I'm almost certain it's not the best of impressions. Normally, I wouldn't give a shit, but I need to win him over if I'm ever going to have a chance with Patience and completing my task.

"Have you heard the mayor's daughter is back?" my grandmother says to God. "Such a good girl. And such a good heart. Off rescuing Ethiopians from ISIS or something I heard."

This time, I do bark out a laugh, which is greeted by

icy stares from both the mayor and her, though there's no denying the grin on God's face.

"I believe it was building wells and orphanages in Uganda, Grandmother. I think ISIS might require something a little stronger than a teenage girl," I say with humor.

She blushes and fluffs her over-the-top hairstyle. "Yes, well…"

"And where is the lovely Patience tonight?" I ask.

The mayor glares at me. "She decided against coming in once she saw who was in attendance," he replies sourly, and my grandmother almost pisses herself in exasperation.

Well…fuck.

I only came to this stupid fucking thing to see her, and she high-tailed it out of here when she saw me. It's almost worth it to see the pissed-off look on my grandmother's face. Almost. But it makes things more complicated for me. If she won't be in the same room as me, how am I ever going to get her to fall in love with me?

God's cell beeps again, and he plucks it out. "You'll have to excuse me. My father only forces me to attend one of these things a month, and the two hours I agreed to is up." He smiles and nods at all of us before leaving the three of us in an awkward triangle.

The chief of police decides to join our trio, and the tension thickens at his presence. Mayor Noelle nods his head and greets him with a tight flex of his jaw. There's friction between them, but I'm done fucking around at this shit gathering, especially since the only reason I came isn't even here.

"I need to go speak to my sister. Good evening," I say,

exiting the conversation.

I head back out into the hallway where I spotted Sabella. Grabbing her gently by the elbow, she turns in surprise to look at me.

"Sammy?" her eyebrows pull in in concern. "What happened? What did you do?"

"Thanks for the vote of confidence, Sab," I huff. "I'm fine. Everything's fine. I just need to get out of here. Cover for me?"

She rolls her eyes. "What's going on?" she asks warily.

"Nothing. Nothing bad anyway."

"No fighting?"

"Jesus Christ, Sab. No, no fighting. I promise." I gesture around us. "It's just this isn't really my thing, you know?"

"And you think it's mine?" she says with wide eyes. "I hate these things, and these people, just as much as you." I cock an eyebrow, and she smiles. "Well, maybe not quite as much as you, but my point is, sometimes you just have to suck it up and get on with it." She groans at her own words, and I smirk.

"Thanks, sis." I finish off my whisky sour and hand her the glass before leaning in and giving her a kiss on her cheek. "And stay away from these pretentious pricks tonight, yeah?"

She rolls her eyes at me, and I turn to leave. She and I know there's no way in hell I'm ever going to kiss anyone's ass, and she knows she lost the argument as soon as she said it.

I head back out of the house with my hands in my pockets. The evening is warm, and the air humid, like another storm is on the way. I have a feeling Patience would

WRATH

have left and gone back home when she saw me, so that's where I'm going. I'm just pulling my cell out to call for an Uber when the throaty purr of a cherry-red Ferrari pulls up.

"Need a lift?" God says, looking out from the driver's seat.

I jog down the white marble steps to his car and climb inside. "Sure, but I'm telling you now, don't be pulling in behind any dumpsters, no matter how bad you wanna give it me." I wink, and he shakes his head and laughs.

The car is fucking exquisite and drives like a dream, taking sharp corners with ease, her engine fucking purring like a catcall.

"Goddamn. She's a beautiful car," I say, smoothing a hand across the dashboard.

"Like I don't know," he replies arrogantly. "And she's a he," he says with a wink. "Where are you going?"

"The mayor's house." I grin.

"Oh, he's going to fucking love that."

"I aim to please."

"You got your shit handled?" By shit handled, he means do I have my task in hand. But I don't know how to answer since Patience is starting to become a royal pain in my ass. A royal pain in my ass who's stirring up memories I've long since forgotten about.

"Always," I finally reply. Because one way or another, I'm going to get her in my bed.

"Good. I might need some help with my task when I get it." He takes another sharp bend, going way over the speed limit, though it feels like we're doing much less with how he handles the road.

God pulls up outside Patience's house, and I unbuckle

my belt and open the door. "I'll be around whenever you need me," I say as I step out of the car. I look back in with a smirk. "That sounded weirdly like a fucking Hallmark card. Don't go getting the wrong idea, man."

He snickers, and I slam the door closed and walk away.

The lights are on outside the large colonial house, and I stuff my hands in my pockets, feeling awkwardly overdressed now that I'm away from the party. I've always been self-assured, unafraid of anything, but something changed this past week, and I'm not sure I like it. Memories I've tried to bury deep begin to surface. Thoughts of the future, of being out from under Maxwell's grasp, and of reaching the place I've worked so hard to get were all within my grasp. And yet, the anger I wear like armor is dissipating right when I need it most.

I reach the large, white front door and ring the bell, half expecting her to open it wearing pajamas and a robe while eating from a tub of Haagen Daaz—that's what most girls do to get over me. Instead, the door opens, and Patience stands there looking like a fucking beauty queen.

Her body is accentuated by her figure-hugging silver dress. Diamonds are scattered across the plunging neckline, drawing attention to her chest. Her hair is loose around her bare shoulders, soft curls trailing toward her waist. I blink, stunned by her once more.

Her eyes narrow in on me, and her tongue darts out to wet her full pink lips.

Jesus. Fucking. Christ.

My jaw drops as my dick hardens, which is right about the same time she reaches out to slap me—*again*.

I grab her arm at the last moment, holding her wrist tight in my grip. "Not this time, sweetheart," I say.

VII
UINCENDUM NATUS

SEVENTEEN

The door slams shut in my face, and I stare at the white painted wood in shock.

What the fuck just happened? And who the fuck does this woman think she is slamming a door on me? I shake off my surprise and hammer my fist against the wood, kicking it when she doesn't immediately come back.

The red mist bubbles inside, burning my esophagus and threatening to make me spew my anger on her doorstep like vomit.

Hello, anger, my sweet friend.

"What?" she yells as the door swings back open. She glares at me, her cheeks red and flustered, her eyes flashing a similar rage. I stare at her in annoyance, but also surprise. Because even angry, she's fucking stunning. "Sam...

what? What do you want?" she yells, propping her hand on her hip.

I blink and jam my foot in the doorway when she goes to slam it shut on me again.

"Stop it!" I yell, fucking furious. "Stop shutting the fucking door on me."

Once more, I have to ask myself, who the hell does she think she is? I'm looking forward to getting her across my knee and showing her who's in charge.

"Then speak!" she yells back, anger vibrant on her face. "Speak and leave. Please."

I see something different then. Something simmering just below her rage and frustration. Hurt, loathing...pain.

"I just came to say hi," I reply, my voice dropping an octave so I'm not yelling like an asshole anymore.

She blinks. "What?" Irritation laces her voice, and I take a deep breath. Fucking hell. I'm well and truly fucked if she doesn't calm down and listen to me.

"I heard you were back in town, so I thought I'd come say hi. Then, you fucking slapped me, twice, and now I'm here to ask why," I bite out.

She scowls at me. "Are you serious?"

By the furious look on her face, the question is rhetorical, so I keep my mouth shut despite wanting to slam her up against the wall, take her mouth with mine, spread those legs of hers with my knee, and...

"Are you even listening to me?"

Fuck. No, no I'm not. I'm too busy imagining fucking you.

"You're an asshole, Samuel. An asshole I want nothing to do with. An asshole I don't want anywhere near me, my house, or my family. You're an asshole, just like your

WRATH

father." She huffs out a breath as she folds her arms across her ample chest, making her breasts push up to the top of her dress. I suck in a breath.

"Well, I'll give you the thing about my father—he *is* an asshole. But me? Seriously, Patience, I'm really not that bad once you get to know me."

Her eyes go wide, and her cheeks go red. If she were a dragon, she would have set me on fire by now. Thankfully, she's just a really angry, super-hot girl who hates my guts.

She goes to slam the door again, but my foot is still there, so it bounces back open. She lets out a squeal of annoyance that makes me grin. Fucking grin. Like I'm a little kid watching Wile E. Coyote get blown up by one of his piles of TNT intended for Road Runner.

"You're cute when you're angry," I state, poking the flames some more. I just can't fucking help myself.

"Oh my God, go away! Just go away."

She turns and storms inside the house, leaving the door open. I guess she's hoping I'll take the hint and fuck off, but I'm Samuel "The Machine" Gunner. I push the door open wider and follow her inside.

I find her in the large kitchen, pouring herself a glass of her father's whisky, then throwing the shot to the back of her throat. Damn, the girl can drink, and she likes whisky too—my favorite. She's almost too good to be true. I have a feeling it's going to hurt me just as much as it hurts her when I break her heart.

"Can I get one of those?" I ask, startling her.

She spins around and stares at me, the bottle in one hand and her empty glass in the other. "How did you get in here?"

I laugh lightly. "I'm not a vampire, Patience. I don't

need to be invited in. Besides, you left the door wide open. I just assumed you wanted me to follow you."

She splutters something and shakes her head, and I have to hold back my smirk. She opens her mouth to talk, and I hold up my hands in surrender.

"All right, all right, I'm sorry."

"You're sorry!"

"Yeah."

"Do you even know what you're sorry for?"

I have a feeling it has to do with the night I kissed her under the tree and called her and her mother a slut, but it's more fun to play dumb than admit my faults. I stay silent for too long, and she turns away and pours herself another drink.

"Just get out, please," she says, her shoulders slumping in surrender. "Please, Sam, I just need you to go."

I take a step toward her, but I know if I push her now, I'll break her. I'm holding all the cards here, she just doesn't realize I've opened the deck and started playing.

I'm not the good guy, and I've never claimed to be. I've surrounded myself with rage and darkness, embracing the hateful side of myself for so long, it's become a living thing inside me.

I frown and turn around, heading back out of the kitchen. Pausing in the doorway, I look back at her. She puts her glass down, her hands flat on the surface of the counter, and looks over her shoulder at me, her eyes glistening with tears.

It hits me then. Like a bullet to the stomach.

I know what I have to do, but it's something I don't do. Not ever. At least…until now.

The Elite better be worth it.

WRATH

"I'm sorry," I say again, dragging a hand through my hair. "For whatever it is I've done to upset you, I'm sorry, Patience."

As the words leave my mouth, I realize with surprise I actually mean them. The look on her face the night I called her a slut still haunts me all these years later. I turn away from her, but her voice stops me from leaving. She mumbles something that makes me turn back to her.

"What did you just say?" I ask.

She stands up straight, her eyes burning into mine. "I said you ruined me."

I frown. "It was just a kiss…we were just kids." I shake my head. "We barely knew each other. You were the one who dropped out of high school and decided to get homeschooled. A normal person would have just gone on with their life like it hadn't happened. Just accepted their first kiss was with one of the hottest kids in school, and that—surprise, surprise—he turned out to be an asshole."

Her shoulders shake as she laughs, and I frown harder. "You arrogant asshole, this isn't just about that kiss!" She scowls at me. "It's about everything. It's about the things you say, the way you treat people. Your actions have consequences, and your actions ruined me. Your friendship meant so much to me, then you ruined it all, Sam."

I glare at her, my gaze unwavering as the anger itches to be unleashed. "This is ridiculous!" I yell, startling her again, done with this bullshit. Beautiful or not, she needs to be tamed. I'm fucking done listening to her.

She chews on her bottom lip, her eyes wary. I can see she's warring with herself—half torn between hatred for me and wanting to cry in frustration, but she's as cool as a fucking cucumber as she walks toward me, her curves accentuated in that tight-as-fuck dress. I want to rip it off her with my teeth.

She stops in front of me, standing toe to toe. We glare at one another in annoyance and hate, but there's something else there too, simpering just below the surface. Heat burns between us. It's like what I felt that night when we were kids. Hell, what I felt all those times when we were kids. There was something between us then, and there's something between us now. Or at least there could be if either of us let it happen. But we're both stubborn and broken and unwilling to back down and be the vulnerable one. I don't believe in soulmates or any of that bullshit, but this electricity between us has been here for so many years, and the closer she comes to me, the brighter the spark is.

"I hate you, Samuel Gunner," she says in defiance, and I know she means it too. Her chin raises, her eyes burning into mine with a fury that matches my own.

"Good," I reply angrily, my nostrils flaring. "I'm fucking worthy of your hate."

She huffs in agreement. "You are."

I shrug. I honestly don't give a shit if she hates me. I don't give a shit if anyone hates me. Right now, she's a task I need to complete. I don't care what's growing between us—what's been there since we were kids—I need to end it—to swallow that shit way down deep and get what I need to done. Because Patience is just a woman, and there are plenty of those in the world for me to seek out and play happy family with once I have my life on the track I want it to be. And if that means breaking her, then so be it.

"I'm serious. You can hate me all you want, Patience,

it won't change anything. Hate's a useless emotion, best saved for revenge."

Her features soften almost imperceptibly. "I won't forgive you."

"Okay," I reply with another shrug. Once I complete my task, she'll understand what real hate is. She'll hate me to her very core, and that hate will burn bright for a real long fucking time.

Surprisingly, that doesn't fill me with any form of satisfaction. In fact, the opposite. Which is strange. I live and breathe on making people feel shit and inadequate about themselves, thrive on it almost.

We remain silent for several minutes, and I reach out almost tentatively to touch her. I only mean to get her attention, but she flinches when my hand comes into contact with the bare skin on her arms. It's like an electric current runs between us, and every fiber inside me flares to life. The hairs on the back of my arms stand at attention, and I lean into her until both of my hands are on her tiny waist, tugging her toward me.

That feeling is there again. The one that's called to me since we were kids. I grip her tighter.

She fights me feebly, her head down so she doesn't have to look at me anymore, but I need to see those eyes of hers. I need to get lost in them. I'm not a gentle man. I'm not soft or sweet or kind. I'm demanding and violent. But when I look in her eyes, I want to be something different.

"We can't do this," she whispers.

"Give me one good reason why not."

She rolls her eyes. "We don't even know each other."

I scoff. "We have always known each other, Patience."

She rolls her eyes at me again, but she's weakening, her resolve breaking.

"This was always going to happen. It wasn't a matter of if, it was just a matter of when. Since we were kids, we've been heading right here, to this moment."

I let go of her waist with one hand to lift her face to mine. We're so close, I can feel her breath on my face. Her sweet vanilla scent is like catnip to me, slowly driving me crazy as we stare into each other's eyes. I tug her body, dragging her against my chest.

"I hate you," she says once more.

"I know," I reply, breathing my words into her hair until she shudders.

"I mean it."

"I know," I assure her.

I put my hand on her lower back, my dick flaring to life when she whimpers. I lower my hands to her ass and grip it firmly, keeping her in place so she can't fight me.

"Look at me," I growl, but she shakes her head. "Patience, I won't ask again. Look at me. I want to see your eyes."

"I hate you," she says, looking back up into my face.

"You already said that," I reply darkly, my tongue darting out to wet my lips. I'm ready to go in for the kill.

She tries to look away from me, but I move my head so I'm still in her line of sight. This moment is everything. It's honesty and truth. It's good and pure, as much as it is pure fucking torture. Feeling her want me like this while knowing she hates me is drenching my soul and burning it up like it's enflamed. Like it's soaked in acid and withering away. She's a target, a task, a mountain I'm going to have great satisfaction in conquering. Repeatedly. Until

WRATH

I'm done with her.

I want to know what she tastes like. Will she be as sweet as she smells? I want to know what she feels like. Will she be the challenge I've always desired—or will she bend to me as I wrap my body around hers?

Claiming her.

Owning her.

Fucking her.

"I can't do this," she whimpers. "Not with you." She shakes her head and pushes at me. It's now or never.

"Patience."

She stills when I say her name.

"You can hate me all you want, that's okay, I'd hate me too, but I'm going to kiss you now, and you're going to kiss me back."

She gasps, but doesn't move, and I know I have her.

"Then I'm going to take you upstairs, and I'm going to undress you slowly. Then I'm going to fuck you relentlessly, until you come so hard, it makes your legs tremble and your knees buckle. It's what's going to happen, so let's not fight it. Life's too fucking short to fight something that feels this good."

She stares at me, pouring her hate and anger and desire into my soul, but my soul is already as black as they come, so I don't care. I reach up, threading my hands through her long, dark hair, and claim her mouth with mine, kissing her hard and soft and everything in between, until we're both breathless and needy and clinging to each other.

It's the most intense thing I've ever felt in my life.

And yet, it's just like I remember kissing her when we were kids. Only now, it's better—it's so much *more*. The pull's *stronger*, the desire *deeper*, the need almost fucking desperate between us.

She may be a task, but there's no denying the way my body comes to life at the feel of her pressed against me.

I steal my kisses from her, until her body becomes weak and pliable in my arms and she gives in, kissing me back with everything she has. Her arms wrap around me, and her body molds to mine, her soft curves pushed against my hard muscles.

We were just kids the first time we kissed, but we're not kids anymore. And I'm more than ready to show her the man that I've become.

VII

UINCENDUM NATUS

EIGHTEEN

Hate.
Anger.
Rage.
Revenge.
Spite.
Loathing.
Contempt.

I feel none of these things as I strip Patience of her dress. The only thing I think about is what she'll feel like wrapped around my cock. I grip the zipper on her dress and pull it down, parting the soft material until I can see her bare back. I scoop her hair up and place it to one side as I lean in to kiss the soft skin at the base of her neck. My nose skims past her ear and down her neck, and her skin pebbles beneath my touch, goosebumps breaking out.

It should be quick and easy to do this—to fuck her and walk away—but I'm going to make sure she has good memories of tonight. Memories that will last her a lifetime, because she'll need them when she eventually has to marry some rich asshole who doesn't know how to please a woman. Tonight is all about her pleasure and showing her how good things can be with the right man, and I'm going to take full advantage of her body. I'll brand her with my cock so she never forgets me.

"I want you to listen to me, and do exactly as I say. Okay?" I murmur in her ear, the base of my voice vibrating against the sensitive flesh at her neck.

She turns her head to my voice, her eyes catching mine for an instant. I let her dress fall to the floor at her feet, and her body tenses at its nakedness. I spin her slowly toward me, my dick straining in my suit pants.

"Eyes down."

She looks confused and opens her mouth to say something, but I put a finger to her lips to silence her. "You speak when I tell you to, do you understand?"

I haven't taken in her body properly yet, because I don't want to break our connection. If I do, she'll either run from me forever or ask questions I can't answer. As my hands roam her beautiful body, I find out quickly she was completely naked under that tight dress of hers and I hum my appreciation out. Clearly, she's not as innocent as she makes out.

"Sam," she starts, but then stops herself, a small frown puckering between her eyebrows. And then, she lowers her gaze. My chest flares in pride at how well she's doing already.

"Get on your knees," I say, my voice firm.

WRATH

Her eyes flit up to me, confusion in them. Her mouth tugs at one side as she tries to decide what to do.

"I won't ask again, Patience. Now, do as I say or I'll have to punish you."

"But why?" she asks innocently. Her insolence should piss me off, but all it does is turn me on even more.

"Because I told you to," I say calmly. "Unless you want me to fuck that pretty mouth of yours until you gag as I come down your throat, I suggest you get on your knees."

Her eyes flare, fight and fire coming to life. Just when I think she's going to slap me and walk away, she lowers to her knees. I swallow the satisfaction as I stare down at her, my hand on top of her head, stroking her hair.

"Hands on your knees, thighs apart, eyes down," I say calmly, still stroking her hair to soothe her and calm me. I'm about to lose my shit with how much I want her.

I watch as she complies, then I take a step back, unbuttoning my jacket while I walk around her, appreciating every part of her body. She was beautiful fully dressed, but it's nothing compared to her naked. Her body is better than I could have ever expected. Like it's been carved from marble—soft curves perfectly proportioned beneath smooth skin.

"You're beautiful, you know that?" I say, and she glances up at me as I throw my jacket over her vanity stool. "Really beautiful." I work the buttons of my shirt. I want her to look back down like I told her to, but I like the feel of her heated gaze on me as she watches me undress.

Placing my shirt on top of my jacket, I kick off my shoes, then work the zipper on my pants, letting my heavy cock be free of them. Her throat bobs as she swallows, her heated stare roaming over my body and landing on my swelling cock. I have to rethink my threat of fucking her mouth because she's practically salivating as she stares at it.

I glance around her bedroom for something I can use, a toy we can play with. The fun we'd have if we were in my house. I pick up her hairbrush from the vanity and smooth the back of it across the palm of my hand. It's no paddle, but it will suffice, for now.

"Stand up," I say, and she stares warily from me to the hairbrush before gradually getting to her feet.

"What's that for?" she asks, her eyes wide.

"I told you not to speak," I reply. "Now, you'll have to be punished."

If she wasn't turned on before, she is now. Her cheeks flush, the pinkness stretching down her neck to her chest. Her nipples are like little pink bullets. I reach over to play with one of them, feeling the hard bud beneath my fingertips. I gently roll it between my thumb and index finger. She whimpers, and my eyes slam to hers.

"Quiet."

I lean down, sucking the nipple into my mouth as my hands find her ass and squeeze the soft flesh there. She moans again, and I release her nipple and look into her face. My breathing is ragged, my chest rising and falling in anticipation of everything to come. She's not like anyone I've ever been with. They were always eager, excited. Patience seems scared and confused. It's enough to give me pause.

"Are you okay?" I ask.

She nods, and I frown.

"Answer me," I press, my tone turning darker.

"You told me to be quiet," she says, her eyes pleading.

WRATH

I chuckle and lean into her again. "Yes, I did. But now you can speak. Are you okay?"

"I'm confused."

"About me?"

She shakes her head. "About me."

I frown again.

"I hate you, Samuel. I don't want you here."

"So, tell me to leave," I dare her, wondering if she'll have the guts to do it.

"I can't," she mumbles, shame blanching her. "I've wanted this for too long."

A smile rises on my face. "So, you do remember the kiss under the tree."

She rolls her eyes at me. "Of course I remember."

I hold her stare, my mouth millimeters from hers, then I admit something to her I've never even admitted to myself. The words slip from my lips like a confession of my sins to a priest.

"I've wanted it since that night too," I admit, throwing myself in the line of fire and making myself vulnerable for the first time in years. She sucks in a gasp at my honesty, and I almost do the same.

This isn't me.

This is some alien who has body snatched me.

The Samuel I know would never admit something like that to anyone. He wouldn't tell anyone he was sorry, or apologize for anything. He wasn't gentle; he didn't show any weakness. Or remorse. Yet, here I am, being the man I never thought I could be. Telling the girl I hurt all those years ago, the girl I intend to hurt all over again, that I've wanted her ever since that moment.

"I'm going to spank you now," I say, cutting into the

heady atmosphere, because I need to change the subject from feelings and emotions and shit I don't want to think about to something I'm the master of. She looks at me sharply. "You're going to enjoy it, Patience. Probably not more than me, so don't get cocky, but I assure you that you will enjoy it."

"Samuel…"

"I said no talking."

I sit down on the edge of her bed and pull her to me, laying her across my knee. Mercifully, she doesn't fight me. I put my hand on her lower back to hold her in place, my cock pressing against her belly. Then I smooth my hand over her pert ass before raising it and bringing it back down. The crack of my hand on her skin rings through the room. She winces, gasping in pain, but doesn't move. My mouth twitches with a smile, my nostrils flaring in desire.

"Why am I punishing you, Patience?" I ask, running my palm over her ass to soothe the stinging. My fingers probe over her cheeks to her cunt where I feel her desire pooling.

"I don't know," she says on a gasp as I press against her entrance.

I raise my hand sharply and bring it back down, the crack sounding out. She whimpers again, caught by surprise by the strike of my palm.

"Tell me," I grit out, all softness gone now as my dick grows painfully hard beneath her.

"Because I talked?" she gushes, the words flying from her lips as I squeeze her ass so roughly, the smooth skin dimples. "Because I talked when you told me to be quiet?"

"That's right." I raise my hand quickly and bring it

WRATH

down once more, and she cries out. "You need to learn to do as you're told," I say, the words rumbling from my chest. "Good girl," I finally appease, rubbing my hand over her ass some more.

I gently lift her up, then lay her on the bed. Her face is red from embarrassment and anticipation. I like that look on her. I see the glisten of dampness between her legs, and that's all I need to know. My cock is hard and eager, and I'm more than ready to fuck her now, but I have to take a minute to look at her—to fully appreciate her.

I push her thighs apart so I can see her pussy. The soft curls of hair are damp with her desire and I part her lips with my fingers before slowly pushing one of them inside her. Her back arches as I slowly slide my thick finger in and out of her. My cock bobs as her body clings to me, holding me tightly, and I'm barely holding it together. The desire to be inside her is too much.

I look up at her face. Her long, dark hair lays over one shoulder, partially hiding one of her pert breasts from me. Her stomach is flat and toned, her legs slim and long. And she's chewing on her bottom lip in an attempt to hold in a satisfied moan as my thumb presses against her clit. She's so compliant to my every touch, yet she still has that spark of defiance I love in a woman. She's fucking perfect for me in every sense of the word.

And I'm going to have to break her, again, and then walk away.

All for the sake of The Elite.

Something akin to guilt flares in my chest, but I push it away. I can't think like that right now. I just need to do what needs to be done, fuck the consequences.

I move toward my clothes and pull my wallet from

my jacket, retrieving a condom, then turn back to her. She hasn't moved or looked away, but sits with one leg propped up, giving me a direct view of her glistening cunt as she waits for me. My chest lets out a growl of appreciation.

Tearing open the foil, I roll the condom down my hard length, then walk toward her and push her back on the bed. She stares up at me with wide eyes, her tongue darting out to lick her lower lip. I groan at the sight, my cock throbbing in anticipation. I wonder for a moment if what Sebastian said is true about her still being a virgin. There's something about that thought I like. Being the first man to ever be here, her pussy lips wrapped hungrily around my dick like a vice. Filling her, taking her, owning her with every thrust of my hips, every drag of my cock.

I lean over her, lining myself up with her entrance before gripping her soft-as-silk thighs and spreading them so I'm seated between them, and then I slowly push myself inside her, letting her warmth envelop my cock.

I groan. Patience gasps. And before I know what I'm doing, I lean down and press a kiss to her waiting mouth, swallowing her hum of satisfaction as I settle inside her. I stroke the side of her face, running my thumb across her lower lip. I swallow and rock my hips gently before placing another kiss on her lips.

Fuck, she feels good.

Too good.

My balls feel heavy, and my dick's rock hard. Once I start, I won't be able to stop. It already feels too good, and all I've done is fill her greedy pussy.

"Sam," she moans, forgetting herself.

I tut and smile darkly, but she lifts her chin in defiance, a flare of challenge in her eyes.

WRATH

"Oh, Patience, what have you done?" I taunt.

And then I fuck her, sliding in and out of her slowly at first. Her body is tight, and getting tighter with each stroke of my cock. She gasps with every thrust of my hips, and I grab her right leg and pull it up to my shoulder so I can move deeper. She throws her head back and calls out as I roll my hips, then thrust inside.

Fuck.

Fucking fuck.

Fucking motherfucking fuck.

I can't take my eyes off her; the way she drags a hand down her flushed face, or the way her dark lashes flutter against her cheeks, or the way she opens her mouth and lets out an indecipherable whimper with each slam of my cock.

The bed thumps against the wall as I drive into her pussy over and over. She suddenly looks up at me, her eyes wide as her cunt tightens.

"Sam!" she calls out, her eyes on mine.

In the next second, I feel her coming around me, her body throbbing and trembling. Her hands clutch at me, and I bring my mouth down to her, rolling my tongue along hers as she cries out my name like I'm her God and she's praying at my alter.

I find my own release seconds later, grunting as I slam into her, draining my cock of every drop of cum. I'm riding a wave of pure euphoria as my climax rolls through me, every nerve igniting and coming alive as we cling to one another.

I stare down at her, brushing the hair gently back as I try to memorize her face like this; flushed cheeks and bright eyes. Because in this moment, I've never seen anything or anyone as beautiful.

"This suits you," I say, and she frowns in confusion. "The freshly fucked look—it's good on you." I smirk.

She grins back.

Thank fuck she didn't slap me again.

VII
UINCENDUM NATUS

NINETEEN

Morning light begins to filter in through Patience's bedroom window, and she stirs, her warm body moving closer to me. She's even beautiful when she's sleeping. I stroke some loose strands of hair back from her face, the ink black locks soft under my rough fingers.

I don't remember falling asleep, but at some point after fucking for the second or third time, we passed out in a tumble of exhausted limbs and satisfied bodies.

And therein lies the problem.

I've never stayed over at a girl's house. Fuck, I barely sleep in my own bed, so sleeping in someone else's was never going to happen. Until last night. Until Patience.

I've been awake for hours now, the better man trying to break out of me not wanting to wake her. She's wrapped around me, one long leg draped over mine, an arm across my muscular chest, and her breasts pushed up against me. I've thought about waking her to take her body again, but then the problem of not wanting to disturb her sleep is still there.

I sigh, my fingers trailing lazy patterns down her arm.

What the fuck is happening to me?

Where's the rage? The anger that burned inside like a fucking dragon waiting to breathe fire upon everything I touched? I feel...calm. No, not quite calm, but my muscles that normally twitch and ache to fuck or break things are...settled, relaxed.

I sigh again and stare up at her bedroom ceiling.

"You're such a loud thinker," she mumbles, and I look down at her with a scowl.

"Excuse me?"

She drags her head out from where it was nestled between my body and the bed, her sleepy eyes blinking up at me. "I said you're such a loud thinker. I can hear your brain running a million miles an hour." She smiles to soften the blow of her tease, and I let my mouth tug up in a half smile.

"So, is this the part where you run for the hills?" she asks, still staring up at me, not an ounce of fear in those dark eyes of hers.

I frown. It's like she read my mind. Though, I'm not running because I'm scared. I'm running because I have to. She's a task—a job—and despite her pretence that she isn't bothered, I can see in her eyes she is. She wants me to stay here, with her.

The bitter part is, so do I.

I'm not ready to leave.

WRATH

To quit whatever this is or could be. I'm not ready to let her go just yet. But I don't have a choice.

She gives me a sad smile and starts to pull away, but I automatically yank her body back to mine.

"It's okay," she soothes. "I'm a big girl now."

I swallow the fucking boulder in my throat that won't go down. She tugs gently, and I let her go, though I'm not sure if it's her heart or mine that breaks as she scoots to the edge of the bed. Every millimeter she puts between us is a stab to my cold, black heart.

"Patience," I say, my voice thick and gruff.

She holds up a hand to me. "It's okay."

But it's not okay. I don't want to let her go. The distance between us is already allowing the rage to consume me again. I can feel it seeping back into my veins. The hate and anger, the darkness that wants me to self-destruct flowing back into me like water from a stream. And I hate it. I hate the way my skin begins to prickle with the all-consuming rage. I hate it, and for the first time in as far back as I can remember, I want it to stop. I just want the peace and the quiet I had five minutes earlier.

"Get your ass back in bed," I demand darkly. *Not yet,* my heart pleads, *don't let her go yet.* "That's an order."

She turns and looks back over her shoulder at me, confusion crossing her beautiful features.

"Do I have to punish you again, Patience?" I say, my tone hardening. "Because if you don't get yourself over here, I'm going to spank you until you come."

Her eyes ignite with desire, and she turns to face me.

"That's better. Now, come here so I can fuck you again."

She moves quickly, coming back into the bed, her eyes

on mine as she looks to me for direction. I rise up to my knees and drag her to me. We face each other, nose to nose, naked, our hearts beating in a steady rhythm. I lean in to kiss her, my mouth connecting with hers in a flurry of lips and teeth and tongue, our hands moving over each other's bodies like we never touched one another before. Like this is our first time.

She pulls out of the kiss and scoots back on the bed before bending down and wrapping her mouth around my dick. I groan as she takes me to the back of her throat before pulling back out and twirling her tongue around my shaft.

"Ahhh, Patience," I grunt, my hand fisting her hair to guide the pace.

My dick is hard, painfully so, begging to be inside her again as she bobs her head up and down on my throbbing cock.

Fuck, she is going to kill me.

Glancing around the room, I spot my tie from last night. I cup her face in my hands and let my dick fall from her mouth as I pull away from her. She stares up at me, her lips shiny from my pre-cum. I groan at such a beautiful fucking sight.

"Fuck, Patience," I mumble. "What are you doing to me?" I suck on my lower lip as I reach down between her legs, finding the moisture at the apex of her thighs. I slide a thick finger inside her. "Stay still," I say with a dark smile, "and be quiet."

Her lips part as I thrust another finger inside her, but she keeps quiet, her gaze locked with mine as I strum her insides. Her cheeks turn pink, and she pants, her hands clawing at her own thighs to keep from moving or speaking.

WRATH

"Is that good?" I ask, and she nods quickly. "Good girl," I say with a smile.

Her cunt tightens, and her chest begins to rise and fall as she starts to climax. I wait for her to call out, to moan or say something, but she doesn't. She stays quiet, her gaze staying firmly on mine, her body rigid as she rides out her orgasm on my hand.

I slip my fingers out of her and bring them to my mouth, watching the needy look on her face as I suck the digits into my mouth, tasting her orgasm on my tongue. My chest flares with pride at her sweet taste. I can't wait any longer.

Gently laying her down, I turn her over, lift her ass up, then climb off the bed to get my tie and another condom. I stride back to the bed, my dick bobbing painfully as I walk, my eyes on the fucking prize with every step I take.

"Hands," I growl as I get back on to the bed, positioning myself behind her.

She lifts her hands behind her, and I bind them together before sliding the condom down my hard length. I rub my hands down her back, smoothing them over her ass, seeing the red marks from my spanking last night. I want to do it again. I want to spank her until she cries out, my name falling from her lips as her ass stings from my hands, but I have to have her now. I can't wait another second. Three times hasn't been enough to fulfil me. I'm hoping four times will, so I can end this with her and move on from her and Maxwell.

I grab my dick and guide myself into her, groaning as her heat envelops me, wrapping me within her tight cunt. Gripping her hips, I fuck her. Hard.

It isn't pretty.

It's fast and brutal.

It isn't making love.

It's fucking at its finest; raw and beautiful and fucking powerful, for us both. She submits to me willingly, simply, almost desperately, and I take her, body and mind, making them both mine. I brand them with my own fucked up version of love. Because I don't love like most. I love darkly, cruelly, and brutally, or not at all.

I hold on to her bound hands and lean over her, wrapping my body over hers so I'm everywhere—in her, on her, around her. So that I'm her everything and her nothing in that moment.

I fuck Patience until she's filling the air with my name and her body is trembling around me. and then I fuck her again. Because with her, once is never enough. I feel like a starving man and her pussy is my oasis. I'll devour her body, feasting on her sweet cunt until I'm sated.

Though my biggest fear is that I'll never have had enough of her.

"Is it always like that for you?" she asks without judgment.

My eyes are closed, embracing the darkness behind my lids as I come back down from the high I'm on. And what a fucking high it is. I'm floating on bliss, moving through calm and diving headfirst into the unknown, and I'm not afraid of it. For once, I embrace the calm and quiet instead of searching for the darkness.

"Yeah," I grunt out honestly.

"Okay," she replies thoughtfully.

WRATH

I open my eyes, letting the day back into my world, and look over at her. She lays next to me, her head on the white cotton pillows, staring at me.

"What?" I bite. She shrugs, and I blow out a breath. "What?" I ask again.

"I'm just wondering why. I don't mind, and I don't care. It's just different, you know? How does a man like you come to being like that?"

Jesus, she's innocent and blind and has no fucking clue who I am. I don't want to reveal that side of me, the part that embraces the dark and distasteful. I don't want her to think anything of me other than good.

Well, after today, she won't think anything of you but hate, my subconscious pipes up.

I groan and sit up, the covers falling to my lap as I drag my hands through my hair.

"I'm not sick, Patience. There's nothing wrong with me," I growl. "I just like to be in control."

She sits up too, holding the covers to her chest. "No, you like to dominate, and that's different from being in control."

"Don't fucking judge me," I snap, though deep down, I know she isn't. And I'm not angry at her for asking either.

I'm angry at myself.

At the fucking world for bringing me into it and taking my mother away from me.

At Maxwell.

And at the fucking Elite for putting me in this situation, because she doesn't deserve this.

"Sam, I'm not…I wouldn't," she soothes, her hand on my shoulder. But I don't need or want her sympathy. And I certainly don't need her judgment.

"What about you?" I grit out. "You saved yourself all this time for the perfect man and all you get is me. How pathetic is that? Was it worth it, Patience?" I sneer with a jerk of my chin.

She stares in confusion before recoiling from me like I'm some sort of monster. Her eyes narrow. "First of all, I wasn't a virgin. I haven't been pining after you all these years wondering if you were going to come find me and take my virginity, you fucking asshole. And second, yes."

I narrow my eyes, feeling like a complete prick for thinking she was a virgin. Fucking Sebastian put that in my head and I ran with it. Patience is a beautiful and intelligent woman. Of course she wasn't going to be a fucking virgin.

"Yes what?" I bite out, feeling the vein in my neck twitching. I am a complete fucking asshole. And an arrogant one, but I still won't back down from this fight.

"Yes, it was worth it, Samuel. I may not have been a virgin, but last night, this morning..." she comes closer to me, putting a hand to my face, "it was like it was my first time. But better because it was with you."

I grab her hand, trapping it within mine, but I don't pull it away. I like her touch.

She runs her thumb across my lower lip, and despite the embarrassment thrumming through me, I suck it into my mouth. Her proximity calms me like only she seems to be able to do.

She moves over, pushing me back against the headboard as she climbs onto my lap, straddling me. She reaches for my hands, holding them to either side of me as she leans in and kisses me, her body grinding down on my rapidly hardening cock. I start to move, to grab her

WRATH

and throw her to the mattress, when she pulls back.

"No, *you* stay still this time," she says with a nervous smile as she lets go of my hands and cups my face. *"You don't move, you don't touch, and you don't come until I say you can."*

She kisses me again, her tongue sliding over mine. My heart hammers in my chest, every muscle in my body tense.

"I can't," I reply honestly, the words coming out hoarse. Because I can't. That's not the way this works. It's not the way I work.

"You can," she says against my mouth. "Because I'm ordering you to. Okay?" She kisses me. "Please, Sam."

I swallow. "Yes, ma'am," I reply, wanting to try for her. She smiles at my words, and my heart beats faster—for her, for this.

She reaches between us and grabs my dick, holding it tightly as she slides herself down on it. I groan as her heat envelops me, her tightness clinging to every inch of my dick. She bucks her body, and my stomach tightens as I resist the urge to push her off me and fuck her from behind. To slide inside that perfect pussy of hers, to spread those beautiful ass cheeks of hers and push inside that puckered hole. My cock swells and throbs.

"Oh, God, Sam," she murmurs as her hips speed up, her core tightening, making it almost impossible to just sit here and obey.

Jesus, this shit is harder than I realized. I suck my bottom lip into my mouth as I watch her ride my body, taking her satisfaction from me, punishing me, devouring me, taking everything she needs and wants. With each thrust of her hips, it becomes easier and harder to sit still.

I want to ravage her, to touch every part of her, to nip and lick and kiss and fuck every hole she has. But I also want this—her on me and in control.

Her hips move quicker, her tits bouncing as she thrusts over and over on top of me, hitting her core as she fucks me, and then she comes like an explosion. Her body thrusts one last time, then squeezes me as she continues to come in a series of moans and whimpers, her eyes fluttering closed. She stills and leans forward, and I give her time to recover.

When she opens her eyes, I'm waiting.

"My turn," I say wickedly.

I grab her and throw her to the bed before climbing back on top of her and thrusting into her in one quick movement. She cries out as I slam myself inside her over-sensitized pussy and begin to fuck her roughly. I wrap my hand around her throat as I fuck her, holding her still so I can take what I want from her. I suck her bottom lip into my mouth, my tongue and my cock working in unison. My hips surge forward as my cock abruptly swells, and then I'm coming in long spurts, dousing her insides as I press my forehead to hers, our eyes connected.

"Fuck me, Patience," I grunt breathlessly.

"I already did." She winks.

I bark out a laugh and kiss her before rolling off her.

We lay on our backs, exhausted, sweaty, and spent.

As my heartrate comes back to normal, I turn to her. She has her eyes closed, but opens them when she senses me looking.

"What?"

"I'm sorry you didn't want to come to school because of me," I say. "I was fucked up that night. I shouldn't have taken it out on you, but I was a kid and hated the world."

If things had worked out differently, I wonder if she would have been there day after day in school. If I had to see the look of hurt on her face every day, would I be a different man now?

She frowns. "I didn't stop coming to school because of you, Sam. I moved away with my mom."

It was my turn to frown now. "No, your dad told everyone you were being home-schooled."

She shakes her head. "He was just embarrassed."

"Embarrassed, why?" I lean up on my elbow.

She sighs. "My mom finally left him, and I wanted to live with her." I cock my head, and she laughs.

"Seriously?"

She sits up, pulling the sheet with her, and I sit up too. "Seriously. Part of the divorce settlement was my mom and I had to come back for special events, and we told everyone she was working away and I was being home-schooled, or working for charities in Europe, or—"

"Building orphanages?" I say, dragging a hand through my hair.

She laughs again. "That I actually did do, but yes."

"Why the fuck did he want that? Wouldn't it have been easier for him to say he was divorced and you were living with your mom?"

She chews the inside of her cheek. "My dad is the mayor, Samuel. The people who put him into office want a good, wholesome family image. A divorced man whose daughter doesn't even want to live with him was not the image they wanted. The chief of police has been after his job for a long time now, so my father couldn't give them any ammo."

"And what's in it for your mom?"

"A lot of money. You can't tell anyone about any of this, though. My dad was supposed to be sworn in as mayor for the next five years in a couple days, but it's gone to a vote because someone is standing against him."

"The chief of police? Fuck, I can't believe I didn't know any of this." Clearly, I've had my head up my ass and missed all of this going on. Or maybe I just didn't care. That Lillian woman, and her brother being all cozy with the chief, then my task to get bribing material on the mayor isn't a fucking coincidence.

She laughs. "No one does. We made sure of it. But look, my mom has been thinking about coming back here. She misses New Orleans—and strangely enough, my dad. But Mom and I…we have a life back in California, and if I'm honest, I don't know if I'm ready to give that up."

I nod. "But she'll do what she thinks is best for you," I say, my head reeling from the information overload. "If you stay, she will too, and if you go back home—"

"So will she," she finishes. "I chose to live with my mom all those years ago because I wanted a fresh start. My dad was drinking a lot, and I had no friends, no future here. But things are different now." Patience entwines her hand with mine before looking at me shyly. "If I had a reason to stay here, I would. I'd give it all up."

I squeeze her hand, feeling the guilt burning in my chest.

"Dad's prepared to leave, though, if Mom won't come back home. He's going to come with us. It would mean kissing his career and family goodbye, though."

Things start to lock into place.

The Elite.

WRATH

The mayor.

The task.

If I break her heart, she won't want to stay. She'll leave, and maybe The Elite are going to expose the mayor's double life and bribe him with the evidence of my task to put someone else in charge. *The chief.*

It all seems too good to be true. Too carefully concocted, and yet I know I'm right. It shouldn't matter—the reason for my task—yet it does.

"Are you okay?" Patience asks, her voice sounding far away.

I nod, but I'm not okay. How can I be knowing what I have to do?

It's worse now, knowing the reason behind it. They're destroying a man's life, Patience's life, and I'll be helping them do it.

It doesn't feel right, any of it.

But what choice do I have?

VII
UINCENDUM NATUS

TWENTY

TWO WEEKS LATER.

"Oh my God!" Patience cries out my name, and pride flares in my chest at my name on her lips.

I run my tongue up and down her sex, spreading her wider so I can devour her sweet pussy. I fuck her with my tongue until she's quivering against me and gripping my hair in her hands. And then, just as she's about to come with my tongue deep in her cunt, I pull the beads out of her ass and she falls apart beneath me.

"Sir!" she screams, her thighs clenching around my head as I suck on her clit.

I let her ride the tidal wave of euphoria from her orgasm until she opens her eyes. I smile wolfishly, and she smirks.

"That was..." She doesn't finish, but that's okay,

WRATH

because I know. I feel it every time we fuck too. It's not just the sex or the orgasm, it's something else. It's our history, our childhoods entwined. Our paths which were always destined to cross no matter how far apart we were.

I put my hands on her waist and practically climb up her body, nipping her every now and then. I bite her thigh. A lick up her cunt. A nip to her stomach. Until I reach her breasts, sucking the hard nipple into my mouth greedily. I'm like a starved man, and I can't get enough of her or her body.

I've had a permanent hard-on for two weeks now, and we've barely left this room other than for me to make it to class, then come straight back here to fuck her some more. She's like heroin, and I'm addicted to her sweet scent.

"Sir," she whimpers as I rub the pad of my thumb over her clit.

She's sore, she's sated, and yet she's always eager for more.

She's as hungry for me as I am for her, and it's fucking killing me.

This isn't me.

I don't even know what I'm doing anymore. I'm playing it off that I'm going to end it with her soon, but every day is the wrong day. Every last time in bed with her is never enough. She's an oasis, and I'm fucking dying of thirst.

I suck her bottom lip into my mouth, and she groans as I drag her arousal from her pussy to her asshole before flipping her over on to her stomach. I probe her hole with my finger and she opens for me like a flower, ready, eager.

Patience glances over her shoulder at me; her eyes are

wide, wary but needy, and I place kisses across her shoulder and neck to calm her.

"It's okay," I mutter against her throat, and she nods.

She nods because she trusts me, and I'm a bastard for letting her.

I should walk away.

Or at least let her walk away with some dignity left intact. But I can't. I need this, her. I need to defile every part of her until I'm branded on her body like a tattoo.

I'm a selfish asshole, but I don't care.

I fist my cock in my hand and guide it to her entrance. I put a hand under her stomach and lift her ass higher, scooping up some of her dampness and rubbing it around her asshole again. I press against her, pushing in just the tip of my cock, and groan into the air, having to count backwards from five because she's fucking perfect.

She grunts as she takes me, my cock slowly filling her up, our pulses felt in our most intimate places.

"You're so perfect," I mutter, biting down on her shoulder as I swirl my hips and grind into her slowly. "So fucking tight."

I'm balls deep in her asshole and she's panting underneath me. It's torture and bliss all wrapped up in one. This is the first time she's had anyone here. She doesn't need to tell me, it's written all over her face, her expression a mixture of pain and desire as she looks at me, her mouth open wide. She hangs her head low and groans as I move in and out of her slowly.

I squeeze her ass cheek in my hand, and for the first time ever, I lose control, squeezing her soft flesh beneath my palm until I know it will bruise. And then I fuck her. Hard.

WRATH

I have no mercy as I slam into her. Fucking her virgin ass until I feel myself swelling inside, then coming in long, hot streams. She grunts and cries beneath me, but I don't stop until I've milked every last drop from my cock.

Patience is trembling, her knees shaking as I slide out of her and lower her to the bed. She's panting and sweating and there are tears in her eyes. I run my hand down the side of her face and stare into her eyes.

"Are you okay?" I ask, my voice rough.

She nods. "That was…" She blinks and swipes at the tears around her eyes. "I've never felt anything like that."

Her body has been used and abused over the past two weeks. I've fucked every part of her. Been inside every hole and spilled myself over every inch of her body. She's swallowed my cum and taken every spanking, every slap of my hand, and every beat of my paddle without complaint.

I don't know how I'm going to give her up.

"Hey, what's going on behind those eyes of yours?" she asks, rolling on to her side to look at me. It's her turn to reach up and touch my cheek now, and I turn my face to suck her thumb into my mouth.

"Nothing. Just wondering what we can do next." I smirk, my lie tasting bitter on my tongue. I never lie, and yet the lies have been coming quick and easy with Patience. I hate it.

She laughs. "I need to shower before anything else. And then eat. And then I need to study."

I climb over her body and grab her wrists, pinning her to the bed. "I have something for you to study," I tease, and she laughs again.

"I'm pretty sure I know the subject well now." She smirks.

I lean down and press a kiss to her mouth, and for a moment, everything is forgotten. But then I pull out of the kiss and my guilty conscience is back, berating me for the lies I've been telling and the pain I'm going to cause her…and myself.

"You're hungry?" I ask, and she nods. I climb off her and grab my pants before pulling them on. "I'll fix you some food while you shower, then we can resume our study session."

She laughs again. Fuck, I love that laugh.

"Sounds like a plan." She gets off the bed and walks into the bathroom, her hips sashaying as she walks. Her ass is red and sore, her body full of bites and brands of my own particular taste. I know I should feel disgusted with myself, but all I feel is pride knowing she bares my mark.

I slip on a shirt and head down the stairs barefoot.

I grab some bread and peanut butter and jelly. As kids, it was what she always made me when I needed comforting. Hell, she was only seven or eight, so it was the only thing she could make.

"Are you okay?" Patience asks, her wide eyes watching me as I devour the sandwich.

"Yeah. Of course I am," I grunt. The truth is, I'm not okay. Far from it. Father hired a new nanny, only she wasn't nice. She shouted at us a lot. She drank and forgot to feed us. But she was better than the last one. At least she didn't hit me.

She did starve us, though. Gave us just enough food to survive. It was why I gave mine to Sabella, slipping my food on to her plate without her knowing and pretending I'd already eaten.

She didn't need to know how bad it was.

She didn't need to know about the monsters that lived in our house.

WRATH

Patience's father is barely ever home, so I don't ever worry about running into him, so it's unfortunate that halfway through making her a peanut butter and jelly sandwich that he walks in.

He stops in his tracks, his briefcase in his hand when he sees me.

"Samuel Gunner." He says my name like a curse. Because it's obvious why I'm here. If the bare feet don't give it away, the just-fucked hair will.

"Mayor Noelle," I say with a tight smile.

I spread the peanut butter over the bread and close the sandwich up. I need to get out of here, away from him. He looks like he's about to lose his shit, and I'm not the sort of man to stand by if he wants any sort of retribution.

I pass him in the doorway, my teeth grinding.

"Bitches in heat always bring the dogs calling," he says to my back, and I stop in my tracks.

"What the fuck did you just say?" I growl as I turn to face him, my hard glare boring into his.

"I guess she turned out just like her mother after all," he bites out.

"Watch your tone." I stare at him, my anger flooding me like adrenaline.

He shakes his head. "What is it about you Gunner men always after the women in my life?"

It's my turn to shake my head this time. "Mrs. Noelle was a slut, but your daughter's a fucking queen. There's no comparison, Mayor."

His eyes flare with fire, but I don't give a shit about him, so I turn and walk away. Halfway up the stairs, I get my reply.

"You Gunners are all the same. You can't keep hold

of your women. They either die, leave you for someone better, or are only after your money. Patience will come to her senses soon enough. Mark my words."

I grip the banister as I try to control the anger roaring inside me. Because killing him seems like a real viable option right now.

Back upstairs, Patience is out of the shower and is brushing her hair in the bathroom. I leave her sandwich on the dresser in the bedroom and follow her in. I step behind her and tear the towel from her body before bending her over the sink.

I pepper her back with kisses as I rub my palms over her back before slowly reaching between us to gather the moisture between her legs and smear it over her pussy. I stare at her in the mirror as I unzip my pants and free my cock. She holds my gaze as I press against her entrance and thrust inside her. I'm not gentle as I fuck her, taking my anger out on her pussy, making her come more times than either of us can count. And when I finally come, I come loudly, slamming in to her pussy so hard, Patience cries out.

My cock spurts, dousing her tender pussy as I pant against her neck. She continues to hold my gaze in the mirror. No anger or disgust in her face.

But I can't look at myself.

I can't catch my own gaze because of the shame I feel for what I just did.

Because I know that had nothing to do with Patience and me, and everything to do with showing her father who owned his daughter now. I am her master. I am in control. And there is nothing he can do about it.

I'm a bastard. Just like my father.

VII
UINCENDUM NATUS

TWENTY-ONE

Waiting in the counselor's office, I check my cell again to see if Sabella or any of my Elite brothers have texted. But really, that's a lie. I'm only really hoping for a message from Patience. I shove it back into my jacket when I see there's no new messages and vow not to be such a fucking pussy anymore. We've had two weeks of fucking bliss, no pressure to fulfil the task. Pride has been caught up in his own shit and has left me the fuck alone. I thought I was well and truly free of having to even see the counselor when an email went out weeks ago informing us of her sabbatical. But now, she's back and wants to see me.

I need to focus on this meeting and on today. Maxwell left me an uplifting note this morning ordering me not to be late to see the school counselor. *Fucking prick.*

It's fucking weird sitting here after I've figured shit out about Lillian after the charity gig a couple weeks ago.

The door is open when I arrive, and Lillian is standing tall, her black hair clipped up high on her head, talking to a gorgeous girl with a mess of blonde curly hair. She looks familiar. I'm sure I've seen her with Lust. She smiles shyly before she walks out, and I can't stop my gaze from following her.

"Ahem." Lillian clears her throat, and I turn back to face her. Instead of the look of disgust I expect, she's smiling widely, almost like she's cheering me on. She reaches out a hand to me. "Samuel Gunner, let's formally meet."

There's something off with this fucking woman.

I take her hand in mine. Her skin is soft, her nails manicured, and on closer inspection, she's older than I first thought. She clearly takes care of herself, and if her brother is any indication, she can afford to.

"And you're Lillian, school counselor, sister of the king of New Orleans, and an Elite player," I say, getting right to the fucking point. I shake her hand with a smirk, and she holds it a beat too long before releasing it, her eyes glinting with something I can't put my finger on before gesturing toward her office.

I head inside and take a seat, and she closes the door behind us and sits at the desk. "I'm Mrs. Griffin, but you can call me Lillian. I believe we're scheduled to meet every other week to discuss your supposed anger issues. But enough of the ruse." She rolls her eyes.

She folds her hands in her lap as she assesses me, seeing how I'll react to the comment.

I don't say anything, waiting for her to continue.

WRATH

"Do you know what it takes to get into a college like this?"

"I'm in it, aren't I?" I grunt.

Narrowing her eyes on me, she smiles tightly making her face look fucking weird. Why isn't it moving?

"Yes, Samuel, you are in it, but don't think what is given can't be *taken away*. We expect the best from our pupils, and for work to be handed in in a timely manner. Insolence will not be tolerated here at St. Augustine."

Didn't she say we were dropping the ruse? Why the fuck is she pretending we're talking about classes when she's obviously talking about my task.

"I understand what's expected of me, Mrs. Griffin, and I've always earned my place wherever I decide that place is." Is she trying to intimidate me, because it isn't working. She's a fucking twig with shiny hair.

Her smile widens, and she stands, making her way around the desk and perching on the edge of it in front of me, her legs crossing at the ankles and making her pencil skirt ride up a little more around the leg. Normally, this would have been hot as fuck, and I would have had her bent over her desk in a heartbeat, but after Patience, this woman's pussy doesn't interest me in the slightest. "Please, Samuel, call me Lillian."

I nod, feeling the muscles in my jaw ticking.

"You look…irritated, Samuel," she croons.

I let my gaze travel up her thigh slowly, and then to her face. "Not at all. I'd just like to get to class. I'm behind and need to catch up. I had a late night working," I say, implying I'm talking about my task.

Fucking Patience instead of breaking her heart will wear anyone out, I think bitterly.

Every minute that's passed since first being inside Patience has left me more and more confused about my feelings for her. She's all I think about. I want to eat, drink, and breathe her, and I have for the last two blissful weeks. To be honest, I haven't thought much about The Elite or my task since that first night with Patience. Every moment has been with her. Either fucking her or thinking about fucking her. I've been lost in Patience, and yet I feel anything but lost for the first time in years. It's confusing and bewildering, but I've decided to go along with it. I'll fuck Patience out of my system if that's what it takes.

Lillian studies me for a couple silent beats. "Tell me, how are you finding your classwork?"

"What do you mean?" I ask with a huff, knowing perfectly well she's talking about my task. My anger spikes. It feels wrong to talk about it with this woman I barely know.

"Have you made any progress, Samuel? Or do you need some extra lessons to help you accomplish your work?" She says it in a way that's almost seductive, and I frown. She crosses and uncrosses her ankles, and I stare up at her completely un-moved by her obvious seduction technique.

"I'm very capable of completing my work load," I reply calmly.

"Oh, I bet you are," she laughs teasingly. She's definitely flirting with me. My dick twitches at the thought, but then the memory of Patience last night comes to mind—her beautiful body tied to my bed and laid out bare for me to nip and suck and take as my own. I tell my dick to calm the fuck down. This is not the pussy it wants. Lillian can have all the Botox and fillers she wants, but she'll never be anything but a speck of dust when it comes between her and Patience. There just isn't any comparison.

I feel out of sorts. Confused by my own tumbling thoughts. I'm trying to control them, but the more I fight to understand what's bothering me, the more stressed I feel.

I'd thought Lillian was attractive, if not a little old, when I first met her, but as the minutes have ticked on, I've realized she's nothing. There's only one woman I want, and it's not this dried up old hag pretending to be something she's not. My friend, my mistress, my fucking counselor. When, in fact, she's Elite, and wanting these tasks completed.

She wants to hurt Patience for the Elite's gain.

Worse, she wants me to hurt Patience, and I can't do anything but obey because I'm her pawn in this game of fucking chess, and that pisses me off even more. I'm no one's pawn, and Patience doesn't deserve this.

She deserves more.

She deserves better. She deserves someone worthy of her body.

And I'm none of those things.

I'm angry. The fury coursing through my veins like dry ice.

It's been two weeks since I felt like this, but it's like the anger never left me.

"Fuck this. I need to go," I say, standing up abruptly and pushing back from Lillian. I have to get out of this shitty claustrophobic office. I need Patience.

"Don't disappoint me, Samuel. I had high hopes for you," she snaps.

I really need to go. I want—no, *need*—to see Patience. I want to feel her naked and writhing underneath me, calling my name and clawing at my back while she comes apart riding my cock.

I'll never have enough of her, I realize with growing anxiety. I'll never have enough of her body or her kisses or her mind. Something has changed in me, and I don't know what. But somewhere in these past two weeks, I've found something more important than my vengeance. I found someone more important than my need for retribution.

I found peace, calm.

I found Patience, and perhaps myself.

I need to speak to my brothers. I drag a hand through my hair, feeling sick.

Lillian doesn't look too happy about me leaving. She frowns and heads back around her desk.

Fuck. I hope she doesn't tell Maxwell I bailed. He'll ask me why I left, and then Sabella will give me shit, and fucking fuck, this is bullshit.

God, when will I be free of him?

When you man the fuck up and do what The Elite needs you to do, my subconscious drawls.

Break Patience's heart…that's all I need to do.

The thought sickens me.

Without another word, I march from Lillian's office.

I jog across the parking lot, feeling a manic sort of hysteria crawling down my spine as the urgency grows. I light a cigarette, inhaling the deathly smoke into my lungs and blowing it out quickly, but it doesn't calm me. I look up as I reach my car, finding Pride leaning against it, my heart thudding in my chest like it does before I go into the ring to fight, the anticipation thrumming in my veins.

WRATH

What are the fucking chances?

"The task. Is it done?" he asks dryly, his expression dark. "I need to know you're getting it done."

"No," I reply shortly, taking another long drag on my cigarette, wishing it was weed. Where the fuck is Sloth when you need him?

"Thought you said it was an easy task?" He looks tired, like this shit is taking a toll on him. He doesn't have to fucking break Patience's heart. I do.

"It is," I bite out, my stare telling him to shut the fuck up before I make him shut the fuck up. I'm really not in the mood to start explaining myself to anyone. "But I don't think I can do it."

"The fuck did you say?" His brows pull down low.

"I said I don't think I can do it." I throw my cigarette to one side and step toward him, daring him to fucking take me on.

Thud.

Thud.

Thud.

"She doesn't have anything to do with any of this," I growl. "I'm not hurting her for the sake of The Elite. It's not worth it—not like this. They can't make me do it."

He shakes his head and looks to one side. "That's where you're wrong, Samuel."

"Am I, though? You think this shit is right? These are people's lives we're fucking with. What the fuck is with the school counselor woman? What is her role in all this, and why are you okay with it all? How can you be fucking cool with this shit?"

He looks back at me, suddenly just as furious as I am. "Lillian isn't some counselor woman. She's fucking Satan.

You think I don't know that what they want from us isn't fucked up? You think this shit is easy for me? For any of us? The Elite owns us. They own you, Sam."

I push against his chest, shoving him, my anger washing over my senses. He falls against my car. He doesn't fight me, though I can see his features contort in frustration. Every muscle in his body wants to shove me back. We're evenly matched in height and build, yet he has better control over his temper, which is lucky, because it won't end well if we get into a fight. We'll tear each other apart and end up killing each other because we're both too stubborn to back down. And all for what? Because we're both feeling the fucking strain of The Elite and their fucked up tasks?

"Get off me before you do something you regret, Samuel," he growls, his hard glare burning into mine. It's then I realize my fists are curled into his shirt.

"Let me make something abundantly clear," I tell him, then let him go. He stands up, straightening his jacket, his nostrils flaring as he breathes hard. "The Elite may have put you in charge like you fucking run this thing, but let me tell you, Pride, no one fucking owns me. No one tells me what to do. I run my own shit, my *own* way."

I push past him and climb in my car before starting the engine. He leans down into the open window as music blasts from my stereo.

"That's where you're wrong, Sam. The Elite owns you now—they own all of us. They make the decisions. They control us and everything we touch. Get it done before they take the opportunity from you and give it to someone who really wants it."

"*I* really want it!" I roar, fury licking up and down my throat like fire.

WRATH

"Yeah?" he goads, his mouth a hard, impassive line. "Do what you need to fucking do and stop being such a pussy about it," he barks out before stepping back and walking away. I slam my hand against the steering wheel, hating him, this school, Maxwell, and this whole fucking Elite bullshit.

Bullshit I fucking need.

No one owns me. Not now. Not ever. I'm beginning to wonder if The Elite is any better than Maxwell holding me and Sabella hostage with their money and power.

I drag a hand down my face and slam my fist against the steering wheel again. "Goddamn it!"

Climbing out of my car, I storm over to him. He stops walking and turns to face me, every muscle in his body on edge. I stop in front of him and reach inside my pocket for my coin, pulling it out.

I stare at it in the palm of my hand, feeling dread and need and anger and the desire to be free burning in my hand. I'm shaking as I look up at Pride, but his eyes betray nothing.

"I need a new task," I say, feeling sick.

"You give that in, you don't get to back out of the next one. And if you think this task is bad, who's to say what they'll make you do next." He sounds almost apologetic.

It doesn't matter, though. He knows it. I know it. From the moment I got this task, I knew I couldn't do it. And that was before I saw her and everything that came after.

I nod. "I know, but I can't do it to her. She doesn't deserve it."

"And you love her," he says, matter of fact.

I don't reply. I don't need to. I've *always* loved her, I just wasn't ready to admit it to myself or anyone else. I'm still not ready to admit it.

Pride holds his hand out, and I drop the coin in his palm. "This is your last chance, Sam."

"It was never even an option," I say, my anger dissipating as the rain starts coming down on us. "Call me when you have my next task."

He sighs and shoves the coin into his pocket before pulling out a white slip of card. "Already got it. You're not as unreadable as you fucking think. Lillian saw this shit coming," he says, like the words are painful. Leaning in close, he slips it inside my pocket. "They're watching. She's a fucking snake, Sam. She slithers into your life and injects her fucking poison. She'll destroy you and everyone you love to get what she wants. You do not want her as an enemy. Trust me, I fucking know," he says quietly, then steps back. "You don't do this task, you're out. No more chances. You've got twenty-four hours, Sam. Twenty-four hours to complete it or they'll fuck up your entire life protecting themselves and their secrets."

I look around us, not noticing anything different, but why would he lie to me? Then what he just said hits me.

"Twenty-four hours?" I say with a dry throat.

Pride nods. "The clock's ticking. Call me if you need help with it." He looks back toward my car, unable to hold my gaze. "For what it's worth, I'm sorry," he says before turning and walking away quickly.

I let him this time, dread sinking into my skin like the rain into my clothes. I climb back inside my car and shut the door, my heart still pounding in my chest.

Thud.
Thud.
Thud.

WRATH

I slowly pull out the card, but I can't look. What if the next task is even worse? What then? This is my last chance. If I don't go through with it, I'm done before I even began.

I'll never be free of Maxwell, and neither will Sabella.

I'll never get my revenge on the man who ruined my life.

The windows have steamed up, cocooning me in my own world as the rain continues to pound down on the car. I turn the card over, my eyes focusing on the words. The dread I've been feeling grows.

"Fuck," I whisper as I swallow, my skin feeling hot. I roll my shoulders and slide my jacket off. The air is too thick in the car, the warmth suffocating.

I throw open my door as dizziness overwhelms me, desperate for fresh air. For freedom.

The rain drenches me in seconds, but I barely feel a thing because all I can think about are the words on the card.

WRATH
Your task is one of sacrifice.
One girl you love for another.
Trading grades for sexual favors is frowned upon.
Catch Dean Griffin in the act of being seduced.
St. Augustine's sweetheart, Sabella Gunner, will be your tool.
Only then will your place will be secured.

You've gotta be kidding me!
"Fuck!" I yell into the sky. "Fuckkk!"

VII
UINCENDUM NATUS

TWENTY-ONE

I screech out of the parking lot and start to drive, letting my hands and feet do the work. The roads move beneath my wheels and I get lost in the motions. I drive dangerously, furiously, my heart pounding in my chest like it's trying to escape.

The roads are slippery and my tires scream as I take the bends too sharply, the wheel spinning wildly beneath my hands. I regain control, my breathing ragged as I start to drive again. The world outside my windows is a blur, like trying to look at the moon through an unfocused telescope. As the lights pass and the rain continues to pour, I feel more and more sick—a stirring in my stomach that won't go away.

My cell phone rings—it's been ringing for the past hour—but I can't bring myself to answer it. Not yet. I just need to keep driving. Keep moving. Keep passing through the rain-drenched roads and pretend I didn't just fuck everything up. Completely blown my chances of getting out of this town, away from Maxwell, my cunt of a grandmother, and being free—finally.

Sabella will be stuck in this family, this fucking hate-fuelled family who despises us both, for good. And there's no way in hell I'm letting her be in The Elite. She's better than this—than all of them. She's too innocent for such a corrupt society. The Elite will strip her of her purity and poison her mind. I slam my hand against the wheel, my eyes burning. I squeal to a stop and dive out of the car. I can't fucking breathe.

I'm gasping.

I'm drowning.

I'm suffocating on my own misery and disappointment.

I stagger away from the car, falling to my knees before standing back up. My clothes are soaked through and clinging to my body by the time I'm at my mom's grave. I sit down, and put my head in my hands, not finding the usual comfort from being here. The flowers I laid last week are dead, dried up, and freshly soaked through—just like me. I pull them out of the vase, feeling guilty for not bringing new ones with me. I know it's stupid and I shouldn't feel guilty because she doesn't care.

She's dead.

She can't see the flowers I lay here each week, or hear the words I speak, or see my actions—the way I try to defend her honor, or protect Sabella. We're the children of the damned, and she doesn't know, or care, because she's fucking dead.

I stand up, needing to be away from here—away from her and her unforgiving arms that give me no love. But I don't know where else to go or what to do. Home doesn't seem like an option right now, because who knows what I'll do if Maxwell starts tonight. I'm a loose cannon waiting to explode. I can feel it in my chest, the swelling of anger and pain and bitter disappointment.

I walk back to my car, feeling lost, but my anger is all burned up. When I get to my car, Sebastian and Sloth are there.

"How did you find me?" I ask, my jaw clenching.

Sloth is smoking a joint, and he hands it to me. I take it instantly, feeling better as the weed hits my system.

"Pride said you handed in your coin," Sebastian says, his usual jittery nature absent for once.

Sloth throws him a confused look. "He said you might need our help. He didn't mention your coin."

"Didn't he?" Sebastian replies without hesitation.

I swallow, feeling sick to my stomach. "I couldn't do it," I admit, because what's the point in denying it? It is what it is now. "I like her."

Shit.

"I really like her." I flinch at my own words.

"For the man with no heart, you sure seem to have a deep well of affection for this girl," Sebastian replies with a cocked eyebrow.

"Who says I don't have a heart?" I bite out.

Sebastian laughs like my question is a joke, which only angers me further.

Sloth leans back against the driver's door. "You got a new task yet?"

"Jesus, what is it with these fucking tasks?" I grumble.

WRATH

"I'm so sick of all the threats and promises, the glory and the destruction. It's all fucking bullshit."

Sebastian nods. "Yeah, he got a new task." He reaches out to take the joint from my hand. "You need some help with it?"

I shake my head.

No, because I don't think I can go through with this one either.

"You want to talk about it?" he asks, then takes a hit.

I shake my head again.

Because I can't tell anyone about my task. It's more disgusting than the last one and I feel sick even considering it.

Fuck, I'm so fucking tired. Like I haven't slept in years. My bones ache from the weariness I feel in my heart.

"You wanna get out of here?" Sebastian asks.

I stare at the graves surrounding us—graves full of lonely, grief-filled bones, suffering eternally knowing they led unfulfilled lives. I belong in one of these graves. Surrounded by dirt and worms. Death and bones and misery. I belong with my dead fucking mother. I'm just as unfulfilled and lonely as she is.

"You gotta do whatever it is, Sam," Sloth says. "Hell of a fucking waste if not."

His words come across like he actually gives a shit, but one look on his face shows me nothing but emptiness. His mask is a blank canvas.

"Maybe it's just not meant to be for me," I say, dragging my hands through my hair. The rain has stopped, and I'm cold, shivering, my teeth chattering. "I need to change," I say, gesturing to my car. "Care to get the fuck out of my way."

Sloth steps to one side and Sebastian heads to the

passenger side. "Need you to drop me off somewhere." He glances at Sloth, who betrays nothing.

Sebastian and I climb inside. I really don't want to drop him off anywhere. I want to be alone, but I don't have the energy to argue with him. So I start the engine and crank the heat all the way up as I start to drive.

"Where are you going?" I ask Sebastian, keeping my eyes on the road. My thoughts are another story, though. They are everywhere. Sabella. Maxwell fucking Gunner and the power he lords over us all. My dead fucking mother. The grandmother who never thought my mother was good enough.

But mostly, my thoughts are on Patience.

I can't help it. She's fucking consuming me from the inside out and I don't know why.

She was your first, my dark thoughts whisper. *She was your first introduction to the pain and pleasure you could give. The power you could yield.*

I hate it, but it's true. I'm just like the father I despise so much. Sebastian still hasn't answered me, and I turn to him with a frown.

"Where am I dropping you?"

He's looking at his cell, his fingers pressing buttons and expression serious. He looks up at me, his green eyes sparking with something akin to irritation.

"Sorry. The mall," he says, shoving his cell back in his pocket. His hand moves to his watch and he starts twisting it over and over. "Women, man, they're complicated fucking creatures, don't you think?" he says with a sigh. "One minute they're hot, the next they're cold."

"The fuck are you talking about?"

He smiles. "That girl of yours, Patience, she's a good

girl. Loyal. Honest. She's got a good heart. She's not all bullshit and lies like most girls, leading guys on to get what they want, you know?"

I have no idea what he's going on about, but I go along with it because it's easier to listen than trying to decipher his lyrical ramblings.

"I can't help but envy you, Sam," he says with a shake of his head. "You've got it all."

I scowl. "How do you figure that? The way I see it, I don't have shit."

He laughs lightly. "Like I said, you see, but you don't really understand," he tsks.

"You're talking in riddles, man," I grumble. I don't have the time for this shit right now.

"So, you're really blowing this whole Elite thing off?" he says, changing the subject.

"I don't see what choice I have. I can't do what they want me to do." The heat is finally filling the car, yet the chill I feel is bone deep and doing nothing to warm me up. Even my rage can't keep me warm today.

"The way I see it, this is about The Elite screwing with the dean. Nothing else is really of interest to them."

I slam my breaks on quickly, almost crashing into a lamppost. I screech the car to a halt, ignoring the beeping horns behind me, and turn to him, fury running through me.

"How the fuck do you know about that?" I bite out. "And I don't want any more bullshit riddles, Sebastian. You tell me right now before I knock your fucking teeth out. I don't take kindly to people sticking their nose in my business."

I expect him to recoil, to deny or at least have the

decency to look fucking worried. Instead, he laughs and unclips his seatbelt.

"Always so hot-headed, Sammy. I'm trying to help you. How about you just listen to what I'm saying and shut the fuck up for a damn minute instead of thinking with your fists." His smile drops, his expression turning dark. Even his eyes seem to lose some of their brightness as they pin me down. "The Elite needs the dean caught with his pants down. It doesn't matter who gets him there, not really."

I force myself to calm instead of lashing out like I normally do. If he has a better plan than walking away from this bullshit, I need to listen. I've got the good sense to see that, even if I don't like it.

"What's your point?" I grit out.

A slow smile creeps up his face. "That girl of yours, she really fucking cares about you, perhaps even loves you going off the texts she's been sending her girlfriends."

"I'm not even going to ask how the fuck you managed to hack her phone. Or why."

He taps the side of his nose. "That's for me to know. All I'm thinking is, if you give her a gentle nudge in the direction you want her to go in, you could still have it all. Get her to help you with the dean problem and no one has to get hurt."

"The card said it had to be Sabella," I say coldly, the words feeling putrid in my mouth.

He shrugs. "I think the point of the task is for Dean Griffin to be kicked out of his position, not who actually gets him there. That's just to fuck with *you*."

Could I do that?

Trade Sabella for Patience?

WRATH

My sister for the woman who's made me feel more things in the past two weeks than I've felt my entire life?

Patience is strong-willed and determined. She comes across like she's all shy and sweet, but below is a woman built for more than what people give her credit for. She could handle that shit. But Sabella, there's no way she could cope in that sort of situation. She's strong, no doubt, she's a Gunner after all, but she's too innocent. This would break her. That is…if I can even convince her to do it.

I open my mouth to tell him I don't think I can when he opens his door, the damp New Orleans air winding its way into the car and sending cold shivers down my spine.

"I mean, you only need him to *look* bad. Patience doesn't have to go through with it. A camera, a low-cut top, and a pervy dean. It'll all play out how you want it to. You just make sure to show up before it goes too far. A little cry for help will go a long way into showing the world exactly who he is. Better than just being a dirty dean sleeping with his students. Think about it." He gets out and closes the door before walking away.

I look around me. I'm nowhere near the mall. Where the hell is he going? It doesn't matter. His idea is good, strong. There's no guarantee The Elite will agree to let me in if I get Patience to do it and not Sabella, but he's right, this would work out better for them—and me.

I have to try it. A spark of hope ignites in me.

Now, all I have to do is convince Patience.

VII
UINCENDUM NATUS

TWENTY-TWO

I head straight to Patience's house. I need to see her, feel her. I need her goodness to wash off on me, and then I need to ask her to do something so disgusting it's making me feel sick.

I knock and knock until one of the housekeepers answers the door. She looks fucking terrified when she sees me, my hair sticking out at all angles and eyes wild.

"Is Patience here?" I bark out.

She wipes her hands down her apron nervously before fluffing her black hair. "She's studying, *señor*. She doesn't want to be disturbed, but I can take a message."

I scowl and push past her. No one is keeping me away from my girl, not even Patience herself.

Fuck, my girl. How did that happen?

I storm through the house, laughing darkly at the

WRATH

so-called family portraits hung on the white walls and placed perfectly on sideboards for any guests to see. This house looks like a picture of happiness when it's anything but.

The maid is following after me, her little legs struggling to keep up with my large strides. *"No señor! No entre!"*

I find Patience in the library, her head low as she reads a book and makes notes. The library is impressive, I'll give the mayor that. It's wall to wall books, a fireplace at one end and a couple sofas in the middle. The large desk Patience sits at is in front of a stained-glass window. As the sun shines through it, it casts reds and yellows over Patience, making her look like a fucking rainbow.

She has earbuds in and doesn't hear me come in. The maid rushes past me to get to Patience first, tapping her on the shoulder and pointing to me.

I'm a bad man.

The fucking worst.

Yet…she looks at me like I'm an angel sent down to her from heaven.

She nods at the maid and stands up, giving me a smile so beautiful, it makes my heart ache. If she knew how bad I am, she wouldn't look at me like that. If she knew my original intentions, she'd never look at me like that again. If she knew what I'm about to ask her, she'd think I'm disgusting, and she'd be right.

I turn to leave. I can't fucking do it to her. I can't ask her to do this.

"Sam," she calls out, but I ignore her in favor of the guilt beating at my insides.

I hear her moving, and then she's in front of me,

reaching out to touch me, but I can't let her. She deserves more than me. She's so much better than me. She'd never ask something like this of me or anyone else. She's good and pure. She builds orphanages for God's sake.

"Sam, what is it?" Her eyes move over me, examining me. "You look like you've seen a ghost."

She reaches for me again, and I try to dodge her, but I'm not quick enough. I can dodge a punch coming at me full force, but I can't dodge her touch.

"Is it me? Have I done something?" she asks, sounding like she might cry.

"No, it's me," I reply, my words short and clipped.

Her fingers slip from me, and she nods, her concern turning to sadness. "I see."

I scowl. "Do you?"

She smiles now and starts to walk away. "It's not you, it's me. I've heard that speech before, Samuel. Just do us both a favor and get out. I don't need an explanation, I—"

"No, it's not like that," I say, feeling annoyed when she rolls her eyes at me.

"Yeah? Then what is it like?" She shakes her head. "In fact, like I said, it doesn't matter, I don't care. Just get out."

She's taken what little I've said and ran with it, coming to her own conclusion in her mind. If I was half the man she thought I was, I'd let it go. I'd let *her* go before I broke her again, because surely asking her to do this for me was going to make her hate me. Be disgusted with me at the very least.

But I'm not that man.

I'm not good. I'm bad.

I storm toward her, grabbing her by the hips and slamming her body to mine. "I said, it's not like that and I mean it. I have shit going on in my life that I can't explain right now."

"Why?" she snaps, clearing not buying my bullshit.

I take a breath. "Just trust me on this, you don't wanna know."

"I do. We're in this together, whatever it is." And fuck me, she sounds so sincere, like she believes her own words. I wish I could believe them too.

I shake my head. "Just go back to studying, Patience."

"Samuel Gunner, don't you do that!" she yells suddenly, slapping my hands away from her. Her eyes spark with a fire that goes straight to my dick. "Don't come here soaking wet and looking like you've just had to sell your soul then make out like it's nothing. Now, tell me what the hell is going on, right now, or so help me!" Her hands go to her hips, and I can't even think straight. I can't think about the task or The Elite. All I can think about is taking that mouth with mine.

So I do.

I take her face in my hands and slam my mouth to hers. She doesn't resist me, not even a little. She melts to my touch as I walk us both back toward the bookshelf and push her up against it. She jumps up, wrapping her legs around my waist, her hands on my body and in my hair, kissing me, fucking devouring every doubt I've had about her and us.

She clings to me as I reach for my jeans and unbutton them, shoving them down my thighs. I pull her dress up before pushing her panties to one side and press my forehead to hers as I grip the shaft of my dick and guide it into her. My hands are back on her, holding her up as I slam into her.

She grips the shelf behind her, her thighs clinging to me as I rock back and forth, my dick swelling with each slam of my hips, until she's crying out.

It's quick and brutal, yet still deeply loving on some carnal level.

We're both giving and taking. I've never had sex like this, where it's both of us working, where I'm not solely in charge. She cries out against my mouth, sucking my lip into her mouth as she comes, her cunt clinging to me, milking me until I come with a loud grunt. Books are falling from the shelves around us as her body clings to my dick.

I kiss her again, stealing her air as she breathes new life into me. I feel grief-stricken and lost as much as I am happy. None of this makes sense. It's confusing how much she means to me already. How much I need her and want her. How much she owns me with every kiss. With every stroke of her tone and touch of her fingers. I'm scared by the intensity I feel for her, but know that there's no way I can ever be without her again.

But then, I guess, love is confusing. Blinding and breaking as much as it is all-consuming. Painful and beautiful in equal measures. It breaks us apart before putting us back together.

And that's how I feel about Patience. She's my band-aid. My medicine. My bandage. She's pieced me back together after feeling broken for so long. Just like a wound, I'll never be the same again after Patience. And that's fine by me.

VII

UINCENDUM NATUS

TWENTY-THREE

"I'm surprised that little maid of yours didn't come barging in here." I smirk and Patience slaps at my arm with a shake of her head.

"Are you going to tell me what all of this was about?" she asks softly.

We're sitting on one of the small sofas, her head on my chest. I swallow, the sound comically loud in our silence. She lit the fire to help warm me up, and it crackles in the hearth.

"I can't," I say, honestly. "You'll hate me, and I don't think I could live with myself if you hated me."

She's silent for a minute before replying. "I don't think I could ever hate you."

I kiss the top of her head, confused by my own gesture. It's so far from who I am. "You did once. In fact, I do believe you said you would always hate me."

She laughs a little and sits up, her eyes finding mine. "I never really hated you, Samuel. I hated me. I hated our parents. But mostly, I hated that I wasn't enough for you. But I never hated you."

Jesus fucking Christ. She thought she wasn't enough for me. I shake my head. "You were always enough for me, Patience, that's why I fucking ran from you. I felt something in that one kiss that I'd never felt in my life, and it scared the shit out of me. I was a coward."

You're still a coward.

"I'm not going to lie; your words that night stung. You ruined our friendship. You took something from me that I didn't even realize I'd come to depend on, but I've come to the conclusion that it had to happen."

"Why's that?" I ask, genuinely curious.

"Because like you said; this was where we were always supposed to end up. Here, together. Maybe we had to go through all that stuff to get us to the right place for us to work." She shrugs like it's that simple. "So, now will you tell me what's going on?"

I frown and look away, dragging my hands down my face. But I have to tell her. I have to take that leap of faith, or I'll never be free.

"I have to get away from my father," I say with a heavy heart. "I have to get Sabella and I away from him and his family."

"Why?" she asks. "Is it really that bad?"

I give a dark laugh. "You have no idea."

"I remember the nanny," she says, her hand gently laying on my arm.

Of course she does. I drag a hand through my hair,

not wanting to talk about this shit, but I decide to anyway. If she's ever going to consider my offer, she needs to understand the stakes. "He hates us. Mainly me. I fight against him constantly and I don't accept his rules."

"That just sounds like you're some spoiled brat." She frowns.

I pause and take another deep breath. Neither he nor I have ever said the words out loud, but I know they're true. "He blames us for her death. He thinks we killed her."

She looks horrified and disgusted. "Sam—"

"Don't. Don't tell me he doesn't. You don't see him. The way he speaks to us. The way he refuses to talk about her. He hates us because we killed her, and he's right, we did—I did. It was my fault, Patience. I broke her when I was being born and she lost too much blood. She never woke up, and it was my fault."

"Oh God, Sam, you were just babies! It wasn't your fault." Her eyes are damp as she tries not to cry. "Is that what you really think? What you've thought all these years, that you killed her?"

I reach over and wipe the tear trailing down her cheek. "There's so much more to it, Patience. You can't even begin to understand."

"So help me to, please," she begs.

I swallow and look away from her. "Growing up, he was always working away. It was like he couldn't bear to be in the same house as us so he just worked and worked and worked. We had live-in nannies all the time, but they never lasted. He'd hire them, then go away for months at a time, come back, fuck them, fire them and then hire someone new."

"That sounds messed up," she replies.

"It was. But the worst part was that they hated Sab and I."

"Sam," she scoffs. "You think everyone hates you."

"Yeah, well they did. They'd be cruel to us, Patience. Each new nanny had their own special way of showing us that they wanted us out of the picture. That they knew that if it weren't for us, our father would have stuck around and they would have had a real chance at becoming the next Mrs. Gunner." I shake my head and drag my hands down my face.

"They wouldn't have even had a job if it weren't for you and your sister," she says, finally sounding angry for us.

"I know that, but they clearly couldn't see that. Each one of those bitches had their own way of showing us we were nothing. That we were unloved and unwanted. Some would be physical, pinching us where the marks couldn't be seen. Or taking our favorites toys away. others were worse, telling us how little we meant to the world. How no one would care if we were gone. I quickly learned that sitting and putting up with it didn't stop them, so I began lashing out, making sure that their attention was on me. I took all of their jealousy and anger so that they'd leave Sabella alone."

Patience is quiet and I turn to look at her. Tears are pouring down her face, her eyes filled with so much pity it makes me feel nauseous.

"And he did nothing to stop it?" she asks quietly.

He let out a dark laugh. "He never even noticed it was going on, but the nannies always had great satisfaction in telling me all the dirty little things he did to them. It was their way of showing me that they meant more to him

WRATH

than I did." I sigh. "I tried to tell him once, but he refused to listen. I guess I was fucked up by then and was constantly in trouble, so it sounded like bullshit."

"I don't know what to say, Sam," she says, her hand squeezing me gently.

"I have a way to get away from him and that house. Between the horrific memories trapped within those white walls, and my father who couldn't give enough of a shit about his kids to hang around and take note of what was happening under his own damned roof, to our cunt of a grandmother who always treated us like lepers that didn't belong in her thoroughbred family tree. There's nothing left for me here. I need to be free of him or I'll go mad."

I watch her straighten her shoulders and get her shit together. She swipes at her tears and looks me in the eye. "Okay, so what can I do?"

I purse my lips. "It's bad. So bad, I can't ask it of you."

She frowns, looking a little bit frightened, but she swallows and tucks her hair behind her ears. "Sam, I told you, we're in this together. Let me help you. You and Sabella."

My heart and head feel heavy. Burdened by the guilt and anger I've kept with me. Not just anger at Maxwell, but at myself, because I killed my mom. It was my fault. But maybe if I can get us both away from Maxwell and this shitty family with all its secrets, I can learn to forgive myself. Living under his roof, seeing the way he looks at me, I'll never be able to.

I take Patience's hands in mine and bring them up to my lips before kissing them.

VII
UINCENDUM NATUS

TWENTY-FOUR

I climb back in my car, and Patience gets into the passenger side. I expected her to crumble, to hate me and call me any number of names when I told her what I needed her to do. I wouldn't have blamed her—I would have deserved it. But she didn't. She listened, nodding and waiting for me to finish, and when I had, she stood up and left the room without saying a single word to me.

I hated myself more in that moment than I had my entire life. And I carried a lot of self-hate around with me.

I sat with my head in my hands, my heart pressing against my ribs for God knows how long, before she came back in. She was dressed in a thin cotton top, the front of it low, too fucking low because it revealed her full cleavage. Her skirt was short, short enough to make my dick hard even in my current misery. And then she told me to take her to school. That she'd emailed Dean Griffin and asked him to take a meeting with her to discuss her current grades.

And now here we are, on our way to school.

Patience reaches across and takes my hand in hers and I feel sick from the love swelling inside me.

Maybe Sebastian is right. Maybe I do have everything.

"You're sure about this?" I say gently, my eyes leaving the road to look at her.

Her features are strong and determined, but her pale complexion gives away her fear. "You'll stop it before it gets too far." She squeezes my hand.

"I will," I swear. "And then I'll fucking kill him."

She gives a nervous laugh, but it's forced. "There'll be no need to kill anyone. It won't get that far. I trust you."

I'm not sure who she's trying to convince, herself or me. But there isn't anything that is going to keep me away from killing that motherfucker if he lays a hand on her.

My cell rings in my pocket, and I pull it out, putting it on loud speaker before I realize who it is.

"Samuel," Maxwell's voice booms out, "where are you?"

I groan. "I'm busy," I snap, and reach to hang up on him.

"Sabella's missing," he says abruptly, and I stop, my hand poised in front of the end button.

"What do you mean she's missing?" I pull into the school parking lot and turn the ignition off. "Since when do you pay attention to her whereabouts?" I bite out angrily. "She's probably at the Humane Society or at the mall or some shit."

I hear him breathing heavily, like he's running.

"Despite what you think of me, I do actually give a shit about you both."

I bark out an angry laugh. There aren't enough words to describe how much of a lie that statement is. "She was due home and didn't arrive."

Thud. Thud. Thud.

"Have you called her? I'm going to call her. She's never late. There will be a good reason. She will be fine."

His words race around my head bouncing of my fucking skull. Sabella is fine. I'd feel it if she wasn't. I'd know. I'd fucking know.

"They found her car, Samuel," he says ominously. "They found her car, abandoned, the door wide open. Where are you? I'm coming to get you so we can look for her."

"Maybe she broke down. Who is they? Who fucking found her car?"

"The police. The police found her car."

No. It's just another one of Maxwell's fucking mind games. Or she's just broke down and walking home. I'll call her and she will answer. I'll tell Maxwell he's a fucking asshole and everything will be normal again.

I turn to look at Patience, all prettied up for the dirty dean. "I'm going to call Sab. Don't come for me I'm busy right now," I say.

"Samuel! This is your sister! Where the fuck are you?" he roars. And his urgency sets off a buzzing in my head.

Patience reaches over and puts her hand on my leg before nodding at me. "I'll handle it," she says quietly, sounding scared and timid.

"Absolutely not. Sab is fine. She's not missing," I grit out.

WRATH

A sharp knock comes on my window, and both Patience and I jump. She gives a little scream as Sebastian's face comes into view. He pulls open the door, looking breathless.

"Told you it was a good idea, right?" he says, moving from foot to foot. He seems more wired than usual, his gaze skipping from Patience to me and back again.

My father is still yelling, the sound of his Ferrari echoing out as he orders me to tell him where I am.

"He's at St. Augustine's, Mr. Gunner," Patience finally says, cutting in through his ranting.

I snap my eyes to her, and she nods.

"I'll be there in less than five minutes," he replies, then hangs up.

"What the fuck are you doing?" I bark. "You're not going in there alone, Patience."

Her gaze moves to Sebastian. "I won't be alone. He'll be there to stop it."

We both look at Sebastian, who looks like a jittery fucking train wreck coming down from a high. Whatever he did between me dropping him off and now cannot have been good.

I climb out of my car, and he takes a step back, his hands twisting that fucking watch of his, his eyes darting side to side.

"You think you can do it?" I ask him, and he nods automatically.

"Yeah, of course. I've got your back," he says. "Anything for you, Sam."

The sound of Maxwell's Ferrari is loud as it comes into the parking lot and he screeches to a halt beside mine. Patience puts a hand on my arm as my father rolls down his window and looks on in surprise.

He looks worried, his normally immaculate appearance anything but. His hair is stuck up at all angles, like he's been pulling on it, and worry crowds his features.

"I'll be fine, won't I?" she says to Sebastian.

She doesn't know him, yet she's trusting him. Maybe I should do the same. I turn to him, gripping him by the front of his shirt. He smells weird, familiar almost. The scent of something I know hangs from him like a slap to the face, but I can't place it.

"You don't let anything happen to her, you hear me?" I growl out, and he nods, giving me one of his fucking creepy smiles. "I'm coming for you if he lays even a finger on her. Do you understand?"

"I've got your back, Sammy," he says, his eyes darting to Maxwell. "You better go, though."

I let out a heavy breath, holding his gaze for a couple more seconds before releasing him. "You film that creep coming on to her, then you walk in. It doesn't go any further," I say. I look at Patience, then back to him. "She is everything to me," I say in warning, "I'll destroy anyone who harms her."

He nods. "I've got it, Sammy. I've got your back. Always."

"Samuel, we need to go. Now!" Maxwell yells from the car. He's on the phone, his features blanching.

I pull Patience into my arms, kissing her mouth roughly. "You're going to be fine, I promise."

She smiles up at me and nods. "I know. Now, go find Sabella."

I head around the side of Maxwell's car and climb into the passenger side, feeling sick to my stomach. The two

WRATH

most important people in my world are in danger, and I can't be there for any of them. What kind of man am I?

Maxwell hangs up and looks at me, his eyes shining. "They found blood," he says, his tone dripping with grief.

Thud. Thud. Thud.

No, she would have caught herself on something, probably trying to look under the hood when her car broke down.

I look out the window, watching as Sebastian walks Patience toward Dean Griffin's office, disgust, shame, and fear crawling through my body. How the fuck can this be happening? I'm leaving her to do this alone, without my protection. And Sabella is out there in the dark trying to get home. I'm a shit big brother. I drag my phone out and check for missed calls... but I know that she would have called me if she broke down.

We've been driving in silence for ten minutes, just the roar of the Ferrari and my panicked thoughts keeping me from going insane. Maxwell looks distraught, but it's fake, just like his words earlier. He doesn't give a shit about me or her, he never has, and I hate him even more for trying that bullshit on.

We're heading down the interstate toward St. Louis Cathedral when he finally speaks up, cutting through the tension.

"She was supposed to be going shopping," he mutters. "I don't understand why she would even be up here."

I turn to him sharply, my gaze scathing as his meets

mine. "You can drop the act now, Maxwell. No one's here to see your fake tears."

He frowns at me and shakes his head. "For God's sakes, it's not an act, son."

"Don't call me son," I reply coldly, enjoying the look of hurt and shame on his face. "And you're not fooling anyone. Like I'm supposed to believe you suddenly grew a fucking heart overnight and decided you give a shit about either of us."

The Ferrari comes to a screeching halt, smoke billowing from the tires as Maxwell slams the breaks. He turns to me, and I lift my chin, my hard gaze meeting his.

"I have *always* cared about you both," he says calmly, but his white knuckles on the steering wheel betray him. "You're my children. It just took me a long time to get my head out of my ass and be a father. Too damn long, I know," he says. "But you, Samuel, you make it so fucking hard to love you."

His words hang in the air between us like a fog. It takes me a moment to catch my breaths so I can reply.

"Love?" I finally sneer. "You don't know what love is. Move this fucking car before I get out and walk."

"I have given you everything. Everything I have! And yet you still hate me. You still throw it all back in my face time and time again."

I laugh. "Given me? The only thing you've ever given me is a black eye and a black heart, now move this fucking car!" I roar.

The day is too bright, the sun glaring down now that the rain and clouds have moved on. It's giving me a damned headache as it reflects back off the red hood of the Ferrari.

WRATH

Maxwell slams his fist against the steering wheel and roars in anger. "It was one time, Samuel. One really, really bad fucking time. It wasn't right—goddamn it, I know it wasn't. I've been ashamed of myself ever since, and I ended things that night. I know I deserve all your anger and hate for that, but I've done everything since that night to make it up to you, yet you continually throw it back in my face." His voice breaks on the final words, and I shake my head at him. "You hate me, I get it. You want out from under me, I get that too. But don't take *her* from me." His words sound strangled and painful—painful enough for me to notice. I scowl at him, enjoying his pain.

Hate and pity bubble to the surface, and I grit my teeth at him. "I won't be taking anything away from you. She's going to leave all on her own. Because that's what you do, Maxwell, you push everyone away. You make people want to leave you. Me, Sabella...Mom."

The last part is a killer that hurts me to even say. I know it's a lie—the biggest lie I've ever told. It was me who killed her and made her leave us. But it has the desired affect regardless.

His face goes red, and he sucks in a sharp breath. I think he's going to lash out and hit me, or get out of the car, or yell at the very least, but like a deflating balloon, the color leaves his face and he opens his mouth, a gust of air leaving him as a sob claws up his throat.

"Get out," he says, his words sticking in his throat. He looks away, unable to bare looking at me. "Get out of my car, Samuel."

"What's wrong, Maxwell? Can't take the truth? I don't blame you, I'm sure it's a bitter pill to swallow. Just like when you said it was our fault she died," I grit out, reaching for the handle. I hadn't mean to say it out loud, but the words can't be taken back once they're out.

"What did you just say?" he says, his voice a whisper.

I look back at him. "I heard you that night with Grandmother. We both did." He looks confused, and I sneer at him. "It went something like: I can't even look at them. Every time I do, I feel angry. They're killers. They killed her." I blink, watching him as his expression turns to horror. "Yeah, it isn't nice hearing that, is it? It wasn't nice to hear as an eight-year-old kid either. Sab cried herself to sleep for a week after that, scared half to death you were going to call the cops and she'd go to prison."

"I'm sorry," he says, dragging a hand down his face. "I didn't mean it. I was so full of grief, even after all that time. I miss your mom so much. She was the love of my life and I couldn't bear to be without her."

I shake my head, because I don't care anymore. I don't want to have this conversation with him, not now, not ever.

"Just drive," I say, closing my door.

Maxwell swipes at the tears on his face. "I still love her so much, Samuel," he says, his voice sounding strangled. "I love her so much, and she was everything to me, and then—"

"Do you think I care?" I yell, feeling like I might explode with rage at any moment. "Just fucking drive, Maxwell. Nothing, absolutely nothing you say, will ever make up for what you've done. I can't forgive you, I fucking can't!" My own voice breaks as sadness and anger engulf me. I sling open the door and get out, unable to sit there with him for a second longer.

"Samuel," Maxwell calls after me. I hear his door open

WRATH

and close as he follow me out. "Samuel, wait. Just listen to me for a minute."

His suit jacket flaps open as he runs around the front of the car. He reaches for me, his large hand landing on my shoulder, but I don't hear what he says as I swing back around, my hand closed into a large fist. I slam it into his face, and he stumbles back under the force of it.

"Yeah, I'm not a little kid anymore, Dad!" I shout, smashing both my hands on to his chest as I push him backwards. He stares at me wide-eyed as I push him again. "I'm not a little kid and I'm not in a jail cell and I'm not cuffed. You and those cunts you called nannies can't fucking bully me anymore! Grandmother can't bully or belittle me anymore!" I swing out and hit him again, catching him in the temple. He calls out in pain and stumbles again, but I can't stop myself.

I rear back and hit him again, and again, and again, my knuckles burning with every punch. I ignore every cry of pain, and I push and punch and push and punch until he falls. I drop to my knees, straddling him as I grab his shirt in my hand and lift him.

My father, the great Maxwell Gunner, stares up at me, his face bloody and bruised, tears streaming from his eyes as I rear back with my fist again.

"I'm sorry, son. I'm so sorry," he cries.

"Stop calling me son!" I bellow. "I'm not your son!"

"You are. You're my son, and I'm sorry I did this to you. I get it, I know it was my fault. All mine, Samuel. You're not to blame. Not you or Sabella. This is all my fault," he cries.

"It is." I let go of his shirt as I stagger backwards. "It is your fault. All of this is your fucking fault." And then I start to cry. Tears like I haven't cried since the night I heard him say we'd killed our mom pour from me, the weight of blame lifting from my shoulders. "It is your fault," I sob.

Maxwell climbs to his knees and reaches for me. I push back at him. I fucking hate him. "Get away from me. I hate you. I fucking hate you!"

"I know, son. I know," he soothes, his arms wrapping around me and pulling me to him. "I know you do, and I deserve it all. Every last drop of your hate and anger, I see that now."

All of my energy is gone. Every muscle sucked dry. I don't have the energy to push him away anymore. I hate him, but I'm broken. I've been filled with anger for so long that now that I'm finally feeling something else it's too much.

My father holds me like a small child for the first time in his life, and for the first time in my life, I find myself clinging to him, desperate for his love.

VII
UINCENDUM NATUS

TWENTY-FIVE

We separate at the sound of my dad's cell phone ringing and run to his car to answer it.

"Hello!" he barks, wiping away the blood from his mouth with the back of his hand. "Yes, yes." He goes silent, his gaze flicking to me. My heart sinks as dread blooms. He hangs up and leans against the car like it won't hold his weight up.

"What is it?" I ask, the words barely making it out of my mouth.

"They want us to go home and wait there."

"What?"

"They want us to wait at home until they know more."

My eyes narrow. "And you said no, right?" My teeth grit together, my jaw feeling like glass that might smash at any moment. "Right, Maxwell?" I bite out. "Because we need to get there and look for her."

Shaking his head, he climbs into the car, and I slam my hand down on the hood, not giving a shit if I damage it. I throw open the passenger door.

"Why?" I yell.

His eyes look empty of life, devoid of anything other than grief. It scares me half to death seeing that look on his face. "Because it's a crime scene now. No one is allowed in. They're sending an officer to talk to us. They said the car is a crime scene."

His words echo through my mind. Not words at all, but noises, sounds that bounce off the hollow inside my head and reflect back out of me.

"What does that even mean?"

"They've found more blood."

"She's not dead," I say, my legs too weak to hold me up. I stagger and sit down in the car and close my eyes so I don't throw up. I feel the car move and my door shut, and then we're moving again. He's trying to say she's dead I know he is.

She's not fucking dead.

I'd know if she were.

Who would fucking hurt her?

No one.

It's just a misunderstanding.

She's going to call any minute.

Silence descends upon us. I can't even think about Sabella being dead. It isn't possible. Not now, not ever. She's alive, somewhere. She has to be. I fucking insist on it.

I send out a group text to brothers. They'll help me

WRATH

look. We'll find her together.

"Do you want me to drop you back at your car?" he asks, his words barely making it through to me. I look up at him and nod, and several minutes later he pulls into the parking lot of school again.

I was here less than an hour earlier. Things were fucked up then, but nothing like this. This is something I won't recover from. I glance across at Maxwell Gunner, my father, seeing the total terror on his face that Sabella might be dead. He pulls up next to my car, his gaze is out of the window. His jacket is torn, his pants full of dirt and blood is smeared down his chin and temple. Small bruises are beginning to form under his skin, purple and green bruises from each fist I had hit him with.

He's empty and broken, just like me, and he'll never recover from this either, I realize.

I open my door and get out, closing it with a small click.

I lean down to look in his open window. His eyes meet mine sending searing pains through my gut at the anguish I see in his eyes. He does love her.

"She'll be okay, Dad," I say with a nod before standing back up.

He leaves a moment later, no screeching tires or smoke billowing. He's calm and collected.

I watch until his car is gone, then make my way to school. I don't see Sebastian's car anywhere, so I guess they already left and Patience either went through with the task or not. It all seemed so important before, and now it means nothing—nothing at all if I don't find my sister.

My phone lights up with a text, and my heart nearly stops at the possibility it's Sab, but it's not her, it's one of my brothers.

LUST: WE'RE ON OUR WAY. ENVY SAID YOU'RE AT SCHOOL. HE MENTIONED LEAVING YOUR GIRL THERE BECAUSE SOMETHING CAME UP.

What the fuck?

I race up the stone steps toward the dean's office before heading down the wood-paneled corridors like the devil himself is chasing me. The office doors are all closed on either side of the corridor, but I hear music coming from the last one. I go lightheaded as the world around me slows. My feet pound down the corridor, but my steps sound hollow on the hard floor.

My knuckles are still bloody and raw from hitting my father, and I find I'm clenching and unclenching them the closer I get to the music.

I've been here before, in a moment just like this, following the sound of music. It hadn't served me well then, and the dread building in my gut makes me think it won't serve me well now.

I squeeze my eyes closed as I stand in front of the wooden door, my hand on the handle.

"Sebastian was here," I murmur to myself. "He would have helped her."

But I know in my gut something is wrong. He left her.

I turn the handle on the door, just like I had as a child, and push it open. And just as I had as a child, I watch as a man fucks into a woman, his big white ass moving at rapid speed as he grunts and groans, pulling his pleasure from her body.

As a child, I had watched, transfixed by what I was seeing, unsure, uncertain, and a little afraid. I had thought it was wrong and dirty, when it hadn't been. It had only

WRATH

been wrong because Patience's mom was married.

But this…this is wrong.

He shifts, moving to the side, and I see his hand is on her throat, his fingers wrapped tightly around Patience's beautiful skin. Her face is devoid of anything. It's just empty. Her eyes are squeezed closed as tears slip between her lashes.

Pain like I've never felt tears through me. Every thrust of the dean's hips is like a stab to my heart. Every grunt he gives is a nail in my coffin.

Without thinking, I grab the first thing I can, a long black umbrella, and I stalk toward him, raising it high and slamming it into the side of his head.

He cries out and staggers away from Patience, blood trailing down his cheek as he turns to look at me. Patience is crying, wailing as her tears pour down her face and she hurries to cover herself back up.

I glare at the dean. "I'm going to kill you," I speak calmly.

The rage I normally feel, the anger that burns, the fury which grows, is nowhere to be seen. It's just him and me. Just the calm in the center of the storm.

"I'll have you expelled," he snaps, reaching down to pull his pants back up. "You'll never get into a college again!"

"You think I give a shit about being expelled, you rapist piece of shit!" I roar.

His bushy eyebrows furrow. "No," he says with a shake of his head. "No, I didn't rape anyone. She agreed to this." He throws a hand in her direction, his gaze still on me.

"Here's a fucking clue for you: if the woman is crying,

she ain't happy, so you get the fuck off her!" I'm going to beat him senseless, and then I'm going to snap his fucking neck.

He shakes his head again. "She wanted to get the grades!" he pleads. "It was her idea, not mine. She came to me, offering to drop her slutty little panties for an A." His gaze flits to Patience, and something inside me snaps. How fucking dare he look at her after what he just did.

I charge forward, grabbing him around the waist and throwing him back over the desk he'd just been raping my girlfriend on. He stumbles and falls, the chair crashing down on top of him as I storm around it. He's scrambling under the desk, his eyes wide as he tries to get away from me, but there's no escaping me and my wrath.

I grab his ankles and drag him out, ignoring his yells and cries as he claws at the carpet to try to stop himself from being moved. I flip him onto his back and begin pummeling him with my fists. Blood gushes from his nose as I slam my fist into it again and again, pushing his hands away as he tries to protect himself.

"I will fucking kill you!" I roar in his face, the red mist of hate drowning me.

"Stop!" Patience screams. "Samuel, stop, please!" She grabs at me, and I push her away, only content with making this man suffer and pay for what he's done. His cries fall on deaf ears. Nothing is stopping me from killing him. Fucking nothing. "He's not worth it."

But he is worth it. His death on my hands is worth everything. I roar as the fury envelopes me completely, wrapping me in its fiery embrace. I'm going to tear him apart, limb from limb.

I raise my fist high once more as Patience comes over

WRATH

again and grabs my arm. "Stop," she begs on a scream. "Just stop, Sammy."

I stumble from her words, Sabella's pet name hitting me in the chest like someone's thrown a rock against my heart. I gag and let my arm fall, my chest heaving with exertion as I stumble away from the dean. He's a mess. A bloody, broken mess. As I move away from him, he staggers to his feet and runs from the room, leaving a bloody trail behind him.

Patience stands behind me, her entire body trembling in shock. I look up at her through angry, tear-filled eyes, feeling like half a man. I shake my head in apology.

The anger is gone, the rage that fueled my fire finally dampening. All that's left is the misery of realizing what I've done to Patience. Despite what I promised her, I broke her again. She'll never be the same after this.

And it's all my fault.

"I'm so sorry," I say, the words getting lost in my throat and coming out a whisper. My hands are shaking, warm blood still dripping from them. "I'm so sorry."

VII
UINCENDUM NATUS

TWENTY-SIX

The sound of sirens finds their way to us in the dean's office. I look down at Patience in my arms. Her eyes are glazed over as she stares into the emptiness in front of her. I kiss the top of her head again and again, pulling her closer to my body for warmth and comfort. She whines and it's like a knife to my heart.

I hate myself more than I've ever hated anything or anyone before. I'm a weak, pathetic coward. I left Patience here to deal with my mess. I fucking left her. The thought makes me feel sick. I drag my hands through my hair, my fingers grabbing at it and pulling.

"Fuck," I mumble, the sickness inside me growing by the second. "Fuck." I hit my fists against my head over and over.

This is all my fault. This happened to her because of me.

WRATH

I am spinning, spiraling into a hate-filled pit. Sick and bile rise in my throat as the image of the dean on top of Patience, rutting away like she was nothing to him, forces its way back into my mind.

"Fuck," I mumble again, my mouth filling with saliva. I'm going to vomit.

Blue lights refract off the old stained-glass windows and bounce around the room. It's too beautiful for such an evil room. I want to smash every one of the windows with my bare hands and then set fire to it, removing anything beautiful from this evil fucking room forever.

"The police are here," Patience says quietly.

It's the only thing she's said to me since the dean ran from the room, his blood still warm on my knuckles. I sat with her in my lap, trying to stem her tears while I feebly attempted to control my bloody-thirsty anger, begging for her forgiveness over and over.

She's in shock and still trying to process what just happened to her, but it will hit her soon, and then what? Then she'll hate me as much as I hate myself, and I won't blame her. In fact, I want her to. I deserve her hate.

The clatter of shoes echoing in the corridor outside the door has Patience's fingers gripping me tighter. The door swings open, and two police officers stand there, their feet wide apart and hands on their guns as if I'm a wild animal who needs to be put down. Shit, maybe I do. Maybe it would be better for everyone if I were dead. All I seem to do is ruin things.

Ruin *people.*

I recognize one of the officers, the female from when I was arrested after my last fight for Daniel. And she clearly recognizes me too. She shakes her head, disappointment showing on her face.

"Samuel Gunner?" the first officer, a black man with a hard glare that says he knows what a piece of shit I am, asks, and I nod. "You're under arrest for the attempted murder of George Griffin. I want you to stand up, put your hands on the back of your head, turn around slowly, lace your fingers together, and wait."

I nod again, but Patience holds on to my arm. I'm not sure if she needs me or if she knows I need her. Either way, she has to let go of me now.

"Please," she whimpers, her eyes beseeching me to make them go away. I want to tell her I will, but I can't. I can't lie, and I know it's not going to be okay.

"It's okay," I say, my voice gritty and painful from yelling. She won't let me go, not even when one of the officer's orders her to. I have to pry her shaking hands off me. "It's going to be okay. I promise."

She starts to cry louder, her gaze going to the police. "He didn't do anything wrong. He was just trying to protect me," she sobs. "It was the dean! He was raping me!"

The last word cuts me to the bone. I squeeze my eyes closed at the pain of it, wishing I hadn't stopped punching him when she begged me—wishing I fucking choked him until he was blue in the face.

The police officers look between each other, but their guns aimed at me don't waiver. I don't expect them to. The police already know me with my extensive history. This just looks like I finally fucking snapped. No one can save me now. No one wants to.

No one will believe Patience over the dean. It's his word against hers and mine, and everyone knows I'm an asshole.

WRATH

"It's going to be okay, Patience. Just do as they say," I soothe—anything to make her feel better.

She finally lets go of me, and I do exactly as they've asked before turning to face the window. They move toward me quickly, gripping my hands and cuffing them behind my back.

"She needs to see a doctor," I say. "Please," I beg when they ignore me.

"There are plenty of paramedics downstairs who can take a look at her," the female officer says in a scathing tone that tells me everything I need to know. She doesn't believe either of us.

The cuffs are tight, too tight. The metal bites into the skin on my wrists as they lead me down the corridor out of St. Augustine's to the waiting police car. Lillian is waiting at the bottom of the steps. She holds a hand up to the officers, and like toy soldiers, they nod their heads and step aside, offering me a tight smile. She leans in to my ear. "Good job, Samuel, task complete. Welcome to The Elite."

"Fuck you," I growl. Does she honestly think I allowed it to get to this point? She's the fucking dean's wife and gives zero fucks what he's done. "He's a rapist," I snarl, and she tuts and rolls her eyes, folding her arms under her tits.

"Is he? Or are these little whores spreading their legs to further themselves?" she goads.

White-hot fury takes over me, and I jerk my head forward, my forehead connecting with her nose in a sickening crunch. The officers grab me and drag me backwards as Lillian stumbles, almost dropping like a sack of shit. Blood pisses from her like a fountain covering her white blouse. Her eyes snap up to mine, the pupils swallowing the color as she pins me with a sinister glare.

"You little fucking brat. How dare you." Her finger pokes into my chest. "I was going to tell them to release you after you calmed down, but you've just crossed a line. I'm all about teaching you boys how to step in line and know your place." With that, she nods to the officers. "Take him away."

Patience runs up and walks alongside us crying, her arms wrapped around herself. I think she's in shock. Too traumatized to speak or comprehend what's happening right now. But she'll figure it out soon.

We pass another police officer waiting by the front of his car, and I bark out, "Get her a fucking doctor! Now!"

He sneers at me and turns away. "You're fucking done!" I yell, fighting against my restraints as my anger flares again. "You're all fucking done if you don't get her some help!"

The dean sits inside an ambulance as paramedics tend to him, acting like he's done nothing wrong. Motherfucker's making it out to look like this is all about a student losing his shit and turning psycho on him because of bad grades. It fuels my anger.

It must have done the same to Patience too because she finally loses it and begins screaming obscenities at him until they close the doors of the van.

"Ma'am, step back!" another policeman orders, grabbing her arm and pulling her away.

"I want to press charges against him!" she sobs, and the officer frowns.

"Get the fuck off her now!" I growl, fighting against the officer again. I'm going to fucking kill them all if they

WRATH

don't get off her right the fuck now.

My anger seems to calm her down. She turns to me, her face red and tearstained, her hands curled into small fists. She takes a breath. "It's going to be okay, Samuel. I'll tell them what happened. You're going to be fine," she sobs, sounding distraught. "My dad will clear this up."

Jesus, I completely fucked everything up. She just went through something traumatic, and here she is trying to make me feel better. I don't deserve her, or anyone else.

I duck my head as they push me into the back of the car, smiling sadly at her and nodding. I don't have the words to tell her it doesn't matter what she tells them. I'm fucked regardless.

I'm in the mercy of the fucking Elite now, of Lillian.

Which means I'm fucked.

She's shaking, trembling from head to toe, and I'm crushed because I can't do anything to make things okay for her. So, I nod and place my forehead against the window when the police slam my door closed.

Patience places her hands against the glass, tears trailing down her face. "I love you," she sobs.

I shake my head at her. "Don't. Not like this," I reply.

Because I love her too, but I won't be declaring it while I'm in the back of a police car. She deserves better than that.

I tear my gaze away from her as several cars pull up next me. Maxwell's bright red Ferrari and God's Escalade screech to a stop. I hang my head in shame as my father gets out. It's then I notice my other brothers have arrived and are gathering around to find out what's happened.

My father looks exasperated. This is the last thing he needs right now with Sabella missing.

Fuck...Sabella. I still don't know where she is.

I want to tell him I'm sorry. I want to explain what happened, because for the first time in a long time, perhaps ever, I don't want him to hate me. But I don't say anything. Instead, I sit there in silence, feeling sick with guilt and shame.

For some reason, it bothers me that he looks one hundred years old. He drags a hand through his short hair, and I realize that's where I get the same gesture from. He begins barking orders for them to get me out of the cuffs when a police officer intervenes, telling him what I'm being arrested for. His stare turns hard and cold as he listens, and then it's like he can't even bear to look at me. He shakes his head and steps back, like he can't believe what he's hearing. He says something to the officer, walks back to his car, and climbs in. And even though we hate one another, and I've never wanted or needed his help in my life—even when I've never given a shit what he thinks of me—I still feel something break inside as he gets back in his car and drives away.

His message is loud and clear: he's finally done with me.

It doesn't feel like I expected it to, like the biggest win of my life. It's painful, like driving a nail into an open wound and then pouring acid inside. I feel numb, empty, and so fucking alone, I can barely breathe.

"Samuel!" Pride's voice booms from outside the car, and I look up sharply at him. He's standing with the rest of my Elite brothers, each of them wearing the same grim expression on their faces. They know I traded in my coin and they don't know how to get me out of this mess.

God nods at me. "I'll handle it," he says, and I nod back.

WRATH

I want to believe he can do something about this, but doubt pours over any hope I have. This is an attempted murder charge, and one I'm not even going to deny. Why would I? If Patience hadn't stopped me, I would have killed him, and then I would have taken out my cock and pissed over his fucking corpse.

God's father is one of the richest men in the world, but I doubt even he can make something like this disappear.

The police officer climbs in the front seat and starts the engine as Pride comes toward the car. He says something to Patience, and she nods at him and starts to cry all over again, her words tumbling from her mouth, fast and furious.

Pride's hard gaze meets mine. "We'll sort this, brother," he says as the car starts to pull away.

I nod, my gaze narrowing in on Sebastian, who's practically hiding behind the rest of my Elite brothers. His expression is calm, but cold. The sickness I've been feeling intensifies, making me dizzy from the anger and hate I feel.

I nod at him as I sit back, the metal of the cuffs biting my skin even more painfully. I hold his stare as I speak to him like I'm fucking telepathic and he can hear my thoughts. And maybe he does, because his features blanch.

I give him a warning.

A threat.

A motherfucking promise.

I am fucking coming for him.

VII
UINCENDUM NATUS

EPILOGUE

The sound of my cell door rolling open has me cracking my eyes open as much as I can. It stands to reason I got into a fight as soon as I got here. I am Wrath, after all. My given sin is still haunting me even in my incarceration. It's almost laughable. At least it would be if I didn't think I have broken a rib.

"Gunner, you've got a visitor," the guard barks out. I roll onto my side and sit up. He chuckles darkly. "Looking rough there, son. You pick a fight with a wall?"

I stand up and crack my head from side to side, the sound of crunching coming from my neck as I stalk forward. My arm is still wrapped around my middle, but I'm standing tall—all six-foot-five of me—as I stare him down. Stupid motherfucker looks worried, but not worried enough. That's a huge mistake. I'm a man who's lost

WRATH

everything and everyone I've ever cared about. They can lock me up and throw away the key for all I care. I have nothing left to lose and a gut full of rage begging to get out.

I won't even blink at kicking this sorry son of a bitch's ass.

Another guard shoulders up to the first one. "Prescott, I'll deal with this," he says, and the first guard sneers and walks away. I make a mental note of his name. I always make a point of remembering my enemies' names. The second guard, who's name badge reads Michaels, takes a deep breath and looks at me. "Hands through the bars. Clasp them together, Gunner."

I glare at him, unmoving, more than ready to tear him apart, limb from motherfucking limb. I have no desire to see whoever is out there. Probably a lawyer The Elite got for me. He'd get me off so long as I admit I was in the wrong, and I won't do it again—or maybe it's Maxwell coming to tell me he's done with me again.

It's all bullshit, and I don't give a shit. I certainly don't need to see his smug face again. I saw all I needed to when he listened to those cops and walked away, not even giving me a chance to explain.

As for whether I'd do it all again? Fuck yeah I would, and I wouldn't stop. I would end the dean and his perverted ways. That's the only thing I regret.

"It's up to you. You want visiting hours, you do as your told." He raises an eyebrow at me when I still don't move. "Real pretty girl out there waiting to see you."

I scowl. Now he's got my interest. More than got my interest. "Sabella?" I ask, my voice coming out throaty and raw, betraying my emotions. My heart thumps heavily in my chest with excitement and relief that she's okay.

I haven't heard anything about her since being in here. No news was good news, I assume. It hasn't stopped me from worrying though, the anxiety of her disappearance eating away at my stomach and mixing with my fury, turning me into a ticking time bomb ready to explode. Hence the state of my face and ribs.

Michaels shrugs. "No idea. Long, dark hair, beautiful, looks real sad. Be a shame if she didn't get to see you."

The world seems to slow, as my thoughts collide and spin. I pushed my hands through the small rectangular space in the bars, clasping my hands together as Michaels cuffs them, then step to the side so he can lead me out.

Dizziness washes over me as I walk. The sickness I've felt in my gut since this all happened begins to dissipate. Sabella is alive. Thank fuck for that. Nothing else matters right now, as long as she's okay. A lump forms in my throat as emotion grips me.

She's safe.

She's okay.

She's *here*.

Guilt starts to mix with my relief. I'm in here—prison. And probably going to be doing serious time. The look on her face is going to be like a knife to the heart. Fucking hell. Just take a blade and slice my throat open now. She'll never forgive me for this. Despite the circumstances.

I should have kept my cool, but instead, I lashed out, lost control, and almost killed a man. And now, I'm not there to support either of the women I love.

Less than five minutes ago, I thought I wouldn't change a damn thing about what I'd done, but now, I

WRATH

wonder. Being locked up in here, I can't keep either of them safe.

Michaels leads me down the hallway, shouts and jeers coming from the other prisoners in the cells we pass. It doesn't matter—*they* don't matter. My one good eye glares at them, and they snarl like fucking dogs as they back up. Even broken like I am, they know I'm dangerous.

Michaels stands to one side and uses a key to open a door leading down another long corridor. At the end, he stops and unlocks door, then brings me into a visiting room full of families, prisoners, and guards. The room is noisy, bustling with people who are angry or sobbing, grief and shock, annoyance and boredom on all their faces. A mixture of every emotion, but all with the same grim expression.

I scan the crowd, looking for Sabella, desperate to see her. The knot in my gut tightens like a noose, making it so I can't speak and I can barely breath. I just need to see her, then I'll deal with the rest of the shit. I'll let The Elite help me, if they can. I'll even beg Maxwell.

I don't realize I'm looking down, the burden of my guilt forcing me to stare at my feet, until we come to a stop.

"Hands to yourself, no shouting, no kissing, no touching," Michaels barks. "I've got a soft spot for you, Gunner," he says quietly, "but don't go pissing me off."

He pushes me into my seat as I finally raise my head, my eyes meeting Patience.

Patience.

Not Sabella.

"Where's Sab?" I ask, the hairs on my arms standing to attention. I look around the room like I might see her standing somewhere, but I already know by the anxiety shining through on Patience's face why Sabella isn't here. She's still missing.

Patience shakes her head, her shoulders slumping farther than they already are. "We still can't find her, Sam."

I shake my head. "No," I mumble, dread engulfing me. I squeeze my one good eye closed, clenching my hands into tight fists. "Fuck, fuck!" I growl.

"It's going to be okay," Patience says, and I glance at her. She looks just as broken as I feel. Dark rings circle her eyes, her lips are dry, and her hair is scraped back into a low ponytail. She looks like she hasn't eaten in a week. Her hands are on the table in front of her, one picking at the nails on the opposing one.

"How?" I say with a shrug. "How is any of this going to be okay?"

I want to reach out and touch her, feel her smooth skin under my rough fingertips, before pulling her into my arms. I want to smell her peach shampoo as I kiss the top of her head. I want to feel her clinging to me, knowing I'm her rock. Her strength. Fucking there to protect her.

But I'm not there. I'm here, on the opposite side of the table with my life screwed up.

Patience has gone through hell because of me, and I'm not there for her.

Sabella is still missing, and I can't even help look for her.

I'm fucking nothing—less than nothing.

"Because God promised me it would be," Patience soothes.

I look up to her sharply, a frown puckering my

WRATH

forehead. "You're talking about Baxter Goddard, right? You're not having a Jesus moment?"

She lets a small smile flit to her face before it vanishes. She glances from side to side, making sure no one's close enough to listen. "God—The Elite—they're fixing this, all of it. It's all going to go away."

I shake my head. "Tell them not to bother. I deserve to be in here, Patience. I let this happen to you. It was my responsibility to protect you—you trusted me—and I fucking blew it." I point to her. "This is all my fault."

"Don't say that, Sam. You can hate yourself all you want, but this isn't your fault. And I *need* you." Her words falter as she tries to control her emotions. "Please, Sam, if not for me, do it for Sabella. We both need you right now, so don't give up."

My heart squeezes painfully, so painful, I can't quite catch my breath.

"I cashed in my coin," I say to her, and she frowns in confusion. "We each get a coin to cash in when we need help. I cashed mine in to protect you." I snort and shake my head. "For all the fucking good it's done because I didn't protect shit."

Our hands are on the table, inches apart, but it might as well be miles for the distance separating us. She stretches out a finger to stroke the side of my hand, and my heart squeezes again.

"He says this help is from a friend, Sam. Not from The Elite."

It sounds too good to be true, but I can't help the spark of hope. It didn't bother me if I rotted in this place before, but knowing Patience needs me, that Sabella is still missing—it's all I need to keep me going.

"Just have a little hope," she pleads.

"I'll try." And I will. For her. For Sabella. I'll try. I've never had hope before, but right now I need to dig deep and believe that God can get me the fuck out of here. That I can find wherever Sabella is and bring her home safely. I need to have hope that I'll get the chance to spend the rest of my life making it up to Patience and Sabella, because I'm a piece of shit and they deserve more—better, than me.

"You've got to stop this, though," Patience says, pointing to my fucked up face.

I laugh darkly, pain shooting through my ribs. "You should have seen the other guys."

"Guys?" she puts a hand to her mouth, her eyes filling with tears.

"Three against one. And all three are in the infirmary now looking a shit load worse off than me." I feel proud of that fact. The other guys are older than me, bigger than me, and they were together in jumping me—and I fought them all off and walked away. All pride vanishes when I see the look of horror on her face. "Okay," I concede, "no more fighting."

"Just stay safe. We're getting you out of here. I'll be waiting for you, Sam." She strokes my hand again, but this time Michaels see it and he slams his hand on the table.

"I said no touching!" he barks loudly, drawing attention to us.

Patience gasps and pulls her hand away, and I snarl up at Michaels. "She's been through some shit, yeah? Just give her a fucking break!"

"It's okay," Patience says quickly. "I need to go. My father doesn't know I'm here."

WRATH

"Will I see you again?" I ask as she stands.

She smiles softly and nods. "Every time you close your eyes, I'll be there, Sam."

"Then I'll be a blind man so I can see you all the time," I reply.

We stare at each other across the table, a thread connecting us, bound together despite everything. I love her. Deeply and unconditionally. I want to tell her, but now's not the time or place. She deserves better than this. She deserves better than me.

Patience stands and smooths down her pastel skirt. "One last thing, Sam." She purses her lips together, like she doesn't want the words to come out. "They're not pressing charges against George."

A bomb goes off inside me as I process her words. Everything implodes. My walls break down and collapse around me. Grief and rage, misery, fury—they twist and combine into a ball of destruction until I'm gasping for breath.

"They say I went there looking to seduce him, and I'm old enough to consent, so…" Her words trail off, and she closes her eyes. When she opens them, they're glassy from the tears she's trying to hold back. "He's on leave for now, so he can't do this to anyone else. That's what's important."

I shake my head, my body trembling with the rage I'm trying to control. "No, that's not what's important."

She leans down, placing her hands on the table so she can stare right into my one good eye. "They're right though, Sam, I could have stopped it—I should have stopped it!" A tear finally lets loose from one of her eyes and makes it's slow descent down her cheek. "I just kept thinking that someone would be coming and it would all be over, but then it was too late and when I tried to stop him he told me I was a tease and playing games, that he'd flunk me anyway if I didn't just go along with it."

Anger flares in my gut, and my hands instinctively curl into fists.

"I'm going to kill him," I grit out.

She swipes at her cheek, wiping away her hot tears. "My father will deal with the dean. He'll make sure he never works again."

"And Sebastian?" I grit out. "What about him? This is his fault. He was supposed to stop it from happening. I trusted him to protect you and this is what happened. One way or another, I'm going to make him pay."

She shakes her head, her eyes flaring with defiance. "Forget him. I need you to get a grip and come home to me."

She reaches out to stroke my face, but Michaels is there again. She glances across at him, then back to me with a sigh, her hand dropping to the table once more

"I have to go."

I nod. "Are there any leads on my sister?" I ask, the words sticking in my too dry throat.

"Me and your dad are heading up a search party to look for her. We have half the town out looking. God's financing some private detectives too. We'll find her, Sam. She's going to be okay." She bites her bottom lip, and I know she doesn't believe that. *I* don't believe that. People like my sister don't just disappear, not unless someone makes them.

The sick feeling in my stomach returns, and it takes all of my control not to lose it myself. I need to be strong—I

WRATH

have to be, for Patience.

"Come home to me," she says. Then she turns and walks away.

My head pounds as I try to process everything she just said, like I might actually vomit on the table right now, but all that would come out would be my emotions and perhaps a broken rib or two. Everything hurts. My body, my mind, my heart. My fucking soul feels shattered into a million pieces. I'm empty, destroyed. I'm fucking nothing.

I stand to leave. I need to lie down. I need to do what she said and control myself. To get the fuck out of here and get home to her and Sabella. Because I will find her. I have to.

"Got another visitor," Michaels says, pushing me gently back into my seat.

I look up, watching as Sebastian walks over to my table and takes a seat opposite me. "You," I grit out with barely contained rage.

He swallows. "I brought her to see you," he says by way of explanation. "No one else would bring her, they thought you'd lose it if you saw her."

My hands knot together in front of me. I have to force myself to pull them back and place them in my lap so I don't do something stupid. I hear Patience's words in my head like a mantra as I breathe in and out slowly.

Come home to me.
Come home to me.
Come home to me.

"What do you want?" I manage to grit out, aware Michaels is still close by. Tension rolls off me in waves.

Sebastian drags his hands through his hair, his eyes looking to me, then to the side. He can't keep still. I can feel the vibrations of his foot tapping on the cold linoleum under the table. His watch is missing, and his hands keep going to touch it, to fiddle with it like he normally does, but it's not there.

"I asked you a question," I say, and he finally looks over at me, wincing when his gaze connects with mine. "What are you doing here? If it's to apologize for letting Patience get raped by that sick fuck then apology *not* accepted. When I get out of here, I'm going to tear you limb from fucking limb. You're a dead man walking as far as I'm concerned. So I'll ask you again, what are you doing here?"

"I wanted to see you. To explain."

"Explain?" I scoff bitterly. "You wanted to explain why you left my girlfriend there all alone to be raped, motherfucker? There's no explanation necessary. No excuses. No forgiveness."

"I'm sorry," he pleads, his green eyes staring into my rage-filled ones.

"Sorry isn't good enough. Sorry won't change what's happened."

"I know."

"It won't change what you let happen."

"I know!"

"You can't take back what you've done, Sebastian, and when I get out of here, I'm coming for you."

He nods in understanding, his hands dragging through his hair again. "I just wanted her to love me," he mumbles, his gaze on the table. "That's all."

"What?" I scowl. "What the fuck are you talking about?"

"It's Sabella." He looks up at me again, his face pinched in frustration and pain. "I just needed her to love me. She's

WRATH

so pure, so innocent. I wanted her." He stands up abruptly, his chair falling back. "I fucked up, Sam." Michaels moves quickly to my side and grips my shoulder to hold me in place as I try to stand up too. "I'm sorry, Samuel," Sebastian says, backing away from me, his hands tugging at his hair and pulling it out in all directions. "I didn't mean for any of this to happen."

I can see it in his eyes—something I've never seen in another person before—a look I see so often in the mirror. It's something worse than despair and grief. Worse than self-destruction and guilt. It's every emotion rolled into one.

It's insanity masked as humanity.

It's anguish and heartache and self-loathing.

"What did you do?" I ask, my stomach falling to the floor at my feet and my heart pausing in its frantic rhythm. "Where's Sabella?"

He shakes his head and turns from me, his hands shoved deep in his pockets and shoulders hunched as he moves quickly through the visiting room. He darts between chairs and tables, oblivious to the angry people around him. All he cares about is getting away—from me.

"Sebastian! Sebastian! What the fuck did you do?" I try to go after him, but Michaels grabs me. And when I try to shrug him off, ignoring the lancing pain through my ribs, another guard comes over. Both guards grab at me, shouting at me to calm down, but all I can do is kick and yell and lash out with all my strength to get to Envy.

In the doorway, Sebastian looks back at me, our eyes connecting across the room. "Envy! What did you fucking do?" I roar as both guards drag me away. "What the fuck did you do to Sabella?"

ENVY IS COMING MARCH 25^(TH)
ARE YOU READY?
ENVY #4 The Elite Seven Series

It was temptation that broke the sinner.

People say I have everything.
They're wrong.

I may have looks, money, and privilege, but I don't have the one thing that really matters, the one thing I crave: a woman with eyes only for me.

I'm searching for my woman—one who will fall to her knees because I'm her king. She'll wear the crown of my tarnished name, and long for me when I'm not near. And when I am close, she'll be naked across my lap, feeling the sting of my palm across her milky skin.

You could say I'm a sinner because I'd do anything to have the perfect woman—compliant to my every need and whim—and I'm envious of every couple who walks around naive to the luxury they have.

That's why I joined The Elite, the most prestigious brotherhood in the south.

It's the one place that will give me what I cannot have.

Only…the task assigned to me is too much for my jealous eyes.

Accept your sin wisely, for the tasks given to earn your place are not for the weak… they're for The Elite.

Those who envy have no peace.

My name is Sabastian Westbrook.

I am *Envy*.

ABOUT THE AUTHOR

Claire C. Riley is a *USA Today* and International bestselling author.

Claire is a genre hopper, because life's too short to pick favorites. Plus, she's a fickle Gemini. She likes to write about alpha males, psycho stalkers and the end of the world, to name a few.

She lives in the United Kingdom with her husband, three daughters and extremely naughty rescue beagle who keeps her company by staring at her like her own personal stalker while she writes.

She can be found most days going a hundred miles an hour while she chases round after her kids, husband, puppy, and of course her dreams!

Never miss an update!
Website:
www.clairecriley.com

Claire C. Riley FB page:
www.facebook.com/ClaireCRileyAuthor

Cee Cee Riley FB page:
www.facebook.com/CeeCeeRileyBooks/?ref=br_rs

Amazon:
amzn.to/1GDpF3I

Group: Riley's Rebels:
www.facebook.com/groups/ClaireCRileyFansGroup

Newsletter Sign-up:
clairecriley.us14.list-managecomsubscribe?u=eda86431d680985
39defc1e7b&id=4e6a3dd390

MORE FROM CLAIRE C. RILEY

Post-apocalyptic romances:
Odium the Dead Saga Series
Odium Origins Series
Out of the Dark

Paranormal romances:
Limerence (The Obsession Series)
Twisted Magic

MC romances:
Devil's Highwaymen Ride or Die Series
Devil's Highwaymen Nomad Series:
#1 Crank
#2 Sketch
#3 Battle
*#4 *Fighter*
*#5 *Cowboy*

ROMANTIC THRILLER SUSPENSE:
Beautiful Victim

Horror:
Blood Claim

Co – Authored Books with Madeline Sheehan:
Thicker than Blood
Beneath Blood & Bone
Shut Up & Kiss me

ACKNOWLDGEMENTS

With thanks

To my fellow sinners; love you bitches.

Huge thanks to Ker Dukey for bringing me on board with this project. I feel hugely privileged to be a part of it. Love you.

Thanks also to my amazing betas for reading the early copy and helping me to polish Wrath to perfection. Especially Ashley who had to read it more than once! Sorry, Boo. But thanks.

And finally, thanks to my family, but especially my husband. You put up with my insane plot ramblings, late nights, early mornings, emotional breakdowns *and* you have a great ass.

What more could a girl ask for.

Love you all.

Claire xox

Printed in Poland
by Amazon Fulfillment
Poland Sp. z o.o., Wrocław